Most Improved Sophomore

A NOVEL

KEVIN KILLEEN

Blank Slate Press | St. Louis, MO

Cover design Kristina Blank Makansi
Interior design by Kristina Blank Makansi
Cover art: Adobe Stock

Library of Congress Control Number: 2017939477

ISBN: 9781943075300

PRINTED IN THE UNITED STATES OF AMERICA

For Jim

Most Improved Sophomore

Chapter 1

TONY VIVAMANO stepped out of the shower—steaming hot naked—and covered his face with shaving cream. He reached for the razor, but his eyes fell on a half-eaten roast beef sandwich he'd left on the sink. The meat sang to him, red and tempting. He knew he should shave first, but he was hungry. So, he grabbed the sandwich and took a bite.

"I am a hedonist," he told the mirror, practicing a new word from sophomore vocabulary.

Chewing and nodding, he rated his muscles and chest hair. Not bad, not bad at all. A handsome Italian face, too. And look at those eyes, brown and sincere—and eyebrows that, with one twitch, could make a girl forget her curfew. It was clear to him that he was a millionaire in biological gold, and he should be prepared to share his riches. What a shame to put on clothes. What a shame to be banished Monday through Friday to that all-boy high school, St. Aloysius—without a girl in sight. What a shame to suffer another weekend waiting to find out what it means to be fully alive with a woman on his favorite planet, Earth.

"I *will* find a woman," he told the mirror, tearing off another bite, "and she will be proud of me when I show her my—" He stopped. Something was wrong. The bread had dragged shaving cream—with its penetrating menthol formula—inside his mouth. His throat was closing up. He reeled around gagging and spit it all in the toilet.

"She will be proud of me," he said flushing.

Wrapped in just a towel, he hurried to his bedroom, where the most beautiful woman on Earth was waiting for him. Sophia Loren, the movie star, watched him from a black and white poster above his dresser. Because of her, the room came alive whenever he flipped on the lights. He looked at her. The cut of her blouse plunged low to reveal almost the full glory of her voluptuous breasts. And it was not just her breasts. Her wild dark hair, her full lips, and flared nostrils—and the look in her eyes: Such desire for him. Tony could sense it. Sophia Loren needed him. Badly. He could almost feel her warm breath. She wanted to step out of the poster and flop on the bed with him and enfold him with her love. Oh, Tony, Tony, Tony . . . He felt sorry for her that she could not join him. He stood before her and blew her a kiss as he put on aftershave.

"Hiya, babe."

Then, whipping his legs into black underwear and blue jeans, he stepped out into the hallway, bare-chested and barefoot, ready to make a phone call. Tony dialed the avocado rotary phone on the wall and started performing leg squats to limber up. He was calling his longtime accomplice in all matters criminal and social, Patrick Cantwell. Together, they could find some women.

"Hello?" Patrick's mother said.

Tony had dropped the phone and couldn't hear her, but Patrick's mother could hear him—his heavy breathing, his grunting and enormous sigh at the completion of his leg squats. He picked up the phone.

"Hello?"

"Who's this?"

"It's me, Tony."

"What's going on over there? I hear . . . terrible sounds."

"I'm exercising. A man should be ready, Mrs. Cantwell."

"Ready for what? Patrick can't go out."

Tony thought quickly about what to say. A woman of many births and baptisms, Patrick's mother was an obstacle to hedonism. Somehow, he had to maneuver around her. Recently, she had caught them watching Bobby Goldsboro on TV, singing, "Summer (The First Time)," a song about a young man who makes love for the first time with an older woman. It was a beautiful song, Tony had thought.

But Patrick's mother—when she'd heard the song—stormed into the room and slapped off the TV. "Boys!" she said, "that young man committed a mortal sin! The devil laid a trap for him before his wedding night, and now he's ruined. Don't let it happen to you, boys, or someday the devil will say to you, 'You damned fools!'"

Tony cleared his throat and spoke into the phone. "Mrs. Cantwell, it's good to hear your voice." Actually, he couldn't stand her voice. "I was thinking me and Patrick should go out after a long week at school." That should work, he thought. Surely she must have noticed how overworked Patrick was at school, what, with all those fool questions the Jesuits asked. Questions like: Can a man conquer himself and become a new man? Can a Catholic wait until his wedding night? Is there more to life than the five senses? Tony shook his head. Such nonsense.

"I'm sorry," she said, not sounding sorry at all, "but Patrick can't go out tonight. I won't let him. He told me he's working on a paper for school."

"Tell him it's Friday night," Tony said with the same charming chuckle he used on all women. "Tell him life is waiting . . . and I'm coming over to rescue him."

"No, that's out of the question. I forbid you to come over, because—"

"But Mrs. Cantwell . . . the night air is good for a man's blood."

Before she could answer, he laughed and hung up, knowing the Big Guns of her Catholic Mom Logic were too much for him.

Chapter 2

TONY GOT DRESSED and jumped behind the wheel of his mother's station wagon, an oversized Plymouth, all gassed up and ready to run. A car he proudly called, "The Love Machine." A sturdy, eight-cylinder battlewagon, The Love Machine was capable of doing a hundred-miles-an-hour easily.

Tony parked outside Patrick's house and looked up to the second story windows. Patrick's desk lamp was on. Tony could see the chinks of light around the drawn shades. He squared his shoulders and walked in the front door without knocking. That was his custom. He could walk into Patrick's house, and Patrick could walk into his. They were like twins, only living with different families. Immediately, Friday night chaos was all around him: the dog barking at him, little kids running by, rock music from Patrick's older brother blaring from the basement, a TV in the backroom belting out the theme song to the *Brady Bunch*.

Patrick's mom darted to the front hallway with a baby in arms to intercept him.

"Tony, I told you not come over tonight. Patrick is working on an important paper." Her eyes were commanding and she nodded toward the door, signaling Tony to turn around and get out. But Tony laughed. A deep, bluffing laugh that made Patrick's dad rustle his newspaper and peer over the top of it from his chair in the living room. That's what Tony wanted, a second opinion. Mr. Cantwell smiled and waved him in.

"Why, Tony, how've you been? Pull up a chair."

Mrs. Cantwell huffed into the kitchen, while Tony pulled up a chair to talk with Patrick's dad, man to man. The living room walls were covered in dark paneling, with a beamed ceiling and Civil War Battle prints here and there, and not much light, except for the side table lamp—a man's room.

Mr. Cantwell put down his *Antique Trader* article on the baseball cards of his youth, flopping it atop his corporate briefcase stuffed with the concerns he was trying to escape. He looked at Tony and ran through the usual adult-to-teenager questions: "How's school? How are your folks? What's new with your family?"

Tony knew how to play it—short and easy answers. "Fine. Everything's fine. Nothing new."

Then Mr. Cantwell took a sip of his Old Fashioned, set the glass down, and leaned forward to get down to the point.

"Tony, I'm concerned about Patrick. Does he seem *all right* to you?" Tony detected a hint of worry over Patrick's mental stability.

"Oh, he's fine, maybe just a little . . . introspective lately."

"Introspective. Yes, you're right . . . that's the word."

Tony jabbed his chest with his thumb. "They taught us that one in vocabulary class, along with 'procrastinate'."

Mr. Cantwell rubbed his forehead. "He's seems to be under a tremendous strain. He's been reading a lot of heavy material up there in his room this year. I gave him a book on the Marx Brothers and told him to relax, but I don't think he even cracked it open. Do you like the Marx Brothers?"

"Yes, sir, I'm a Chico man myself."

"Well, at least you can name one of them. I don't think Patrick could. I'm not sure *what* he's thinking about up there."

"Maybe he just needs to get with some girls, *if* you know what I mean." Tony wiggled his eyebrows like Groucho Marx.

Mr. Cantwell drew back. "What exactly do you mean?"

Afraid he'd gone too far, Tony conjured up a sincere look on his face. "You know, good Catholic girls."

That was the right answer. Parish girls. Girls who make curfew. Girls who would make a good wife someday.

"All right." Mr. Cantwell patted Tony on the knee. "Go see if you can get him out of the house. You're a good man, Tony."

Upstairs, Patrick, sat hunched over his student's desk. He wore an old bathrobe, the hood cupped around his head. The only light in the room from a plaster, desktop lamp—a Portuguese Man-o-War tossing in the waves. Strewn about the desk were various books: a Freudian primer, Carl Jung's essays on archetypes, the biography of St. Aloysius, and another book he had just checked out but not yet read, *What is Man?* by Mark Twain.

Amid the clutter sat a cup of tepid tea and scribbled notes on key passages he could use in his paper on wisdom, which wasn't due for another week. But, he wanted to understand it more for himself than the grade. Human nature, good, evil, self-improvement—man's search for something more—the whole thing was overwhelming in its complexity. If it were a physics problem, he would have had a chalkboard in his room filled with equations from top to bottom, with no resolution. Head down, he ripped out the notebook page on which he had been trying to draw a perfect circle without a compass and threw it in the trashcan. The paper landed atop a copy of the morning newspaper folded open to an ad for Famous Barr bras. He went back to the book in his hands, *Good News for Modern Man*, and wrote down a possible passage for his paper:

I do not understand what I do; for I don't do what I would like to do, but instead I do what I hate . . . Who will rescue me from this body that is taking me to death?

There was a knock at the door. Tony burst in grinning, an unlit Camel non-filter in his mouth, and disco-danced over to Patrick. "Hey, bathrobe boy, are you ready?"

Patrick looked over his shoulder. "Ready for what?"

"Life."

Life—the source of all his problems—which along with death, were the two main things for which he was not ready. "I need to stay home tonight."

"No you don't."

Patrick turned back to his book. "Yes, I do. I've made up my mind."

"Your mind! Your mind needs some rest. And you can only find rest in the arms of some beautiful girl, who right now, this very minute, is out there somewhere waiting to meet you. We can't procrastinate." Tony slapped Patrick on the back and leaned over the desk to see what he was writing. "What are you working on? A love letter?"

Patrick closed his notebook and moved his chair around to face Tony. "No. I'm working on a paper."

"On a Friday night?" Tony covered his face with his hands and opened his fingers a crack to peek at Patrick. Poor Patrick. There he was, his face hooded in the bathrobe. He looked pale and feverish. Tony clapped his hands together ready to reason with him, to pry him free from the desk with his animal charm and logic. "What paper?"

"For Father Murphy's class."

"A religion paper? Hell, that's not due for a while. C'mon, really, what are you doing up here? This room stinks." He opened a window and the cool October air swept in, lusty with fallen oak leaves.

"Why are you bothering me? What do you want?" Patrick said.

"What do I want? I want what's good for you."

Patrick laughed. "*You* know what's good for me?"

Tony lit up his cigarette and blew the smoke out the window. "You want one?"

"No thanks. I quit, remember?"

"Oh, I forgot . . . how long?"

"Since last weekend." Patrick stared at the cigarette as Tony took a drag.

"Five days? Ha! A tobacco person should never quit. It will only make you smoke more when you start up again. Here . . ." Tony turned the butt-end of the cigarette and offered it to Patrick.

Patrick turned away from him. "Can't a person change?"

"Only his underwear. Hey, look out the window; The Love Machine is waiting. Remember that time—"

"I remember."

"What were their names?"

"I don't think they gave us their names."

"That was the beauty of it. No names. Just two males and two females . . . a meeting of the species. You in the back with yours; me in the front with mine. They only went *so far*, but it was better than sitting in your room writing a paper . . . on what? What's so important on a Friday night?"

Patrick straightened up his desktop, aligning some books in a neat stack and putting his pen in a cup full of more pens. "I'm trying to write a paper on . . ." Patrick's voice trailed off to a whisper on the last word: ". . . on wisdom."

"Wisdom?!" Tony choked on the cigarette and laughed so hard he leaned on Patrick's dresser to keep from falling over. He yanked open the top drawer. One after another, Tony threw white Fruit of the Loom briefs at Patrick. In seconds, underwear covered the floor and the desk.

"Stop it! You're acting like a fool."

"Hey, we're all fools in the end," Tony said.

"*Another line* you stole from a movie. Don't you want to know for yourself what life is all about?"

The underwear drawer now empty, Tony looked out the window, inhaled the cigarette until it glowed orange and hot. He was getting impatient. He blew the smoke out the window again and came to the point.

"Look, Patrick Cantwell, you need to stop playing with yourself and all these books up here in your room." Tony reached over and plucked the hood from Patrick's head. His shoulder length brown hair fell down, uncombed and sweaty. "Look at you, sipping tea like a monk, when you know you should be out enjoying cold beer and girls. Who do you think you are? St. Aloysius?"

There it was. The problem exactly.

Patrick nodded in agreement. Choir music from a school Mass echoed in his brain, mocking him. Who was he kidding? St. Aloysius, the namesake of their all-boys prep school whose plaster statute stood by the entranceway drinking fountain, gazing at them piously every morning as they arrived. Aloysius, the boy saint, who had renounced his riches and took a vow of virginity, only to die tending Bubonic Plague patients at the age of twenty-three. How did he do it? What was his strength? It seemed everyone else at the school—including Patrick—wanted only to find riches and lose their virginity as soon as possible.

"What do you want?" Patrick asked Tony, his green eyes staring at the underwear dotting the floor.

Tony softened, shrugging. He turned his hands upward to show Patrick he was not trying to be harsh. "Look, man, I don't want to take you away from wisdom and all your studies. I just think that God wants you go with me tonight."

"Ha! He does? Did God phone you? Did he call long distance to send you over here to get me?"

"You know what I mean. . . . God wants to forgive you for everything you've ever done, right?"

"I guess."

"Well, if you never get out of your room and do something big, well, how can you have any proper sins to confess?"

"You're crazy."

"You're right. *And* I'm 'a fool.' But maybe you can learn something for your paper by going out and spending time with me. I'll wrestle you for it." Tony grinned. "Unless you're afraid."

Patrick sprung from his chair, tromped over, and jammed his elbow on the dresser top. Tony stuck the cigarette in his mouth and said, "Now you're talking." He plopped his elbow down next to Patrick's and grabbed his hand. Smoke squiggled up between the two boys.

They were an even match: back and forth, up and down—grunting and squinting at each other through gritted teeth. Tony, still smiling, struggled to pin Patrick's hand onto the dresser. Patrick was winning, but then he began to ease up. Maybe, he thought, it would be useful to see the world on a Friday night. Maybe, just maybe, in the midst of some Friday-night revelry some truth would leap out, perhaps the missing part of his paper. He gave in.

With one last snap, Tony forced Patrick's hand down on the dresser and laughed. Patrick sighed and looked out the window at The Love Machine, a warm harem on wheels waiting in the driveway.

Chapter 3

PATRICK SAVORED a Camel non-filter while Tony drove and they listened to the song "Space Cowboy" throbbing from the dashboard of The Love Machine. He was clean-shaven and combed down now, with nonchalant weekend clothes on—a clean blue-plaid shirt and some khaki pants, and sneakers, along with a windbreaker. The night air from the open car window felt cool and snappy. Still, Patrick felt uneasy. Maybe he should have stayed home, he thought. He felt withdrawn and unable to make small talk with Tony.

"So how is everything?" Tony said, smiling.

"Everything? Whew, there's so much to consider when you include *everything*."

"You know what I mean. How the hell are you?"

Patrick thought deeply for half a block and gave an honest answer. "I have no idea."

"Well, never mind. We'll meet some girls soon."

Tony's plan was to go back to school for the Friday night football game. He hated to go near the place before Monday. "But that's where the girls are," he explained. Girls from all around. Girls looking for guys who know how to chat it up and make them feel at ease. "You know," he'd added, "to lay the ground work for later in the night, when the smart ones will drift to the parties for the beer and sofas and necking. And who knows? There might even be necking at the game." Then he cut his eyes over at Patrick. "Just be yourself; keep it *light*. Be pleasant. Smile. Nod and laugh at their jokes. Girls like that sort of thing."

"OK, I'll try."

When they got to the school, the dark hills surrounding the field were crowded with fans, the field bright as daylight. St. Aloysius was tied 7-7 with Ladue High School. The marching band bellowed from the stands, and the crowd cheered in response. The air was chilly enough to see your breath, which Tony noted was a tactical advantage. They bought a couple of hot chocolates and walked along the crest of the hill looking for girls. Tony spotted two girls wearing Ascending Path Academy sweatshirts sitting on a quilt. He stopped mid-stride. "Target acquired. Ascending Path babes. Nine o'clock."

Patrick stopped and looked. There they were—a blonde and a brunette—two girls from the strict, all-girl school run by nuns, probably hoping to meet some nice boys with good manners. They were both good looking. The brunette had French braids. But the blonde had bigger breasts, which Patrick tried not to notice. "I've always wondered about Ascending Path girls. You know, how their homework load compares to ours."

"Homework load? Forget about homework. Look at the load on that blonde."

As they approached within earshot of the girls, Tony pretended to laugh at something to get their attention, and to announce that someone fun had arrived to save them from a boring evening.

"Ladies, how ya doin'? Who you rootin' for?"

With one eye shut, the blonde looked up at Tony, wondering whether he was from one of the finer zip codes. "Ladue," she said.

"Ladue? So are we," Tony lied, backslapping Patrick's chest. "Mind if we join you on this chilly night? We brought a couple of hot chocolates to share."

"Well, as long as you're from Ladue," the girl in French braids said. She had seen the big homes in Ladue, the kind she'd like to live in some day when she got married. "I guess we can share some hot chocolate. As long as you're not sick."

"Naw, we're burning with health. I'm Tony, and this is Patrick."

The two boys bookended the girls on the quilt, Tony diving next to the blonde.

"Here, have a drink." Tony handed his hot chocolate to the blonde. She whiffed the steam to check for booze or anything weird. Then she looked at Tony, still wary of him. Tony sent out love beams with his brown eyes and flexed his eyebrows.

The girl with the French braids studied Patrick and waited for him to speak.

He was awfully quiet. Just staring at the field. When was he going to say something about her hair she'd spent so much time twisting? She waited.

Patrick held his hot chocolate between his hands and pondered what was before his eyes. The game down on the field. The white yard markers. The rules, the time clock. It must have some deeper meaning. It must be some external expression of man's inner condition. He glanced at the St. Aloysius school building in the background and thought of some of the concepts he'd been studying and how they might apply to the game. *Think, Patrick, think*, he demanded of himself.

"Hey, aren't you going to give me any?" the girl in French braids finally said.

"Sorry . . . here."

"Thank you," she said as she took the cup from Patrick. She brushed his hand on purpose to get his attention. But he didn't seem to notice. Then she looked over to see how her friend was doing with Tony.

Tony's date took a sip of her hot cocoa, leaving a red lipstick mark on the cup. She handed it back to Tony, politely turning it so he wouldn't get her germs. But Tony turned the cup around so that her lipstick mark would face his lips. He was sending a signal that their lips should be together. He drank deeply.

The girl next to Patrick saw what Tony had done, so she pressed her lips onto the cup and smeared a big lipstick mark and thrust the cup back to Patrick, to see what he would do.

"Thank you," he said lifting the cup to his lips— but he paused—wondering what Swiss psychoanalyst Carl Jung might think of the action on the field. Patrick had been reading a book on Jung. He lowered the cup and studied the players jostling and fighting over the ball. Of course! The ball must be some archetype. But what? Maybe the ball represents the self, he thought. *That's it*. Old Jung would be proud of him. The realization made him smile inappropriately as his date was studying his face.

Tony handed the hot chocolate back to the blonde, and watched to see where she would land her lips on the cup. Tony decided if she put her lips where his had been, then that was her signal—that he should kiss her right away. The question was—*What kind of kiss should it be?* He decided on a lips-only kiss. But lots of lips—so she'd know he understood. Oh boy, did he understand. She raised the cup and Tony watched her lips, but just then—

"What's wrong with you?!" the girl next to Patrick said. "Aren't you gonna drink some hot chocolate?"

Everyone paused to look over at Patrick. He was deep in thought, considering that if the ball did, in fact, represent the Jung's concept of the self, the players on opposite teams represented opposing forces in a person's life, the ones trying to control the self. Sometimes the good team you're rooting for controls the self, and other times, the bad team grabs the ball and takes the self in a different direction. It was a tense game . . .

"Hey Patrick! Drink some damned hot chocolate," Tony said leaning over the girls to jab his knee.

"Sorry," he said, absentmindedly drinking from the very spot where the girl with French braids had laid her lipstick mark. Her pupils widened with desire.

Tony's date drank from the same spot where Tony's lips had been, and no sooner did she lower her cup, when Tony's lips met hers, pulsing and puckering, pleading for her to get in the game, to run across the field, to tackle him. She dropped her cup and they sank back onto the hillside quilt kissing.

Patrick's date saw what was happening, so she grabbed the cup from his hands and drank from the same spot where his lips had been. She closed her eyes and lowered the cup from her lips, waiting for his lips to find her.

But Patrick didn't notice any of this. His eyes were fixed on the Ladue coach, an older man, who was yelling obscenities from the sidelines. Patrick wondered: What if the players on the field—the ones suffering to control the self—think they are doing what *they want*, but really they are just being controlled by the coaches? Perhaps all of society was being coached along, by the priests, the bosses and generals yelling from the sidelines. But who's to say the coaches are right? Why, think of the Soviet May Day parade with the troops marching beside long erect missiles, a kind of pep rally before the game. How can any of us know at any moment that the thing we "want" for ourselves is our own idea? It was troubling.

"Hey, shithead, snap out of it!" Patrick's date said, snapping her fingers right in front of his face.

"I'm sorry . . . what?"

Tony and his date stopped necking and bolted upright. Tony thought maybe Patrick had grabbed the girl's breasts too soon.

"What did he do?" Tony said.

"Nothing!" Patrick's date said, throwing the rest of the hot chocolate on the grass. "This guy's on pot or something. I thought he was watching the game, but he's not even reacting to what's happening on the field."

They all looked at Patrick. He knew he had to fake some awareness of the game. Fast. Just then, a St. Aloysius player ran the ball out of bounds and tumbled into a row of Ladue tuba players. Patrick clapped, as if it were a great play. "Way to go, St. Al, *Whoooooo Hoooooo!*"

The girls looked at each other, and then at Tony.

"I thought you were Ladue guys," the blonde said. "You said you were rooting for Ladue."

The girl in French braids raised her nose up. "Yeah, where do you go to school?"

"Why, right over there," Patrick said pointing to St. Aloysius.

Both girls stood up.

"Get off the damn quilt," Patrick's date said.

Patrick and Tony stood up, and the girl's snatched their quilt and walked away to the other side of the hill in search of Ladue guys.

The game ended. The marching band played, and the cheerleaders ran out onto the field. Patrick looked at the field and thought of how in the winter it would all be covered with snow and quiet. The events of the game by then would be meaningless and forgotten.

"Well, crap," Tony said. "Patrick, you're not yourself tonight."

"I know, I'm sorry. My mind—"

"Forget your mind. We need to find a party and drink."

Chapter 4

TONY FOLLOWED a caravan of cars winding through the streets of Ladue, not knowing where he was going, but hoping some great party lay ahead. He was right. The Love Machine idled behind a row of sports cars on a street of enormous lawns, an enclave of mansions with lighted columns, manicured shrubs, and gurgling fountains. This was not a street where you had to turn off the bathroom faucet while you brushed your teeth. You could let the water run down the drain until it was time to spit, with no concern for cost. Tony parked the car and they got out. Rock music and laughter from a crowd in the distance filled the air, along with the scent of a bonfire and the bouquet of chlorine from swimming pools out there somewhere in the night.

"God, isn't it all beautiful?" Tony beamed.

"Yes, it is," Patrick agreed, looking around as they walked toward the music. He thought of his paper and wondered what St. Aloysius might think walking toward this party, maybe in his early days when he was struggling with whether to give up his riches. Not a stone of these mansions will be left unturned, young St. Al would think. Yes, someday the swimming pools will all be drained, and the laughter and music will stop. They'll be throwing their oil paintings in the street and begging for bread.

"With these Ladue babes, you have to play like all of this is nothing," Tony said.

"All of this is nothing," Patrick repeated blankly.

"That's right. That's a good attitude. We'll do all right. I can tell."

Tony breathed deeply, while admiring the lawn as they walked up the long blacktop driveway to the mansion. They walked around a three-car garage and under an arching trellis of roses into the backyard. A harvest of teenagers, the restless rich, filled the rolling hills, hundreds of them, everyone holding beers or smokes. There was a rock band playing under a tent. The silhouettes of girls dancing by the bonfire gyrated to the music.

Tony grabbed a burning cold can of beer from a tub filled with ice, drank it straight down, then pulled out three more. He tossed one to Patrick, opened his second, and put the extra one in his back pocket. They walked along through the crowd not knowing anyone, Tony bobbing his head to the music. The band cranked out "I Can't Get No Satisfaction" by The Rolling Stones as Patrick followed Tony toward the glow of the swimming pool lit beneath the water, the surface calm as glass. Three girls sat at a pool patio lounge table, their eyes flickering in the shimmer of orange candle jars on the table. They were playing a card game and drinking wine from a bottle.

"Hello, ladies! What's the game?" Tony said, finishing his second beer.

The girls looked at each other and then back at Tony.

Then the girl dressed all in black—silky black blouse, slacks, and black riding boots—stared at Tony as she shuffled the cards. "Strip poker." Tony caught his breath as the girl slung her long, black hair over her shoulder. "Whoever gets naked first has to jump in the pool."

Tony laughed, stalling for time, thinking that maybe they were just bluffing to flirt with him because of his muscles. "Is the water cold?"

"No, it's heated."

"OK, deal us in," he kidded. He took his third beer from his back pocket and sat down. "I'm Tony, and this is Patrick."

They all nodded, but didn't give their names. Patrick didn't sit down, but stood and watched.

"The game's five card stud." The girl in black started dealing. "Sunglasses, shoes, watches, and belts don't count, only fabric items."

"I didn't know you were serious. Hey, Patrick, sit down," Tony said, "These girls are after our fabric."

"I'd better not. I'm no good at poker."

"That's all right. Poker is a game of chance, not skill . . . right ladies?"

The girls laughed and looked at their cards. Tony re-arranged his cards, as if he had something great. "It's not fair for a man of my skills to take advantage of three delicate ladies like you," Tony said. Patrick peeked over Tony's shoulder at his cards. He had nothing. "Give me three," he said confidently. As Patrick wandered away, Tony was playing his first hand. For the time being, he was wearing four fabric items: his black t-shirt, jeans, his underwear, and socks.

There must be some truth here tonight, Patrick thought, as he wandered through the crowd. Something I could see that's hidden in the open, something for my paper. He drank more of his beer and walked through groves of girls, making sure to keep his head down to avoid temptation, just as St. Aloysius would have done. Ah, but their scent, he could smell them, their perfume and shampoo, and the sweet drinks on their breath in the night air. Still, he focused on the beer can in his own hand. The fine print on the logo intrigued him. Thank God for the printed word . . . for linear type. Thank God for language, the saver of civilization, the handing down of wisdom from generation to generation. He pulled the can closer to his face and tried to read the tiny letters to learn what they said, but it was too dark. That made him wonder: What if each beer can were like a fortune cookie—only true—with a unique message divinely printed for you at the factory, telling you exactly what you needed to know that night? Oh, if it were only that easy. Patrick walked closer to the house to catch some light from the windows, so he could read the message that had been prepared for him at the brewery. This would be the answer to every question bothering him.

You have chosen von Bierhart beer. No other brand worldwide can compare. Our patented Black Forest bark brewing technique makes von Bierhart beer the most delicious, thirst-quenching, and satisfying beer ever to touch the palate of man on Earth. Zum Wohl!"

"Worthless," he said, "worthless." He drank the rest of his beer and looked around for a trashcan.

"You seem to be lost . . . or looking for something," a voice from somewhere said.

He looked toward the house. Standing there, backlit in the sliding glass, basement door, was a fat man in black pants and a red sports coat—the man of the house.

"Come in for a visit," he said, "I want to tell you something."

Patrick looked back behind himself. "Me?"

"Yeah, kid, you."

Probably some drunk with war stories, he thought. What message could he have? Patrick started to pivot toward the pool, but he saw Tony was now shirt-less and none of the girls he was playing with had lost one single piece of fabric. He turned back toward the house and went in.

"Come in," the fat man said, sliding the door closed. Patrick took in his surroundings. The basement was finished with a red shag rug, a leather sofa, and matching chairs. To one side of the room was a bar, where two teenaged guys were mixing liquor. To the other side sat a magnificent mahogany floor TV, the sound off, but the screen lit with a show about the Pyramids in living color. In the center of the room, a girl with thick glasses sat, her hands flying over the keys of a cherry, baby grand piano, its lid up. Boogie-woogie shook the room.

The man motioned to the sofa. "Have a seat. How about a drink?"

"No, thank you."

"I insist."

The guys behind the bar brought both him and the fat man vodka martinis, dressed with olives. Patrick's first ever.

"What's all this about?" Patrick said taking a tentative sip. It was warm and soothing, like cough syrup on a desperate night.

"I was looking out the window at all the youth . . . enjoying their revelry, forgetting their problems, when I saw you, a boy immersed in his problems."

"Well, I was just thinking—"

"Don't even tell me what it was, because the answer is the same to all such questions young men have." The fat man took a swig and chuckled with con-fidence.

Patrick tested him. "What kind of questions do you mean?"

"You know . . . Who am I? What should I do with my life? How will I find true love? The usual questions."

Patrick took a sip and nodded to humor him. "So the answer is the same?"

"Yes."

The boogie-woogie piano player was filling the room with seventh chords, and lost loves and disappointments laid out like railroad tracks.

"So what's the answer?"

He held up his glass in a toast. "It'll all work out." Then the fat man took a deep gulp and studied Patrick's reaction.

"I'm afraid it's not so simple as that. I'm afraid—"

"Don't be afraid. You see, you gave yourself away with your own words. You're *afraid*, and of what? Life, death, homework, sex? Don't be. It's all nothing." He started laughing and coughing, then drank a slosh of his martini to settle down.

"Well, thank you for the advice and the drink, and now I must be going." Patrick got up.

"Sit down! I haven't told you the secret yet."

"The secret?"

"Yeah, the secret."

Patrick sat down and the fat man looked over at the guys behind the bar and wagged his head toward Patrick's glass. One of them came over with a pitcher and refilled his martini, which was still mostly full, and then the fat man's.

"Let me tell you what I know," he began. He paused to call out to the piano player. "Hey, Hathorn, play something pretty."

She stopped playing and looked over at him blankly. "What'd you want?"

"The St. Louis Blues . . . and sing it. I know you can sing it."

The piano player shrugged and sang the lyrics like she was the star attraction on the *Goldenrod Showboat*.

"Now, what's this secret you're talking about?" Patrick asked.

The fat man put down his drink on the coffee table and looked Patrick in the eyes. The girl with the glasses continued playing the St. Louis Blues, Patrick slowly sipping his martini, while the fat man weaved the story of growing up poor, in a coal-heated house, with only a high school education, and now, here he sat in one of the finest mansions in the county, at ease, in comfort, listening to good music.

"You want to know how I got here?" he asked.

"How?"

"By opening the yellow pages."

"I really have to go."

"No, wait; here's the secret—I opened the yellow pages one day at random and just took a chance. I put my finger blindly on an ad for some company and went there to ask them for a job. I've been at it ever since."

"What job?"

He leaned forward with pride and pointed to the TV. "Selling Magnavox TVs."

Patrick glanced at the TV. An Egyptian princess was bathing in the Nile. She was beautiful. Patrick looked back at the fat man who was still talking. "I worked my way up from nothing, and now I own four stores. Don't you see? Don't you understand? It's all chance . . . and hard work, but you have to take a chance."

The two guys tending bar went over to the piano and started to sing with the girl quite loudly.

Patrick downed the rest of his martini and rose to give his rebuttal. He was determined to counter this nihilism with clear Jesuit logic. He felt dizzy and the rug seemed to sponge beneath his sneakers.

"That can't be right. I was always told that God has a plan for our lives, and our mission is to discover it somehow." He had to shout over the piano player and the singers, whose voices drowned out his own. "You make it sound like there's no design. Why, if I wanted to fall in love, I suppose I could just walk out there and kiss the first girl who says hello and she'd be the one, just by chance."

The fat man clapped his hands and smiled in delight. "That's it! You've got it. That's exactly what I'm saying. You go out there and kiss the first girl who says hello and I'll watch from the window."

"No . . . thanks . . . I have to go." Patrick turned and started to walk toward the door, but the fat man grabbed his arm.

"Don't be afraid of chance. You're a student. Think of this as a project. Just go out there and prove me wrong. I'll be watching from the window while you prove me wrong. Unless, that is . . . *you're afraid.*"

Patrick's face burned red hot. "Afraid?! I'm not afraid to show you there's more to life than Yellow Pages and Magnavox TV's. Just watch. I'll kiss the first babe who says hello."

They shook on it and Patrick staggered out into the night, the chilled air cooling his face. The fat man rocked three times like an elephant before he was able to get up from his leather chair. As Patrick walked away from the house, the man leaned on the sliding glass door, watching. Patrick kept his head down, like St. Aloysius, knowing that no girl would say hello to him with his head down. He took about ten steps when he bumped into a girl. Her drink sloshed onto her pants leg. "Dumb shit!" she said. Shocked, Patrick looked up. Right into her eyes. This was it, he thought. She was going to say hello. "Why don't you watch where you're going?" she snapped.

Looking back down, Patrick said, "Sorry," and kept on walking. All he could see were legs, some bare, some covered in pants, and shoes, such cute little sneakers with white laces on the feet of the young ladies probably all on the verge of saying hello. Whole grape clusters of girls waiting to be picked. That's when he realized this could be great material for his paper. He could prove the fat man wrong, and write a paragraph on the experience.

But, when he reached the pool and looked up in search of Tony, he spotted trouble.

20

Chapter 5

TONY WAS NAKED. Almost. He was only wearing his black speedo under-wear. There he sat by the pool, at the strip poker table, with three, fully-clothed girls. Evidently, he had been losing steadily. Beside him, neatly folded on the pool deck were his pants, shirt, and socks. As Patrick learned, Tony would have been naked and tossed into the pool already—were it not for having won an argument over his socks counting as two separate items of fabric. He won this argument by chance, because on this particular night, Tony had worn two socks that didn't match.

Patrick approached Tony and tried to see his cards, but they were cupped tightly in his grip.

"Hey, Tony, you ready to go?"

"You kidding? You're just in time to see me win."

"Show your cards," the girl dealer said.

"I will, I will. But first, I want to raise the bet." Patrick looked at Tony again to see what he was wearing. Nothing but those fool black speedos.

The three girls at the table traded grins. "You haven't got anymore clothes on to raise the bet," the dealer said.

Tony pointed to Patrick. "I'll bet his clothes, too. Both of us. Against all of you . . . and your clothes. That's fair."

Patrick took a step back, but Tony grabbed his arm and pulled him over to look at his hand. Patrick saw Tony was holding four kings, four beautifully solid, steady-eyed kings with an eight high. The girls saw Patrick's reaction. Two of them folded, but the dealer hung in. "So, if you lose," she said, "both you and your friend have to jump in the pool naked . . . that's the bet, right?"

"I'm not playing the game," Patrick said. "Let's just go."

Tony turned to Patrick with the stare of a twin, arguing, warning, *begging* him to yield. Patrick was disgusted with Tony, ashamed of Tony, ready to walk away from Tony. But how could he? He was Tony. They were a unit of shared disasters. "This will be the stupidest thing we've ever done."

"We can't lose."

"Are you in?" the dealer asked Patrick.

Patrick nodded OK.

"We're in," Tony said to the dealer, "but just so you know the bet, if you lose, you have to take off all your clothes and jump in the pool, right?"

She nodded.

A crowd of onlookers had gathered, hearing the stakes, including the dealer's older brother, a tall guy with perfectly trimmed yellow hair and wearing a green shirt with the letters VB monogramed above his heart.

"Wait a minute," he said to his sister. "Show me your hand first."

"I play my own hand."

The whole crowd turned their heads to see how the older brother would handle her.

"Virginia, you always do," he said, shaking his head.

"Show your cards," she said to Tony.

Tony laid down his kings one at a time, like thousand dollar bills in a homeless camp. He was so proud. "Try'n beat that!"

The dealer blinked. Everyone watched for her hand. But she held it shut and pushed back her chair. The metal legs squeaked across the patio rock. She stood up and walked over to Tony to show her cards, but Patrick was in the way. She looked him in the eye with a get-the-hell out of the way look and tossed in a sarcastic "hello."

She had said hello. He had to kiss her now.

Patrick's blood jolted. He looked back at the house, the fat man watching in the basement doorway. Patrick hated to do it. She was so annoyingly pretty, her matching black blouse and slacks, her black hair and high cheekbones, her blue eyes bored with looking every day in the mirror at such beauty and symmetry, a slave to her biology, a girl trapped in fashion. His entire sermon of pity and disinterest poured into her from his split-second glance, and before she knew it, he grabbed her in his arms, tilted her back, and kissed her. The crowd erupted in cheers. The fat man at the window danced. Patrick let her go. A fist slammed into his cheek. The dealer's brother.

"What the hell you doing?" the brother shouted.

Patrick teetered and regained his balance. "Nothing."

"Do you even *know* my sister?"

Patrick looked at her again, only for a second, but the answer was in her eyes: They were a couple. How could this be? A strange circle was drawn around them and they were inside it together, inside a quiet, calm, and warm circle. He felt separated with her from the crowd on the patio, from everybody he ever met, even Tony. It was the kind of feeling they write songs about. Something had happened that every teenager who ever went to a party wants: to meet someone who would erase your earlier existence as a bland preparation for this moment. This was not some distant, improbable heaven. This was real happiness. Right now. Real happiness. Something had happened. They were a couple.

"Where the hell you go to high school?" the brother asked Patrick.

"St. Aloysius."

"No wonder! You and this guinea don't belong here." The older brother wound up to punch Patrick again—but before he could swing—Tony leaped to his feet winding up to punch. But before Tony could swing—the girl Patrick had kissed dropped her cards and punched her brother—a lightening shot to the eye that knocked him in the pool with a big splash.

"You ruin everything!" she shouted, jumping in after him.

The crowd rushed to the pool's edge to watch the brother and sister fight, thrashing and splashing in the lighted, blue water. Patrick jabbed Tony to leave. "Let's get out of here!"

Tony was furious; his nostrils flared. "Are you kidding? We won!" Tony, in his black speedo, dropped down on his knees, searching for the cards she had dropped. Beer slopped on him from above as he yanked cards from beneath people's shoes, checking each card, adding them up. *Damn!* She had a straight flush. That beats four kings. It only took Tony seconds to get up, grab his clothes, and backslap Patrick on his arm. "Maybe we should go now."

Patrick glanced one more time toward the pool as the girl pulled herself up the ladder, black clothes dripping. He wanted to stay. Instead, hot on Tony's heals, he turned and ran all the way to The Love Machine. Tony jumped behind the wheel, started the engine, and raced up the street.

"You're going the wrong way!" Patrick yelled.

"I know the way. Just watch . . . nobody's gonna call me a guinea."

Tony drove The Love Machine forty-miles-an-hour. In reverse. Up the driveway. Onto the lawn. Then stopped. Tony put the car in neutral, floored the pedal, and grinned at Patrick as the engine smoked and whined and trembled. Then he shifted into gear. It was the most beautiful lawn job Tony would ever give—all heart, well deserved, fifty feet long, the grass stripped down to the mud.

Patrick looked in his side-view mirror and saw her.

Wet hair and wet black clothes clinging to her body.

She stood in the exhaust and watched them race away.

The Love Machine skipped onto the street, losing a hubcap as they bounced over the curb and drove off into the night.

Patrick sat stunned and shaky. Tony, suddenly very hungry, craved something hot and tasty.

Chapter 6

THEY GOT A BAG of White Castle cheeseburgers and ate them in the car as they drove along toward the next party. Fully clothed again, Tony tossed the empty little boxes out the window, one after the other. Patrick put his empty boxes in the bag to throw away later in a trashcan. They said nothing for several miles, only eating and listening to the song on the radio—"The Tennessee Stud." The Love Machine heater warmed their feet, and the cool autumn air blew in the open windows.

"Nothing like salt and grease and chopped-up onions to revive a man and help him think clearly," Tony said. Then he burped.

Patrick was quiet. He kept thinking about the girl. He'd really kissed her.

"And how about that lawn job?" Tony beamed, "a triumph for me . . . and The Italian People everywhere."

Patrick held some ice from his soda on his cheekbone where the girl's brother punched him. He tried to laugh at Tony's jokes. But he knew what was coming. Tony was probably saving it for dessert. He would launch into a big discussion of the girl he had kissed.

Finally, Tony punched Patrick proudly on the arm. "I can't believe you did it."

"What?"

"What? You know what. That girl you kissed. Why'd you do that?"

Patrick ran his hand through his hair, raking his fingernails across his scalp. "I don't know. It was nothing." He wanted to tell Tony what fantastic things he had seen in her eyes, and what he had felt for her. But it was too dangerous to tell Tony anything like that. He would make an opera out of it and tell everyone.

"Nothing? Don't brag. You'll be thinking of her tonight, up there in your room with your books . . . Damn, man, do you know who she was?"

Patrick ate a greasy french fry and gave Tony a shrug. "I don't know. Who?"

Tony stuck out his lower lip and nodded like an appraiser holding a million dollar diamond. "That girl was VVB!"

"Who?"

Tony veered the car around a curve, tires squealing just as he missed a black cat running across the road. "Virginia von Bierhart, you idiot! You know, von Bierhart beer! You kissed VVB!"

Patrick held the ice to his face. He'd heard stories about her. She was the daughter of the brewery baron, Hugo von Bierhart. When other guys had caught a glimpse of her on the highway behind the wheel of her black Corvette convertible with the VVB license plate, they honked to get her attention, but she only gave them the finger and raced off.

Patrick's mother had also once talked about a VVB news story in the paper. She'd been arrested for riding horseback naked—totally naked, and drunk—along Ladue Road at two o'clock in the morning. But because she was rich, the charges were reduced to riding a horse after dark without proper reflective gear. The von Bierharts were royalty, fourth generation St. Louisans from Bavaria, and Virginia was the wildcat of the family.

Patrick replayed the kiss in his mind, her full lips, her gentle frame bending back in his embrace, her smooth blouse rustling his forearms. What a kiss. But what a stupid thing to have done. Not only guzzling martinis with the fat man, but kissing a girl at random. Kissing Virginia von Bierhart. What a fool. Patrick's knees were knocking. He felt as if part of her spirit was still in the car with him, and part of his was still with her, five miles back. Hell, if Tony turned the car around to go back for more card playing, he wouldn't argue.

"You want to go back and get her number?" Tony said laughing.

Patrick choked on a french fry.

Tony laughed. "Ha! We better not, I guess, after my lawn job."

Patrick sighed. "I don't want to ever see her again."

"Don't worry, you will."

"No. I won't. I'll make sure I won't. Besides, she'll forget about it, a girl like her."

"She won't forget. Not in her whole life. Did you see the look she gave you after you kissed her?"

Patrick lied. "No, I didn't. I got punched, remember?" Patrick dug out more ice from his cup and dabbed it on the bruise, eager to hear Tony's full-blown observation, but he was careful not to act too interested. "She was probably bored."

"She wasn't bored. Man, she gave you *the look*."

Patrick scrunched his whole body around in the seat to face Tony. "What look?"

"*The look . . . the look . . .* damn. She wants you."

Patrick faked laughing and asked Tony to pull over so he could pee. He'd heard enough. Time to change the subject.

Tony pulled over and they both peed on some bushes in front of a ranch house while The Love Machine idled at the curb.

"What'd you think of that football game tonight? Our defense was solid—"

"Forget *that* . . . It was a definite look," Tony lectured as he peed. "She was bored with me and all my words, even with me in my underwear. But then you come up and without even speaking, grabbed her and kissed her. That was brilliant. She sure wasn't ready for you. Now she's after you. She'll track you down. So, you'll have to be ready for your big chance."

"My big chance?"

"Yeah, I'm pretty sure she's a non-Catholic. She seems educated." Tony flexed his eyebrows. Patrick thought of the possibilities, how wonderful, but how awful, the dark forces he had dabbled in by taking the fat man's advice. Perhaps the devil and the fat man and VVB were all working together to lay a trap for him so his soul would come to ruin. The devil was sure to laugh at him. "You damned fool!" he'd say. Damn fool is right.

A barking dog spotted them around the side of the house where they had stopped, and a porch light came on. They zipped up and ran for the car. Tony teasing Patrick as they drove off. "Maybe you'll marry right. Hey, I could swim at your pool someday."

"You can't tell anyone."

"Wha—?"

"You can't." Patrick shoved his hand toward Tony. "Shake on it."

After a minute, Tony said, "This pains me, you know." But he reached over and shook Patrick's hand. He crossed the fingers on his other hand as he gripped the steering wheel.

Kevin Killeen

Tony whistled as they drove off, headed to a quiet party with old friends from the parish—all guys—to drink some more beer.

Chapter 7

BACK IN WEBSTER GROVES, where white gravel driveways dotted with weeds led to old houses in need of paint, but full of children, Tony parked The Love Machine on the street and they got out. They walked behind a garage whose backside faced the Missouri Pacific train tracks. They were now in Walsh Country. That's what everyone called the spot behind the garage where Dan Walsh played his guitar around a campfire and everyone drank and talked. The last party of the night was always at Walsh Country.

Parish teens drunk from other parties always stopped by on their way home to prolong the night. As Tony and Patrick walked in the dark to the party, they saw the Gang of Five was there. Bobby Jones, Jimmy Purvis, Steve Bicks, Brian McClandon, and Buck Wilson—five grade school friends who ran away together in the fifth grade. Their escape had made them grade school heroes, boys more alive and sure of themselves than other boys back then who didn't run away. But, that was long ago.

Now they were all in captivity Monday through Friday at various all-boy Catholic prep schools. Life was hard. Get up before dawn, carpool to school, go to classes—algebra, English, western civilization, chemistry, biology, and, of course, religion. And, man, did the Jesuits pile on the homework. At least two hours a night. Sometimes four. The guys all knew they had to make good grades because the parents were bleeding money for the tuition at these schools. After school hours the guys all worked jobs at gas stations, McDonalds, cutting lawns, or raking leaves. Life was work.

Except on the weekends. Life was beer—beer and girls. But the girls were all Catholic, too. Girls with nuns and uniforms in their lives, careful and chaste girls. Girls with toothbrushes in their purses to scrub away their party breath before they went home in time for curfew.

"What? No girls?" Tony piped in as they approached the group of all guys sitting on tree stumps around a campfire in a grassy area beside the train tracks.

"Left at eleven. Curfew. Damned curfew."

Tony just nodded as he and Patrick snatched a beer from the cooler and took a seat with the gang. Dan Walsh, his hair hanging down to his shoulders, was playing "Folsom Prison Blues" on his acoustic guitar. All the guys were intent on the words. It was a song about a guy locked up in prison who wished he was out. And that's the way it felt, Tony thought. For all their homework, moral training, and attempts at hedonism—none of them felt free. Time dragged on and on and on. So, they drank, and they drank some more, and listened to one sad song after another.

"Play something happy, Walsh," Bobby Jones complained. "It's Friday night. Why should we feel so sad?"

"The problem is our sperm count is at an all time high," Tony said.

Two or three of the guys spit-sprayed their beer, laughing.

Everyone looked at Tony. There he sat calmly on a tree stump, like a man who had ripped a hole in the sky and was about to re-arrange the planets. If there was one thing they never discussed, it was their sperm count. But Tony *had* been studying the problem for some time now, and had been collecting and comparing information as he went from biology class to religion class to psychology class. And now, a picture emerged. He took a long swig of beer and laid out the lesson.

"Look, we know from religion class that you're not supposed to have sex until you're married. Or, for that matter, even look at a girl. But nobody can do that," Tony said. "Now, the way I see it—"

"Wait, *which one* can nobody do?" Jimmy Purvis interrupted.

"My point exactly!" Tony said, "Give me another beer."

Patrick sat on the outskirts of the group, still thinking of Virginia von Bierhart, while looking down the tracks, and listening to Tony. He drank another beer.

"Look at the facts of life," Tony continued, "in biology class, they say our sperm count as teenagers is higher than the whole rest of the male population, but then down the hall in religion class, what do they tell us? They tell us there's more to life than having an orgasm."

Dan Walsh quit strumming his guitar. "Bullshit. Did they really say that in class . . . in those words?"

"Those were the *exact* words this old Jesuit told us, and easy for him, he's about sixty! He hasn't got any sperm left to count."

They all fidgeted, and Tony opened his beer and expounded on what he had learned in his sophomore year. "Our biology dee-*mands* that we have sex. And who invented our biology? God! God wants us to have sex when our bodies are interested so that we'll be happy, and, of course, to keep humanity going. And that's the way it was for centuries. Take the Middle Ages, for instance, say, back in feudal times . . . guys like us were already married and having sex all the time, because it was an agrarian society."

"A what?" Buck Wilson asked.

"Agrarian, you know, all farms, no industry."

Patrick thought of Virginia von Bierhart and how much easier it would have been if they had met in feudal times. Why, they could get married right away and she could ride horseback naked around the farm. Patrick would come home from the fields and she'd be there waiting for him, and they could have sex whenever they wanted to. No papers to type out. No reading assignments.

"It was the Industrial Age that ruined us," Tony argued. "In the beginning, God created man and a woman—not man and a factory."

"You're full of shit," Jimmy Purvis said. "The Industrial Age gave us chemicals, and medicine and electricity and cars. . . . The Middle Ages sucked!"

Tony lit up a Camel non-filter and nodded thoughtfully. The blast of a freight train horn sounded off in the distance, coming their way. Tony continued to defend his position.

"OK, so some good came of it. I like electricity and cars, but what has the Industrial Age done for your sperm count? Nothing! Nothing but made you wait about eight years longer, until after college, when society says you're ready to get a job and start a family. That's not right. We're like a freight train loaded with cargo. We have to deliver the cargo or the whole train could derail. And that's bad for business and bad for the railroad."

The freight train came around the corner, lighting the trees. The guys waived at the engineer and he waved back, probably wishing he was drinking beer and watching a train go by, instead of drinking coffee all night and worrying about cars on the crossings, and missing his wife he hadn't seen in Omaha for four days.

Unable to talk over the racket of the train, the boys stared at the tanker cars loaded with cargo, rocking back and forth, a "flammable" warning label on every tanker.

Dan Walsh started strumming blues chords on his guitar in rhythm with the train. Some guys started clapping to the beat. Patrick watched the train wheels racing, and shook his head. Maybe Tony was right—the Industrial Age was at odds with biology, and every teenaged boy was doomed to wait, wait, wait. Maybe God understood the times, just like Tony said. So, what was wrong with obeying your biology? Especially if you felt some higher attraction to a girl as a person—the way he had felt after he kissed Virginia von Bierhart. He replayed the kiss and the look in her eyes as best as he could remember them. Man, what a couple they were already . . . how far could it go? This was beyond sex. How could he throw her away? And for what would he be giving her up? For the Industrial Age? But then his mother's voice whispered to him from the clacking wheels of the passing train. "Don't be a damned fool, Patrick. You can wait."

Patrick drank some more beer. Maybe his mother was right. Why can't a guy in the Industrial Age wait until his wedding night? Can't a modern guy forget about girls and think only of good things—sports, homework, and preparing for the ACT?

Tony finished his beer. He stood up in full optimism for the future and made an announcement loud enough to be heard over the train.

"Guys, I don't know about you, but I've decided. I need to be happy . . . and I can't be happy waiting. I need to have sex before marriage."

"You need a girlfriend first," Bobby Jones said.

Everyone laughed at Tony, flicked lit cigarettes at him, threw empty beer cans at him. Everyone but Patrick, who was staring at the campfire, thinking.

Jimmy Purvis slapped Patrick on the shoulder, laughing. "Hey, what about you?" he shouted over the train, "Are you going to have sex before marriage?"

Patrick poked at the fire with a stick and gave a shrug. "I'll probably just have to wait until my wedding night."

Just then *BOOM*! And then metal crunching against metal. No more than a mile up the line, the engine had struck an empty Ford Pinto stalled on the Gore Avenue crossing. Then like dominoes, the freight cars slammed into each other, *BAM, BAM, BAM*! The petroleum tankers, one after another, skipped off the tracks, sparking a row of fireballs barreling straightaway toward the party.

"Run for your lives!" Jimmy Purvis shouted.

Dan Walsh dropped his guitar. They all dropped their beers. The boys rounded the front of the garage just in time to see an orange mushroom cloud spew upwards above the roofline. No one was hurt. But, Walsh Country was never the same after that. It was no good for relaxing anymore. The train wreck caused a big mess a mile long with fire engines, cranes—and insurance forms. It was a bad night for the railroad.

After watching the disaster for a while, the guys looked at their watches. Time to make midnight curfew. Friday night was over. So, they all went home to lie alone in their own beds and think about the girls they had seen that night. Maybe Saturday night would bring some happiness.

Chapter 8

VIRGINIA von BIERHART rode her favorite horse Applesauce, the one she had once ridden naked along Ladue Road. Only this morning, she kept to the trails inside the white wooden fence that surrounded the family estate. It was a sunny October Saturday, shining with yellow and orange leaves. She wore a smart outfit: brown riding boots and beige riding pants, a yellow sweater, and a tan, corduroy sports coat. Her ponytail bounced as she rode, and she viewed the world through a new pair of sepia-toned sunglasses that made the present seem like an old Kodak snapshot from the past.

Applesauce sensed something was different, because Virginia hadn't kissed him good morning in the stable, and she didn't talk to him as they rode. She rode Applesauce like he was just a horse. Virginia's mind was on the guy who had kissed her last night, and the strange things she had felt when they looked in each other's eyes. She galloped up the final slope toward the stable, through a field of pet elk and buffalo, grazing in bored captivity. She trotted into the walking pen and dismounted. The old stable keeper took the reins and walked Applesauce around in circles to settle his heart.

Inside the house, Virginia's brother, Nelson, the one she had punched into the pool, sat in a dark corner of the living room in his pajamas and mono-gramed bathrobe, with an ice bag on his eye. "She needs to be punished," he told his parents, who stood by the leaded glass window watching Virginia walk toward the house. "I could've drowned."

"All right, Nelson. We'll handle this now." Mr. von Bierhart said.

"Don't let her always get away with this shit. She needs to be grounded for about a month," Nelson said, getting up.

"That's enough, Nelson," said Mrs. von Bierhart, "Your father and I will do the parenting." She sipped her coffee and rested the china cup from one of their carefree trips to Europe back down on the saucer.

Nelson stomped upstairs.

Virginia's parents waited for her. With the sunlight streaming onto the Persian rug between them, and the gold mantel clock with the tiny beer-bottle counterweights chiming ten bells, Mr. and Mrs. von Bierhart took their positions in the big leather chairs. On the wall behind Mr. von Bierhart, a stuffed owl, its talons curled open, as if ready for attack, perched on its makeshift branch.

Mr. von Bierhart wore his Saturday suit, and had just returned home from an eight o'clock strategy session with the marketing team at the brewery. Mrs. von Bierhart was already dressed for a brunch. Her purse and keys ready to go. The couple listened as Virginia came in the back door singing "When Will I See You Again." They heard her rooting around the kitchen and called her in.

"Virginia, please come see us right now," her mother said. Virginia walked in holding a big glass of milk, looking at them through her sunglasses. "Isn't it a beautiful today?" she said.

"Young lady—"

"If it's about punching Nelson, you're right. I owe him an apology. I shouldn't've done that." She drank her full glass of milk and sighed. "I just guess I went a little crazy. I'll go tell him now right now." She started to leave, but Mr. von Bierhart slapped his knees.

"This meeting is not adjourned, young lady."

She stopped and looked at her father. Her father who was always at work. Her father who never had time to help her with homework. Her father who never went to her games or shot baskets in the driveway with her. Or just have fun with her. No wonder her best friend was a horse. Her dad's face was pulsing red. Just like the time he'd slapped her for riding the horse naked.

"Please take off those damned sunglasses in the house and sit down," he said. His voice was pointed, but he was trying to stay calm. He didn't want any more violence.

Virginia looked at her mother, who nodded at the little wooden chair with the carved back chair facing them, letting Virginia know she should sit.

OK, I can do this, she thought. I can sit through another lecture, maybe get yelled at . . . or grounded. No problem. I can sit here and think of *him*, the guy who kissed me last night. She sat down and put her empty milk glass next to her chair on the rug.

Mrs. von Bierhart flinched and stared at the glass, the latest in a series of ten-thousand glasses, cups, plates, and ice cream spoons Virginia had left all over the house her entire childhood. "Don't forget . . . to put that in the dishwasher when we're finished," Mrs. von Bierhart said.

Virginia nodded OK to her mother and looked back at her father, who was pursing his lips and narrowing his eyes to the rhythm of the clock. Virginia knew what was coming. He looked that way when he was about to dispense his fury on a secretary calling from the brewery.

"Virginia, I've just come from the brewery. Do you have any idea what VB shares are trading for these days?"

She shrugged.

Her father got up and began to pace about beneath a large framed lithograph of the brewery from the 1890s that depicted a bird's eye view of the empire, the red brick castle-like buildings with chimneys puffing white smoke, locomotives hauling away beer, and horse and wagons trotting beer barrels off to thirsty neighborhood taverns.

"VB shares are wavering, and if we're not careful, we could be vulnerable to a takeover someday." He paused to remove his handkerchief from his pocket and swab some dust off the gold leaf frame girdling the brewery.

"Hugo!" Mrs. von Bierhart jumped in, "I thought we we're going to talk with Virginia about last night."

"This *is* about last night!" he thundered, turning around and pacing some more as if the board of directors were present in the room with them. "We have to recognize when you smell the beer coming from those smokestacks, you're smelling the breath of a living industry, and we in this room have been given the enormous duty and privilege to run this industry during our short lives and pass it down to the next generation. But how can the next generation run it when he is out getting punched by his own sister into a swimming pool where he could have drowned?" He pointed his finger at Virginia. "Did you for one minute stop to think about the shareholders?"

Virginia picked up her milk glass. She needed to wet her tongue, but there were only a few dribbles left as she leaned her head back and tilted the glass up.

"I'm glad to see you still drink milk on occasion," her father said.

Lowering the glass, Virginia snapped, "What's that supposed to mean?"

"I understand before you punched Nelson, you'd been drinking again."

"Not much."

"Not much?" Her father sighed and sat down. "Virginia, if there's one thing we can't have in this family, it's an alcoholic."

The phone rang and the butler brought in the extension, saying it was urgent. The general manager of the ball team wanted $25,000 more than the agreed-upon salary cap in order to sign a left-handed pitcher.

Mr. von Bierhart took the call quickly, while his wife and daughter watched in silence. "OK, that's fine; don't worry. If he wins games in extra innings, we'll make that up in beer sales." The butler took the phone away, and Mrs. von Bierhart cleared her throat.

"Virginia, dear, there's something else disturbing about last night that I wanted to bring up."

"Yes, Mother?"

Mrs. von Bierhart adjusted her bracelets and rings and earrings. "It's this business about the strip poker." She shook her head and sniffled. "I . . . thought that after that foolishness with the horse . . . that we were through with . . . with nudity. I . . . we . . . thought you understood we all have to live within our proper boundaries."

Virginia pulled on her ponytail and tried to explain. "Mother, I'm sorry. I really am. I am not trying to hurt you."

"You're hurting yourself, Virginia, and your chances to end up with the right kind of man, if you continue taking your clothes off in public."

"I didn't take off any of my clothes."

"But you were in a strip poker game, dear; it's the same thing."

"She's right," Mr. von Bierhart added. "Can you imagine if all this got in the paper? Strip poker . . . fighting with your brother in public." Her father shook his head at the shareholder implications.

"And kissing that boy. Who *was* he even?" her mother said.

Virginia shrugged. "I don't know."

Mrs. von Bierhart gasped and put her hand to her cheek. "I never let your father kiss me until we knew each other's resumes."

"Did you feel something strange and wonderful happen to you, Mother, when Daddy kissed you?"

Mr. von Bierhart looked at his wife to see how she would answer. But she just shrugged.

"That was a long time ago," Virginia's mother said.

"Let's not get off topic," her father continued. "The point is this, Virginia. What if your actions made shares plummet to the point where the brewery fell to a hostile takeover?"

Virginia stood up and shook her empty milk glass at her father. "Father! This is not about the brewery!"

A drop of milk hit him in the face and he wiped it off, almost exploding, but restrained his voice to almost a whisper. "*Everything's* about the brewery. That's what I'm trying to tell you. If a man can't keep his own family from running amok, it sends a signal to the business community and weakens the entire operation. A lot of families with good incomes are depending on you. Don't be so selfish. Think of them."

"But I had a straight flush."

"Virginia, if you must play cards, learn bridge," her mother said, "and in the meantime, we've decided you're going to be punished. Isn't that so, Hugo?"

Mr. von Bierhart was checking his pocket appointment calendar for the coming week, and looked up. "That's right, Nelson deserves an apology from you."

"All right."

"And I don't think you can just *tell him* your sorry. I want it done right. Type up an official memo, so you'll really mean it. Copy your mother and me on that and give the signed original to Nelson."

"OK. Is that all?" Virginia was contrite but weary.

"No, I think you should also be grounded," Mrs. von Bierhart said, looking at her husband.

He nodded in agreement.

"OK, how long?"

"A week."

"Yes, Father." Resigned and sad, she got up and crossed the room toward the staircase, forgetting the milk glass on the rug as her parents watched her go.

It had been a productive meeting, without violence, and they had agreed upon some best practices and important principles. Mr. von Bierhart was satisfied.

Just then there was a car horn outside.

"Now, who could that be?" Mrs. von Bierhart said.

Virginia remembered she was supposed to go with her friend Loretta Sharp to the planning session for the Veiled Prophet Ball, the annual presentation of debutantes by their tuxedoed fathers in December. "It's Loretta. . . . She's here for that VP thing," she said, "I'll tell her I'm grounded."

Mrs. von Bierhart shot a glance at her husband and he nodded in agreement.

"No, wait, Virginia," her mother said. "Why don't you go along with Loretta? It's important you girls help with the VP when you're young. Meet the right people. Maybe someday you can be the Queen of Love and Beauty. You can work on that memo to Nelson this afternoon, OK?"

"OK." Virginia walked slowly out to the yellow Trans Am idling in the circle driveway. Watching from his bedroom window, Nelson fumed as Virginia got in the car and Loretta drove off very slowly at first. He just shook his head.

"I'm glad she's going with Loretta," Mrs. von Bierhart told her husband. "She comes from a good family. She'll be a good influence on her."

"It's not easy raising a daughter."

Loretta waited until the car was out of view of the house, then turned up the music, raced down Ladue Road, and handed Virginia a freshly-rolled joint. A sophomore at Joyous Days High, the all-girls Catholic school, Loretta had been friends with Virginia since swing-set days in the neighborhood. And even though Virginia went to Ladue High, a public school, they shared all their secrets. Like the time recently Loretta's boyfriend dumped her. That was a tough one. But Loretta was strong. She was an actor in school plays. She had wild brunette hair, brown eyes, and a loud voice. She knew how to act on the stage of life. Virginia decided to tell Loretta everything about the boy who had kissed her at the pool and how she *just had* to see him again.

"Who do you know who goes to that all-boys school? St. Aloysius?" Virginia asked, lighting up.

"Hell, I don't know. Why?"

"We need to find a yearbook. I'm looking for a name. Can you help me?"

"I know a girl whose older brother went there, but she's a real bitch. I hate her. We're in the Ping Pong club and she always wins."

"It's a nice day for Ping Pong."

"Shit."

They went to the girl's house and Loretta tried to play Ping Pong while she was high. A serious athlete, the girl who was not high, started laughing when Loretta would mess up. Loretta started cussing and messing up more. And the girl laughed harder and scored point after point.

"You have no game. You have no ball control," the girl told Loretta as they played. "You are going to die a slow painful death."

Sitting off to the side in a wicker love seat, Virginia flipped through a St.

Aloysius yearbook looking for the face of the boy she had kissed. The girl didn't know why Virginia wanted to see her brother's yearbook.

"Just don't get any sweat marks on the pages, or my brother will notice," the girl told Virginia while she smacked another scorching serve. When Virginia found his face, she held her breath and read the name. Her lips whispered it for the first time: Patrick Cantwell.

Virginia exhaled and nodded the signal to Loretta who whacked the ball out of bounds all the way into the living room.

The girl ran after the ball, and Virginia ripped out the page with Patrick's picture on it. She folded it up and put it in her bra. Then she found the picture of Patrick's friend, Tony Vivamano, and tore it out, too. She put that one in her shoe. The girl came back with the ball to finish the game. But Loretta told her they were late and had to get going to the VP Ball planning thing.

"It was fun beating you. Come by anytime," the girl said waving goodbye at the door.

Loretta gave her a stage smile and they drove off.

Chapter 9

TONY AND PATRICK rode The Love Machine across the Mississippi river into East St. Louis. It was Saturday night and they were going to get beer. The legal drinking age in Illinois was eighteen, three years younger than Missouri. And even though Tony and Patrick were only sixteen, East St. Louis was a poor town, and they usually didn't card you. Patrick was holding the cash, about thirty dollars from all the friends waiting back on the grade school steps at Mary Queen of Our Hearts. The Gang of Five was waiting. All the Catholic schoolgirls from last night, who missed the train wreck because they had to brush their teeth and go home early. That's where they always met to start their weekend nights, on the same gym steps where they used to be kids waiting their turn for kickball. Now they were smoking pot there, in the dark, and pooling their money to buy beer. The gold statue of Mary was still on the church roof, but, they'd seen her so often over the years, no one noticed her anymore. And no one talked of the old days of grade school imprisonment. Their eyes were on the present moment. The plan was to get the beer and go back, and drive to someplace outdoors to drink. It was a nice night, warmer than the night before.

"What about this girl you kissed? What's the plan?"

Patrick was smoking another one of Tony's Camel non-filters and thinking the very same thing. He wanted to call her, but was afraid. This was no time to fall in love. He had a paper due. So he lied. "I don't know. I haven't thought about her."

"Who're you kidding? You haven't thought about her. Ha! And you also quit smoking. It's time you bought a pack. I'm getting low supporting you."

"I'll buy you a pack."

"And one for yourself, too. Be honest."

They parked The Love Machine on the gravel parking lot of a cinder block liquor store and got out. It was dark, a lone light bulb over the entrance, graffiti on the wall, a Kool cigarette sign on the side of the building, the metal door, dented, the windows protected by burglar bars. A cowbell clanged over the door as they walked inside. The clerk stood behind a chain-link fence covered with Plexiglas—with all the booze behind the fence— to discourage robberies.

A few locals stood in line ahead of them on the cruddy tile floor. The boys listened as an older black man with whiskers and a raspy laugh bought a half-pint bottle of Southern Comfort and a pack of Kools. He made some joke to the clerk and laughed so hard at his own joke he went into a coughing fit. Then two black women in their twenties bought a bottle of Jack Daniels. Tony admired their tight pants, shimmering party jackets, and hoop earrings. They smelled of perfume and style. While one of the women bought the liquor, the other glanced over at Tony. He gave her his best eyebrow twitches, and she asked him for a light. Without blinking, he whipped out his Zippo and gave her a flame.

"Thanks," she said. "My friend has an apartment. You and your friend wanna party with us?" Tony took another look at her hips. He wanted to go. He looked over at Patrick to see if he wanted to go.

"Oh, thank you, ma'am, but we can't," Patrick said. "I'm working on a paper."

"A paper? What are you in, high school?"

The clerk looked up, as if he was about to card them.

"Hell no, we're college men," Tony said, doing a few leg squats. "Yeah, No-tre Dame rowing team; in town to practice on the river. Gotta stay in shape."

The woman with the cigarette whispered something to her friend and they both laughed and left. Then Patrick paid the clerk for two-and-a-half cases of von Bierhart beer and two packs of Camel non-filters. The clerk slid the mer-chandise in a deep wooden drawer that separated the two worlds and closed it. Tony pulled the drawer open and grabbed the beer.

"Be careful out there," the clerk said, ringing the register.

Tony and Patrick walked out into the night looking around for trouble. But trouble wasn't around. It was a quiet night in East St. Louis. At least right then. They put the beer in the car and drove back across the bridge.

When the boys got back to the playground, everyone was gone. Tony spot-

ted a note with a rock on it sitting on the gym steps, so he got out of The Love
Machine to read it.

"What's it say?" Patrick yelled out the window.

"Says 'Meet us at Copemeister's. Bobby Jones's friend died.'"

"Who died?"

"Doesn't say."

Tony pulled the car onto the parking lot at Copemeister's Funeral Home
and drove around slowly looking for their friends. They spotted Bobby Jones's
Cougar, and Jimmy Purvis's Nova, but not a soul was around. So they parked
the car, tossed their empty beer cans in some bushes, and walked around front
past the lighted fountain and through the heavy black doors.

In the lobby, a puffy man in a dark suit sat behind a reception desk. The
air was stuffy with funeral flowers, and there was the buzz of large crowds down
the hall, out of view in different parlors. Tony wrinkled his nose and the man
looked up at him.

"May I help you?"

"Yes, sir," Tony said, helping himself to a cinnamon mint from the bowl,
"Somebody died and we're here to pay our respects."

"Who?"

Tony stopped to think. "You know, he died so suddenly, I didn't catch his
name."

The clerk sighed and reached for the list. "Would it help if I read the names?"

Patrick nudged Tony and pointed down the hallway. Spilling out of one of
the parlors was Jimmy Purvis, blowing his nose.

"We see one of our friends now," Patrick told the clerk.

Tony thanked the clerk and grabbed a few more mints, to have around, for
later, for making out.

Down the hall they went, and into a parlor where the Gang of Five and all
the girls were gathered around a casket, talking to some man. Jimmy Purvis told
Tony and Patrick the dead guy was a friend of a friend of Bobby Jones who went
to Lindbergh High, a public school kid. They knew each other from soccer
teams. He had crashed his car into a tree coming home from a party. Dead at
the age of sixteen. Patrick and Tony eased up within ten feet of the open casket.
They could see the profile of the guy inside. He was dead all right. The man by

the casket in a suit was the guy's father, pale and worn out from the tragedy. But he was making the best of it, warning the Gang of Five to never put their parents through this, to never drink and drive.

"When you're dead, you understand everything," he said, "but it's too late to do anything about it, because you're already dead."

Some of the girls hugged the father and the guys shook his hand, but Patrick and Tony stayed back because they didn't know the father or the son. And Patrick knew that you can't say or do anything right near a stranger's casket. Tony and Patrick looked at each other and nodded toward the door. They started walking fast. They held their breath like underwater swimmers, gliding past stuffy death parlors until they busted out the front doors into the night air. They stopped to breathe it in.

"A place like this should be closed on a Saturday night," Tony said. He dug the cinnamon breath mints from his pocket and threw them away into the lighted fountain. They watched them sink to the bottom.

"Death," Patrick said.

"Don't think about it. Think about ice cream for a minute."

"Ice cream?"

"Yeah, you can't think about death if you're thinking about your favorite ice cream."

"Is that all you've got to face eternity? Ice cream?"

"Hey, I don't know why, but it works. I've used it at funerals myself. Trust me."

"Let's go."

They walked back to the car and popped open a couple of cold beers and had a smoke. After a few minutes everyone came out and they divided up the beer, and decided to drive out to Castlewood Park, to drink on the bluffs overlooking the Meramec River.

Chapter 10

THREE CARLOADS OF TEENS raced west on Highway 44, drinking beer, smoking pot, and listening to loud tunes. No one wanted to talk after seeing a dead guy on a Saturday night. When they got to the bluffs, they first had to haul coolers uphill through the dark woods along a trail with pine needles whipping their faces. Up top, the trail opened onto a rock plateau looking down on train tracks and the river. The perfect drinking and making out spot. Beyond the river, on grassy hills, a landfill loomed like an historic burial mound, squared off and sloped. Only this one hid all the baby diapers, egg cartons, and milk containers their families had thrown away since 1960. Beyond that—Interstate 44 hummed like a Hot Wheels set in perpetual motion, with all the headlights of miniature cars and tractor-trailer's passing through the night.

Patrick sat on a cooler next to a girl named Jane Sullenbrook. With her blue jeans flush against his leg, she gave off a bit of body heat, which was nice, he thought. But neither of them were interested in each other. Jane had a boyfriend. Everybody knew that. Jane and Nate had been a couple since grade school.

"Sure wish Nate was here," she said. "I sure do miss him." She took three gulps of her beer.

Patrick wasn't sure if she was trying to convince him or herself. But he tried to make polite conversation while he thought about his own problems—his unfinished paper, and the girl he'd kissed last night.

"Where is he?"

"He's working. True Love Pizza. He's *always* working."

"He's a hard worker." Patrick didn't know what else to say.

Jane turned so she was looking directly at Patrick. "You know, Nate and me got married once . . . in a field by the skating rink—"

"I know . . . I know." Patrick and everybody else had often heard the story when Jane was drinking and Nate wasn't around.

"We were in the sixth grade. It was a night I'll never forget . . ." Jane took a deep breath and sighed. "You ever been in love?"

Patrick thought about Virginia, and, that kiss. "Not everybody's that lucky."

"Not everybody . . . but if you have ever been in love, then you know that's the way I feel about Nate. But he had to work. He's always volunteering for extra hours, saving for the future. Guess some day he'll go away to one school and I'll go to another." She leaned over and kissed Patrick on the lips.

"Jane, what the hell?"

"I'm sorry, I was just thinking of Nate. Are you thinking of someone?"

He drank some beer to get her kiss out of his mouth. "Maybe."

"Is she here tonight?"

"No."

"Oh, good! Pretend I'm her for a minute and kiss me again. That way I can tell you how you really feel about her. I'm a lip reader." She didn't wait for Patrick to agree. She kissed him again and this time, he kissed her back, trying to imagine she was Virginia. But it was no good. She wasn't Virginia.

"You must really love her. I can tell."

"How many beers have you had?"

"I dunno." Jane grabbed Patrick's hand. "You want to go for a walk?"

"No"

"Just to talk? I won't try to kiss you anymore."

"I don't want to."

"Me neither. It's hard being a couple sometimes."

"Yeah."

She let go of his hand. "I just love Nate."

They sat there alone, together, watching everyone else necking and groping in the starlight. It was a lonely plateau. Tony was off to the side on a flat rock with Barbara Doglesdorf. His heart was pumping blood to his muscles and he rolled over too far and knocked over their beer cans. Cold beer soaked through her pants leg to her skin and she pushed him away, cursing. The other girls heard the commotion, and a female regrouping took place. A gathering of the

Female-Congress, the girls buzzing together around one set of coolers, and the guys around another set.

The necking had the guys stirred up, so they channeled their lust into a contest to see who could finish a beer the fastest. Jimmy Purvis won, but he had cheated, since his beer was already open, and he'd already taken a few gulps. So, the guys all got out another beer and made him drink it right. It was about a four-way tie. Next, they began to work off their energy by throwing rocks off the bluff toward the river to see who could throw a rock the farthest. Whoever threw their rock the shortest distance had to drink another beer all the way down without stopping. Patrick drank about four beers in fifteen minutes. By then, they were all feeling a little better, despite making out with the girls and having nothing come of it.

Watching all this, the girls shook their heads at what fools the guys were. Drinking so much beer. The guys hadn't learned anything from going to the wake of the dead guy from Lindbergh High. And they told them so. None of the girls knew the guy in life, but they kept on talking about him and drinking toasts to him, and toasts to his girlfriend—whoever she might be. They even toasted his parents, his best friends, and his team. Without planning to, they had brought the wake with them, and Death had crashed their little party. Jane Sullenbrook was the first to sense it. She looked into the woods and started crying.

"What's the matter?" Kim Springer asked Jane.

"I was just thinking Nate might die . . . this place is so dark, it gives me thoughts."

"Drink another beer," Jimmy Purvis called out.

"Shut up, Jimmy! She's right," Cindy Matthews said. "This place— .

"This place sucks!" Kim Springer yelled to her boyfriend, Bobby Jones. "Why'd you bring us to such a sad place?"

"It's not sad. It's peaceful," Bobby said. "Look at the view. Look at the river."

Jane blew her nose. "Maybe it's a sign. Nate almost drowned on a river . . . got a sad feeling tonight. Nate's in danger."

That's when the girls decided to leave. Right then. Cindy Matthews jabbed her boyfriend Jimmy Purvis in the chest

"We need to move ass nowwww . . . Nate's in danger. He almost almost drowned in a place like this."

"Will you relax? He's not gonna drown. Nate's making pizzas," Jimmy said.

Kim Springer jumped up. "Dammit, let's just fucking go!"

Bobby Jones looked up at her. "And if we don't?"

Kevin Killeen

The girls stomped down the trail toward the cars. So, there was nothing the guys could do but grab the coolers and chase after them.

"Women," Tony said. They all agreed.

When they got to the cars, all of the girls except Jane wanted to switch cars and ride with Tony in The Love Machine. They all said they didn't trust Bobby Jones and Jimmy Purvis to drive safe enough, which suited Tony just fine. He liked being the only man in a station wagon of six girls. Barbara Doglesdorf jumped into the front seat next to Tony. And the rest of the girls all piled in the middle seat and the way back seat. It was more girls than a Holy Footsteps Academy carpool.

Patrick hopped into the back of the red Nova with two other guys, and no sooner had he got in, when Jane squeezed through the door onto his lap. "I want to ride with you tonight," she said petting her bangs. He nodded and looked out the window.

Buck Wilson plopped in the front passenger seat of the Nova and shut the door. He opened a fresh beer and handed it to Jimmy Purvis.

Three more guys packed into Bobby Jones's green Cougar. An all-male expedition. All pissed at the girls. And all ready to hit the highway. Bobby turned the key, stepped on the pedal, and revved the engine. Each time he gunned the gas, the car reared up. "Let's get the hell out of here," he said. Then he slammed the stick shift into first and the Cougar took off down the steep street on the backside of the bluffs.

Jimmy jammed the Nova into gear and raced after him.

Tony put on his seat belt and started the engine softly. With the car in park, he adjusted the rear view mirror, first, to look at his own hair, which he finger-combed again, and to enjoy the sea of beauty behind him. This was a chance to not only impress the girl beside him, but all the other girls. Who knows? He might end up with one of them some day.

"Quit fiddling around and catch up with them," Kim Springer said.

"Patience," Tony said. "We want to make sure everything's ready first."

Tony looked over at Barbara beside him. He apologized again for spilling beer on her pants and offered to point the heating vent on the dashboard toward her leg to dry it off, once the car got warmed up.

"Can we just hurry up and go?" Cindy Matthews said.

"OK, here we go."

Tony put the car in gear and gently rolled down the hill. At a red light right before the entrance to the highway, all three cars came to a stop side by side.

48

Kim Springer leaned over and rolled down the middle seat passenger window of The Love Machine. Then she yelled at Bobby, "Don't be an asshole on the highway!"

Cindy Matthews leaned out the window on the other side of the station wagon to warn Jimmy about being stupid. "Don't get anybody fucking killed!"

Satisfied they had their boyfriends under control, Kim and Cindy sat back down and waited for the light to change.

The Cougar and Nova engines growled.

The light turned green.

"Shit, lookat'm go," Cindy said.

"Assholes," Kim said.

The Nova and the Cougar shot up the entrance ramp to the highway like fighter jets taking off from an aircraft carrier into battle.

Tony crawled away from the green light like an insurance salesman, knowing it would impress the girls that he was careful. He looked over at Barbara and turned on the heater for her. "It should be ready in a minute, babe." Tony blew into his fist to warm his hand and reached over to squeeze Barbara's hand.

Cindy Matthews leaned into the front seat between Tony and Barbara. "Hurry up! Don't let'm get too far ahead! They need to slow the hell down!"

Tony flipped the turn signal and merged onto the highway like a student driver.

Up ahead, they saw the Nova and the Cougar swerve into the fast lanes, darting around a tractor-trailer and a car pulling a camper.

The sports cars accelerated up the hill—70 . . . then 80 . . . 90 miles an hour. Bobby Jones opened another beer and played the highway like a race car arcade game, the kind where you can get killed and just put another quarter in and start over. Jimmy Purvis slapped in his favorite Eight Track tape of the Marshall Tucker Band and turned up the volume. "Fire on the Mountain" blared. Jane nuzzled closer to Patrick. Patrick eyeballed the speedometer as it climbed higher and higher.

"I'm glad we ended up together . . . after our talk," Jane said.

Patrick nodded, but his mind was on the two cars, side-by-side, inches apart, hot rubber whining as they fought to hold their lanes around a tight curve. If a tire blows, he thought, we're gonna flip and burn.

"I went on retreat and we talked about death," Jane said, "You ever think about death?"

"No!"

"I think of death sometimes, like tonight. Death is out there." She looked out the window at the speeding Cougar, then back at Patrick. "They told us on retreat that every time you blink, somebody somewhere just died."

Patrick tried not to, but he couldn't hold it. He blinked. "Jane, please stop, I have to ask you—"

"Yes?"

"What's your favorite ice cream?"

"My favorite ice cream?"

"Yes, I need to know right now."

"I dunno, never thought about it."

"Well, please think about it. Now. Think real hard about ice cream."

The Nova dropped into passing gear and car jerked forward, but the Cougar roared up alongside, Bobby honking the horn as they drew even.

"I got it. Butter Pecan," Jane blurted out.

Patrick tapped Jimmy Purvis on the shoulder over and over, like a hotel counter bell. "Jimmy! Jimmy! Jimmy!"

Jimmy ignored him.

"But anyway, on retreat, it's all about death. Death, death, death, death, death . . . They make all the people who love you write letters that you open in your room. Makes you think about what they'd say if you really were dead. Forever. It's very peaceful."

"SLOW DOWN!" Patrick yelled.

Jimmy and the rest of the guys in the car laughed at him. Marshall Tucker's slide guitar laughed at him. Jimmy was finally going to show everyone that his Nova was better than Bobby Jones's Cougar. The highway straightened out long and flat, and both drivers poured it on all the way, the engines screaming like dive-bombers.

"Maybe I'll get killed and you'll survive," Jane said. "If so, I want you to tell Nate how I felt about him . . . after you get out of the hospital. Just let him know that he was on my mind till the very end. Tell him how I would've kissed him, if he were here."

Patrick wasn't listening. He watched wild-eyed as the Cougar and the Nova, still fender to fender, raced at 95 miles an hour.

Without warning, Jane wrapped her arms and legs around Patrick, like an octopus seizing its prey in a death grip. "Tell Nate I loved him." Her lips pushed against Patrick's, trying to drill her tongue inside his clenched mouth.

"Lemmie go!" Patrick mumbled. He squirmed and pulled back away from

Most Improved Sophomore

her, but he still got a cheek full of tongue slobber. Jane only let go when the Nova eased back, and they heard loud honking and laughter.

Tony let up on The Love Machine, now going over 100 miles an hour, just enough to pull alongside the Cougar and the Nova. All the girls had rolled down their windows by now and were shouting obscenities at Bobby and Jimmy to slow down. But their voices bent away as Tony floored The Love Machine, and shot out in front, leading the pack all the way to their exit. His mother's station wagon had triumphed again.

When they came to a stoplight, Patrick looked over and saw Tony lighting a Camel non-filter nonchalantly. As soon as the car stopped, Barbara jumped out of the front seat and slammed the door. The rest of the girls followed while they cussed out Tony for racing like a drunken fool and risking their lives. They all piled in with the other guys in the Nova and Cougar. As the girls got in one side of the Nova, Patrick twisted free of Jane, and vaulted out of the car for The Love Machine. He slid into the shotgun seat, and slammed the door—locking it fast—so Jane couldn't follow.

"How's it going?" Tony said.

"I'm OK now, but I gotta tell you—"

"What?"

"That ice cream shit is worthless."

As soon as the light turned green, all three cars rolled forward like a funeral procession. Not one of them revved their engines, peeled out, or broke the speed limit.

51

Chapter 11

SARA JIBBS was one of the nicest girls in the parish, and she never did anything wrong. She was babysitting two young children in a quiet Cape Cod style house with tidy rugs when The Love Machine, the Nova, and the Cougar pulled up out front and everyone got out. Jane wanted to use a phone to call Nate and make sure he was all right. And, all of the girls wanted to go to the bathroom right away, pinching their legs together and hopping up and down, because they had held it in the whole time back on the bluffs, while the guys just peed in the bushes. An entourage of girls knocked on the back door, while the boys lurked in the darkness of the yard. Sara opened the storm door a crack and looked out.

"Yes . . . who is it?"

"Pssst . . . Sara, it's us," JoAnn Greggerman said. "Let us in a minute."

"I can't. It's against the rules. Besides, I just put the kids to bed and don't want any noise."

"We'll be quiet." The girls hoosiered their way in, promising to only stay long enough to pee, but the boys in back yard didn't hear all the terms of the contract. Before Sara could stop them, they all filed in like a pack of dogs, tracking up the white kitchen tile with their muddy shoes and talking loudly.

"Shhh! Stop!" Sara said. "Don't anybody go past the kitchen, and take off your shoes."

The guys balked. None of them wanted to take off their shoes. But the girls tilted their heads and bulged their eyes, so the guys gave in. The shoes piled up near the back door. Then everyone looked at Sara, who was very sober and in charge.

"The bathroom's right there," she said, pointing to the hall off the kitchen, "Hurry up and go, because I'm not supposed to have *anybody* over."

"I need to use the phone," Jane said. "It's an emergency."

"OK, but don't talk too loud and—"

One of the boys noticed a basketball in a hamper by the back door, and started dribbling with it. Just the sound of dribbling touched off a sudden basketball game with some of the boys passing and tugging for possession and laughing.

"Shhhh," Sara said.

Upstairs, a little girl started to cry for her mommy, and Sara slapped her thighs with her hands. "You guys be quiet, or I'll lose my job!" She stormed upstairs almost crying, and the boys felt bad about it. Some of the girls punched them on the arms, and they took it and quieted down.

Jane picked up a white wall phone by the refrigerator and dialed True Love Pizza.

Tony noticed a gold foiled box of chocolates on the countertop—a Mavrako's assortment—which he opened up and grabbed a caramel. Bobby Jones and Jimmy Purvis, still upset from The Love Machine passing them, also grabbed some chocolate to show Tony he wasn't going to do things uncontested. Some of the girls waiting to use the bathroom, also ate some chocolate, until one of them read the card.

"Shit! It says Happy Anniversary," Kim Springer said. "We can't eat this. Put the lid back on."

The girls managed to cover up the chocolate, but the boys had swung open the refrigerator and were taking swigs of milk right from the plastic jug. Next, it was the meat tray. Tony selected a packet of Oscar Meyer bologna. He pulled off the red string wrapper and put the whole piece in his mouth. The rest of the guys followed suit.

Some of the girls were still in the bathroom, giggling. Sara Jibbs was still upstairs soothing the baby. The guys continued to forage for food and found some cherry Pop Tarts in the closet, along with some Cheerios, which spilled on the floor when they each dug their hands in the box, and a bottle of Christmas wine. Buck Wilson swung the bottle upside down in his crotch, hiding the top of the bottle between his belly and his sweatshirt. Jane hung up the phone and smiled.

"Guys, I have great news. Nate's all right."

The guys all looked at each other in disgust. Of course he was all right, Jane.

"Well, hurry up and pee so we can get out of here," Bobby Jones told her.

By the time all the girls had used the bathroom, the guys were all standing around eating vanilla wafers, Cheerios, bananas, and passing around the milk jug.

"I wonder whose house this is?" Jimmy Purvis said.

"Who knows," Cindy Matthews said. "But it's pretty. Can you see us living in a house like this someday?"

"Cindy, I don't even know what I'm having for breakfast tomorrow."

Nobody knew whose house it was. Except Sara, and she was still upstairs.

As they were standing there wondering this, in the calm throes of nourishment, they heard the front door unlock. Shit! The parents were home. The sound of jangling keys and romantic laughter echoed into the kitchen as the husband took off his wife's coat and hung it in the front hallway closet, and then turned to embrace her. He kissed her like they were young again, before they had a mortgage and kids.

"Not now," the wife scolded. "Remember? The babysitter is still here." The wife straightened her blouse and walked into the kitchen and peeked around for Sara.

The muddy floor had been wiped clean with a dishtowel that was now gone forever out the back door. The little red bologna strings, banana peels, Cheerios, and Vanilla Wafer crumbs had all been all picked up, too. They took the bottle of wine with them. The raiding party had grabbed all their shoes and eased the kitchen door shut and ran across the back yard in their socks toward the cars. The man noticed the box of chocolate and took the lid off.

"Look, honey," he said noticing about fifteen pieces gone.

The wife looked at the half-eaten box. "Poor Sara, she must be under a lot of stress. It's not easy being a teenager."

Everyone got back in the cars and decided to drive over by the golf course to drink the wine and finish off the last dozen beers. They parked the cars on a side street and carried the coolers through some back yards, up a path worn by schoolboys through a thicket of trees, over the Frisco train tracks, and onto the fairway. It was a remote, private corner of the golf course lit only by the stars and the distant windows of the clubhouse where captains of industry sipped mixed drinks and chatted about times gone by when they were young.

"You girls will like this wine," Buck Wilson said twisting off the top. "I picked it out myself."

They all sat down, some on cooler tops, others on the grass, and passed the wine around, all of them wanting to get back the buzz they had before the car ride and the food had ruined the mood.

"Crazy the way those fools drove so fast," Kim Springer said, loud enough so her boyfriend Bobby Jones could hear. He didn't care; he was drinking off to the side with some of the guys, ignoring her. "I got my permit, and when I get my license, I'll drive us safe," Kim said. "Hey, Jane, you got your license. How come you don't drive us?"

Jane took a three-swallow swig of the wine and wiped her mouth. "My dad thinks I drink, so he won't let me drive at night. And, Nate, he says I can't borrow his car, because I don't have experience."

"That's what I've been telling Bobby," Kim said, taking a drink. "I need experience, too, but he won't ever let me have the wheel. These guys are just holding us back. How can we get experience if they don't let us drive?"

Cindy Matthews took the bottle and glugged down a few gulps. "You're right! I've got my permit, but Jimmy never lets me drive his damned Nova, either. Says I'll crack it up."

The girls all grumbled and looked over at the guys with disgust. There was a fight coming. The guys could feel it throbbing like a chin pimple that needed popping. But Buck Wilson knew how to fix it. Without a word he just got up and walked off in the dark toward the clubhouse.

"And another thing," Kim said, "sure would be nice if you guys would spend some money on us to eat, instead of stealing all that stuff from Sara Jibbs's babysitting job."

"You guys ate, too," Bobby called out.

"We didn't want to," JoAnn Greggerman said, taking her turn with the stolen wine.

Tension between the sexes was rising. But just then, they heard a whirring sound and looked around. Coming toward them was Buck Wilson . . . in a golf cart. He sported a big grin, his buck teeth shining in the night.

"What are you doing?" JoAnn asked him.

"Driving lessons. Come on. Hop in. Lots more where this came from. They're all plugged in and ready to go up at the cart shack."

The girls looked at the golf cart, as shiny and inviting as a go-cart could be to anyone who doesn't have their driver's license yet.

"C'mon, let's go," Kim said, grabbing the bottle of wine. All of girls piled into the cart, along with some of the guys who didn't have drivers licenses yet.

Kevin Killeen

As Buck swung the golf cart around, it lumbered away, moaning from all the extra weight.

"I hope they don't get killed," Bobby said sipping a beer. "Those girls are in no condition."

"No condition?" Tony said. "What about us back on the highway? We drove like mad fools." He laughed in a forgiving way—forgiving of himself and all fools everywhere. Bobby Jones and Jimmy Purvis also laughed at themselves, but when Patrick joined in, Jimmy turned on him.

"Hey, what are you laughing at? You weren't driving. You were in the back seat practically having sex with Jane."

This was news to Tony and Bobby. They looked over at Patrick to hear more. "What did you do with her?" Bobby asked Patrick.

"It wasn't me. It was her. She wanted to kiss me like I was Nate, so I could tell Nate how much she loves him."

"Crazy Jane," Bobby said. "Whatever you do, don't tell Nate."

"Crazy Jane?" Jimmy Purvis said. "I thought maybe Patrick was finally showing some manhood with a girl." Then he turned to Patrick. "When was the last time you even kissed any girl?"

Patrick shrugged. "I can't remember."

Tony got out a Camel non-filter and lit it. He narrowed his eyes at Patrick, who was sitting next to him on a cooler.

"Don't let Patrick fool you. He's more of a man than he wants to admit." Tony slapped Patrick on the shoulder. "I've seen him in action. Like last night. A girl I was playing strip poker—I was down to my underwear—and here comes Patrick, cool as Bogart, and he just walks up and kisses her without warning."

Bobby Jones gave Patrick a thumbs-up, and Jimmy Purvis laughed and swigged back some more beer.

Patrick sat trapped between the guys like a defendant on the witness stand in a trial. He wanted to get up and walk home, but contempt of court would only make things worse.

Patrick shook his head. "Tony's exaggerating. That was nothing. I didn't want to kiss her, but there was this fat man—"

They all laughed at him. Fat Man? Ha!

Tony jumped up and faced his audience. "No, guys, listen . . . here was this girl, who—I won't say *who* she was—but let's just say she's from a very wealthy family, and she's so hot she could defrost the refrigerator in the next room."

Patrick listened to the story and relived that moment: the look in her eyes,

56

the feeling of being a couple, the gravitational pull of her tugging at him, even now, to ruin him before his wedding night. He wanted to never see her again, just go back to school on Monday and concentrate on his classwork.

"You're smart," Bobby told Patrick, "going after a girl outside the parish."

"I'm not going after anybody," Patrick said.

"Why not? We'll never get into the pants of any of *these* girls," Jimmy said, thumbing toward the girls who disappeared to drive golf carts.

That was it. Patrick was going to tell them off now—Tony, too. He was going to unload on them with the Jesuit logic he'd learned in school, and some he'd been working up on his own. He jumped up and faced them like St. Aloysius facing hospital patients infected with the Bubonic Plague.

"OK, what if I did go for it and get into her pants? What if we *all* got into some girl's pants? I'll go even further," he said, unleashing a secret idea from his paper. "What if we all had a special watch with a red button on it?"

"A red button?" Bobby said.

"Now he's lost it," Tony said. He leaned forward and pointed his beer at Patrick. "You've been thinking too much."

"And drinking too much," Jimmy added.

"Maybe so, but do you want to hear about the watch?"

"Yeah, what the hell. Go ahead," Bobby said, sipping his beer.

Patrick knit his eyebrows and paced back in forth in front of the cooler, the way he'd seen the Jesuits pace in front of chalkboards when they were trying to make a point.

"I'm talking about a red button right on top of your watch that whenever you wanted to, you could push it and feel all the pleasure in the world. Just press that button and you would feel what its like to have sex, and feel what it's like to have someone love you." Patrick stopped and raised both arms to the stars. "And feel what it's like to drink water when you're thirsty, eat chocolate cake when you damn well pleased, and get birthday presents even if it wasn't your birthday, and find a new car sitting in your driveway . . . get good grades, and all the money you'd ever need . . . and all you had to do was push that little red button and you'd feel all that every time." He dropped his arms down and looked at them. "Can you imagine?"

"Damn. I want a watch like that," Jimmy said.

Bobby pointed to his wrist. "I'd put duct tape on my red button and never let it stop."

They laughed at him, again, but Patrick kept a straight face. "No you wouldn't, because it wouldn't be enough. Don't you see? It would never be enough. Ever. You'd still want something *more*."

He stopped and they were all quiet for a second.

"Something more? What more is there?" Jimmy asked.

Patrick sat down and hung his head. "I don't know that part. I'm still studying it."

Bobby, Jimmy, and Tony laughed and danced around him, pushing a make-believe button on their watches, and pretending they were all swept away in perfect bliss.

Just then, a dozen golf carts came racing across the fairway, driven by laughing and drunk girls. Patrick and Tony, and Jimmy and Bobby opened another beer and watched them loop circles on the grass, going round and round like clown cars in the Greatest Show On Earth. It was pure entertainment, and more fun than any golf course member paying the $10,000 membership fee ever had on those same golf carts. Everything was right and calm. And Patrick was glad for the distraction—ashamed of his talk, and ashamed he'd shown his equation to his friends without knowing the answer yet. Sometimes, he thought, when you're drunk, you say too much. But other times, you get things out that need to be admitted. Maybe he was just playing with words, playing with himself, and playing with life.

Then a car drove into view on the main entrance road up by the clubhouse. Jimmy Purvis spotted it first—the gold star decal on the side door. Renowned since grade school for having the loudest whistle on the playground, Jimmy let go a whistle so sharp that a foursome playing Bridge in the clubhouse heard it faintly and looked up.

"Cops!" he yelled, waving them in. The whine of the electric motors buzzed like a thousand bees when they all floored the golf cars and raced back to the coolers. The patrol car searchlight swept across the fairways like a Nazi guard tower, searching for escaped prisoners. Just as the carts skidded to a stop and they hopped off, the cop car lurched onto the grass, all lights aimed at them zooming forward. The guys grabbed the coolers and ran after the girls, into the bushes, up the embankment, over the Frisco tracks, through the woods, branches snatching and scratching at their faces, and back into their waiting cars.

They raced through some back streets where married couples sat in living rooms reading, while children slept. They zigzagged around, past yards with swing sets, narrowly missing parked cars owned by dads who drove them to work all week to pay the bills. They didn't want any other cops who might be prowling around and listening to radio traffic to pick up their trail. They ended up back where they started, rolling slow and easy onto the parking lot of the grade school by the gym steps. All of them still jittery with adrenalin, and woozy from zipping through all the left and right turns—and the wine.

"I guess we shook 'em," Bobby said. "So, what do you wanna do now?"

"What time is it?" Kim asked. "My curfew's at eleven."

"I know. It's almost eleven," he said checking his watch. "You ever wish you had a watch with a red button on it?"

"What's that?"

"Never mind."

Everyone said good night, knowing tomorrow they'd have to get up early and go to Sunday Mass with their parents, then face homework, and then get ready for Monday morning. Another school week. Monday morning was waiting like an open grave. The weekend just wasn't long enough. You looked forward to it all week, and then before you knew, it was over, and nothing ever happened.

The Cougar and the Nova and The Love Machine all went their separate ways, careful to obey all posted speed limits.

Tony dropped off Patrick in front of his house and apologized for telling the guys about him kissing Virginia at the party. "But remember, I didn't tell them *who* she was, only that she was hot, and you done good, so I hope you're not mad."

"No, I'm not. It's OK."

"What are you doing tomorrow?"

"I gotta work on that paper."

"OK. Maybe I should start mine, too. See you Monday, man."

"See you."

The Love Machine drove off, and Patrick stood and stared at his parent's house. All the lights were off. Still drunk, he walked with John Wayne legs, swinging his arms to balance himself, around to the back of the house. Just as he reached the patio deck, out of the corner of his eye, he spotted something moving in the yard—a white opossum waddled across the grass to get away from the human. He watched the creature and felt some strange compulsion to go speak with him, at least exchange eye contact in search of mutual understanding. He stepped off the deck into the yard and the opossum hopped the fence into a neighbor's yard. Patrick ran after him and hopped the fence.

The opossum climbed another fence into a third yard, and Patrick kept after him, calling out "Wait, wait." Then the animal scurried up a maple tree with branches low enough for Patrick to climb after him. Branch by branch, huffing and determined, he pulled himself up the ladder of the trunk to where the opossum was just four feet above him, looking down, hissing.

"It's all right," he said. "I understand." He held out his hand in a gesture of friendship, the way Captain Kirk might befriend a hostile alien glob on *Star Trek*. The opossum snarled and bared its teeth.

Suddenly, he felt foolish and afraid. What was he doing trying to communicate with a wild animal? You can't tame a 'possum. They'll tear you up. He lowered himself down the tree, stumbled through the yard, and went inside the house to go to bed.

Chapter 12

MONDAY MORNING at 7:55 The Love Machine driven conservatively by Tony's mother came to a stop in the circle drive outside St. Aloysius High School and the guys got out. A petite woman wearing a bathrobe and curlers in her hair, Tony's mother bid them farewell with her favorite slogan: "Don't be fools; learn something today." The car doors slammed and she drove away. It was a cool October morning with orange leaves on the trees, and green spittle on the pavement from guys partying all weekend in the night air. Everyone looked sharp in neckties, white shirts, and brown blazers. Brown was the school color, which was supposed to have a spiritual meaning, but moms were just glad it hid the dirt.

Usually Patrick surrendered without a struggle to the comforts of St. Aloysius Mondays—the smell of books, the dandruff of Jesuits on their black-shirted shoulders, the glory of trying to become a new man. But this morning, the glory had departed. Maybe it was Tony's sermon on the Industrial Age. Were they really just entering a factory turning out white-collar Catholics, whose mission was to not have sex until they finished college and get good paying jobs?

No, that wasn't it. It was something worse.

The first bell was ringing—just four minutes to get to lockers and homeroom before the second bell. The boys burst through the front door, past the trophy case, past the statue of St. Aloysius, whose fervent plaster eyes studied them. He knew what every one of them had done over the weekend. Their drinking. Their pot smoking. Their cursing and impure thoughts. Yes, and he even knew about Patrick kissing Virginia.

There was loud talk and laughter of things done over the weekend, lockers banging shut and shoes scuffing along the shiny floors, students running up staircases to get to homerooms before that final bell that signaled, "Weekend's over, men."

As Patrick and Tony hurried to class, Tony hummed the song, "Tennessee Stud," while recalling all he had accomplished over the weekend: the girls kissed, the lawn job completed, the escape from police. Yep, it was a decent weekend.

But, Patrick was quiet, preoccupied. Not only with his moral collapse in kissing Virginia, and getting drunk, and chasing the opossum up a tree—there was the book. That book. The one he opened up after coming home from Sunday Mass. The one by Mark Twain: *What is Man?*

And from its pages, poured ideas so dangerous, Patrick was afraid to speak of them. He hadn't told anyone, not even Tony. Especially not Tony.

He carried the book gingerly into his homeroom, tucked beneath his algebra binder so no one would see it, or ask him about it. The book was volatile. An atomic bomb that could take out the entire school. A book with ideas that had to be handled gently. He needed to get some Jesuit counseling to defuse its meaning right away, not only for his paper, but for his own peace.

But which Jesuit should he ask?

Father Moore? Their homeroom teacher was a burly, bearded man with a toy monkey on a unicycle sitting on a high wire that ran above the desks. He was the kind of priest who would wind up the monkey in the middle of a test—when everyone was concentrating—and laugh as it rode across the wire clanging symbols in its hands. Father Moore also kept a coffee mug of an old cowboy on his desk. The caption on the cup said: "There's a lot of things about this outfit they didn't tell me when I signed up."

The final bell rang and the school was quiet, except for the sound of the late students making a dash for their desks to avoid a demerit. Every student had to carry a demerit card at all times, or face immediate Jug. Any student who was late, or failed to complete homework, or talked back, or got into a fight, or was overheard cussing—a teacher could demand his card and mark it up with a demerit. Five demerits meant Jug—staying after school mopping bathrooms, or sitting in a detention room decoding speeches of Churchill and Hitler, or subtracting the number two from a large number over and over until you got to zero.

Matt Baimbridge, a student who was often late, ran in after the bell, panting to show Father Moore that he had made a good effort. Father Moore gave him a friendly nod over the top of his *Life* magazine, and Baimbridge sat down. It would take a riot to work up Father Moore enough for him to hand out a demerit.

The loud speaker on the wall came on and hummed, and the voice of the principal and school president, Father Woerstbrauth, filled the school.

"Good morning, men, and welcome back," he said.

What about him? Patrick thought. Could he ask Father Woerstbrauth about the book? As principal, he was a businesslike man with fat fingers and smiling eyes, a man adept at budgets and fundraising. He might nod hello to you in the hallway, but he was always walking fast with important goals on his mind. The only time Father Woerstbrauth engaged the students was freshman year orientation day. He stood before the new boys in the cafeteria assembly wearing his extra large black priest suit coat, and gave them some advice.

"Someday you will all occupy important roles in society," he said. "You'll be in the board rooms making important decisions for Christ, and the public school kids will be on the loading dock unloading boxes. So, don't be a 'Nowhere Man' . . . get involved; be a new man . . ."

Father Woerstbrauth rolled through the announcements: weekend scores from all the school teams that won, while leaving out the ones that lost; congratulations to a few named students who had closed out the previous week with noteworthy progress reports. Same old stuff. And then came the surprise news.

"We'll have a special visit later this week from the Vatican."

Father Moore and all the teachers perked up.

"Two high-ranking members of the Society of Jesus will be coming to St. Aloysius to see how we're doing, and to encourage us. So let's everyone pick up trash and maybe get a haircut."

Loud moaning chorused through the entire school. This was 1974, and long hair was essential to the weekend social status of half the student body.

"Please rise now for the Our Father," Father Woerstbrauth said.

They all stood and mumbled the words, but many, like Patrick, felt their minds drift.

Patrick drifted back to freshman year. He was thinking about the priest who taught religion class. Father Blendon. An easy going priest with a pot belly and thinning hair, Blendon would have been a good one to ask about the book. But Blendon was gone. Fired. Several students had begun to notice his breath smelled like bourbon in the afternoon. Then, one afternoon he got a little chatty and went off lesson. "Men, as Catholics, you might get to heaven some day, but," he said, "it will be *despite* the church, not because of it."

Despite the church—not because of it? Puzzled students looked around at each other for an answer. This was a riddle. Right? What did he mean? He never explained. Somebody must've complained about it; maybe told a parent who made a phone call.

Father Blendon was gone the next day.

No one knew if it was for the drinking or what he said.

Prayer time over, another bell rang, and they all filed into the hallways quietly, carrying the books they needed for the first three classes before lunch.

Patrick's first class was Spanish with Father Ortega, a sixty-five-year old priest with a mouthful of troubled teeth, a Bolivian, who had been raised in poverty.

Now teaching in an affluent North American school, Father Ortega wanted to tell his students the truth: they were poor, blind, miserable, naked, and lazy overfed fools. But, he held back. He tried to have the patience of Christ. It wasn't easy. He was daily offended by students trying to speak Spanish by just adding an "oh" sound to the end of English words: el door-oh, el book-oh, el car-oh. . . . One boy, Matt Baimbridge, had the impudence to suggest Spanish was somehow a lesser language than English.

"How do you say that in real language, Father?"

Father Ortega's face got red that day. "Real language? There is no one real language! Spanish is a real language. Sit down, you damned fool!"

That morning, nursing a sore molar, he sat behind his lecture desk waiting for the final bell to begin his lesson. Patrick studied him. He seemed like a devout man, perhaps a little short-tempered, but maybe he could explain this *What is Man?* book to him.

Patrick raised his hand.

"What do you want?" Father Ortega asked.

"I've been reading a book," Patrick said.

"Is it in Spanish?"

"No."

"Well, what's it about?"

Just then, some students playing a prank on Father Ortega rushed in the door, stopped, and raised their legs as if to step over an imaginary—and invisible—obstacle before proceeding to their desks. Father Ortega flinched and squinted to see what it was.

"What are you doing, you damned fools?" He walked over to the doorway holding his jaw, bent down, and waved his free hand through the area students had been stepping over. "There is nothing there. You are all nothing but ignorant wild men." He sat back down and shook his head.

The final bell rang and Matt Baimbridge sprang from the hallway into the room, tripping over the very spot Father Ortega had just inspected. He landed on the floor spilling all his books. Everyone burst into wild laughter.

"Baimbridge! You silly damned fool! Get up! Give me your card!"

Baimbridge, gathering his books, acted innocent, pointing to the doorway as if something really had tripped him. But Father Ortega took his card and marked it up.

"Jug!"

Patrick decided not to ask Father Ortega about his problem.

After Spanish class, the bell rang and he moved down the hall to Father Murphy's religion class. The room was full of old, ratty couches, bookshelves jammed with pulp fiction paperbacks, and student desks in no formal rows, just haphazard wherever you thought you could learn.

The shepherd of the clutter, Father Murphy, was a tall man in his early forties with long bangs almost covering his eyes, and lamb chop sideburns. He sat behind a messy desk with a shiny brass Sphinx paperweight that stared out at the class. Father Murphy never wore a Jesuit uniform. Just a short sleeve, picnic shirt with his shirttails hanging out over khaki pants. He liked tennis shoes, not the black dress shoes the other Jesuits wore. And when he put his feet up on the desk, students could see his socks didn't always match. Some days he didn't even wear socks. Students loved Father Murphy. He taught religion by taking it apart like a V8 engine—and leaving it up to them to put back together. And, he not only let them know there were many religions out there, he brought in live samples.

One day, he invited in a couple of Hare Krishnas, decked out in their orange robes and drums, and chanting their mantra; the next day, a Salvation Army recovering alcoholic, and, one day, even a young nun—in a mini skirt—who demonstrated how she had chained herself to a nuclear missile site. Everybody got real interested in nuclear disarmament that day. Religion class with Father Murphy was a parade, and everyone was allowed, riding their own float, throwing candy to the crowd.

In fact, it had been Father Murphy who had assigned the paper that Patrick was working on. He'd probably be thrilled that Patrick was digging for knowledge and had found a tough book to crack. If there was one school rule that Father Murphy preached, it was the same rule that every student had heard in every class since freshman year: A good paper should have multiple sources, and never the *World Book Encyclopedia*. Obviously, Father Murphy was the perfect person to talk to.

Or, maybe not.

As Patrick watched Father Murphy teaching students how to throw darts at a dart board blindfolded, he remembered that Murphy was the same priest who once talked about sex and the Industrial Age. That's where Tony got all his ideas. Plus, Father Murphy once said there was no hell.

"Gentlemen," he said, "Hell is just a scare tactic to get people to behave."

"Imagine that! Crowd control," Tony said.

Now, Tony had decided to have sex before his wedding night.

Patrick loved Father Murphy, but these were unsteady days. The blue eyes of Virginia von Bierhart were chasing him down the hallways. He had a paper to finish. And now the whole moral architecture of the school was threatened by a book he had read. How could he avoid Virginia if some sockless priest told him the wrong ideas about *What is Man*? Nope. Father Murphy was out. Only one thing left to do.

Confide his problems to the most boring and pious priest at school: his gym teacher, Father Dunelli.

Chapter 13

THE GYM CLASS OF THIRTY YOUNG MEN wearing brown St. Aloysius sweatshirts and gym shorts ran out onto the football field. The day was sunny and warm; the trees on the far side of the field strummed the death song of fall in chords of red and yellow. Father Dunelli, a short, thin man in his thirties with short black hair, a Michelangelo nose, and brown eyes like a church statue walked behind the boys, his head down. The same way he walked indoors, head always down, in thought, in prayer, no one knew. "OK, men," he called out in a gentle voice, "are you ready to workout?" Without waiting for any replies, he yelled, "Take your positions." The boys laid down in the middle of the field in rows of six, five guys to a row. "Pushups!" he shouted gently.

As Patrick listened to the soothing quality of Father Dunelli's voice counting down from twenty-five, he thought he just might be the right priest to ask about the book. Besides, he looked like a priest.

The guys ran through their drills: pushups, sit-ups, burpies. Burpies were killers. On Father Dunelli's command, they had to lay on their backs and wait for the signal, then lift their legs six inches off the ground, and open and close them like scissors several times before dropping them back to the ground.

"Up . . . apart . . . together . . . apart . . . together . . . apart . . . down."

"Down" was the word every guy longed to hear. A single group sigh—a grunt really—rushed out as they all dropped their rubbery legs back onto the grass. Then, they had to do it all again:

"Up . . . apart . . .together . . ."

Father Dunelli took no relish in their suffering, but he made them suffer, knowing it would prepare them for bigger things—self denial, endurance, and most importantly, becoming new men.

"I can't hold it any longer," someone grunted, letting out a fart. It never failed. Some guy always farted during burpies. A group moan followed. Everyone knowing Father Dunelli would punish them with laps to learn self-control.

"Twice around the field for that indiscretion."

Patrick got up off the grass with the others and started to run around the field. It was the same field as the football game he and Tony went to on Friday night. But that was so long ago, a false dream that had melted into this real world of soreness, farting, and running. The runners circled the field once, passing Father Dunelli, who studied his stopwatch as he called out their times. One more lap and they would be judged. The judgment was how well they had done compared to their last class run. Had they improved? Were they better men today than they were last Friday? Monday laps, like burpies, were always the hardest: lungs stinging from weekend cigarettes, hearts beating hard from too much pizza, White Castle burgers, and beer. And everyone's legs—weak and powerless, wobbling because there had been no real running over the weekend, except for when they'd run from the police.

"What have you been doing all weekend?" Father Dunelli called out. "The world has softened you. Run like Paul! Run for the prize!" Father Dunelli always found a way to bring in Paul.

As he rounded his final lap, Patrick watched Father Dunelli from across the field. Even though he didn't know him very well, Father Dunelli was obviously the right one to ask. Patrick lagged behind and came in last on purpose.

"What's wrong with you today, young man?"

Patrick stopped and put his head down panting, and rested his hands on his knees. "I don't know. I guess I've got a lot on my mind."

"What's the problem?"

Patrick stood up. "Something's bothering me, Father."

Father Dunelli cleared his stopwatch to zero and put it away. "What is it, son?"

Patrick got nervous and stalled. "Well . . . it's hard to explain. But—" Patrick hesitated. "Something happened to me . . . over the weekend."

"Have you sinned?"

"Well, no more than usual."

"You'd better come see me in my office where we can talk. Run in now and take a shower, and I'll be waiting for you."

Patrick jogged into the locker room where some guys were standing around naked, toweling off after a shower. He'd never liked the locker room. This was the same room where Father Dunelli had shown them the film on venereal diseases earlier in the semester. It was a film with true confessions of men who had sex before they were married, men who ended up with diseases that made their penises burn and itch in agony. Patrick had almost fainted that day. Shaking off the memory, he took off his clothes and walked into the shower room where four other naked guys stood washing up, including Tony.

"I've been doing some thinking," Tony said when he saw Patrick. He was standing there with his back to the shower spray, lathering up his chest hair. Tony's "Gift of the Italian People to the World," as he called it, was also lathered up, but at rest. Tony's blood was rushing to his head instead, to coordinate some new plan that always seemed to be forming. "I've been thinking about this coming weekend."

Patrick took the space beside Tony and grabbed a bar of soap and washed his armpits. "What weekend? It's only Monday."

"A man needs to think ahead."

"I don't want to go out this weekend," Patrick said. "I have that paper to finish—the one you interrupted. It's due Monday."

"So write it before the weekend. Look, it comes down to this . . ." Tony whispered, leaning toward Patrick so the others wouldn't hear, "you need to call Virginia right away to let her know you're interested."

"But I'm not."

"Don't lie."

Patrick filled his mouth with hot water and began to gargle as loud as he could to drown out Tony. Tony was right. He *was* interested in Virginia. More interested in her than he'd ever been in any girl. And now, she was practically in the shower with them, naked herself, standing with her back to Tony, pleading with Patrick to reach out to her, to please, please not let her go, to join her in the wet sudsy bosom of the Middle Ages. But for that very reason, he had to stay in control. He couldn't let his sperm count dictate his actions. His body was just a vessel for his mind and his spirit. And this current project—which he *was* going to talk about with Father Dunelli—was far more important than a girl that some fat man had tricked him into kissing. None of this would have happened if he'd stayed in his room Friday night. He decided to forget he ever met Virginia. She was a mirage. He spit out the water he was gargling and started to leave. But Tony grabbed his arm.

"Wait, I have to tell you a secret . . . You know what this is?"

"What now?"

Tony turned his chest into the shower, rinsing the suds off something hanging around his neck. It was a string holding a shiny brass key.

"It's the key to our golden future."

"Whatever you're talking about, I don't want to know." Patrick grabbed a towel. "I have to go talk with Father Dunelli."

"Don't listen to him," Tony called out, "He tried to talk to me once. He only believes in abstinence."

Patrick knocked on Father Dunelli's gym office door and went in. The room was harshly bright with fluorescent light overhead, and the steamy haze of humidity from the showers down the hall. Father Dunelli sat behind his desk holding a book on *Abstinence Through Athletic Activities*. But Patrick had a book of his own ready to go: Mark Twain's, *What is Man?* A crucifix hung on the wall behind Father Dunelli, alongside a school calendar, marked to show all the C-team cross-country track meets. Beside the desk, a short metal bookshelf sagged with books on athletic training and some religious books. Patrick took a seat in the duct-taped vinyl chair in front of Father Dunelli's desk.

"Now, what seems to be the problem?" Father Dunelli asked.

"It's about this book I read," Patrick said handing it to him.

Father Dunelli turned it over, read the title, and skimmed the back cover for the main idea. "What is Man?" he said, "It's not a very thick book for such a deep subject."

"I'm glad to hear you say that, because I was hoping you could read it for me, and, give me your opinion."

"I could, but, I'm confused. Why me? Why not your English teacher, or some other teacher, perhaps the one who assigned it?"

"Oh, it's not assigned. I just found it in the school library. I'm researching for a paper. And honestly, I thought you might be the best priest to explain it."

"But, why me?"

"Well . . . I . . . don't know. I just like the way you look, Father. I mean, you look like a priest."

Father Dunelli leaned back and blinked. "Are you teasing me? Is this some kind of joke the other boys put you up to?"

"Oh, no, Father, no. I mean it."

"Well, I don't understand. What's bothering you about this little book?" Father Dunelli pushed the book back across the desk to Patrick.

Patrick sat forward in his chair and rubbed his hands together, struggling about how to say it—so it wouldn't sound stupid. "The problem is . . . this book makes me feel like a fake. Like . . . I'm just pretending to be something I'm not."

"And what do you think you're pretending to be?"

"It's not just me, Father. And no offense—it's you."

"Me?" He looked at his watch.

"Well, not just you, but you . . . and all the other priests . . . and all the other guys. Maybe the whole school is pretending, but we don't know it yet."

Father Dunelli reached for the book again, and then leaned back and opened it. He rifled through several pages looking for some line to pop out that would explain why this sophomore was so overwrought. "I'm not familiar with this book. What's the main idea?"

"The main idea is . . . the thing that he keeps repeating is . . . that man doesn't really care about anything but impressing *himself.*"

"Impressing himself?"

"Yes, that's it."

Father Dunelli relaxed. He could handle this one easy. He leaned forward. "Nothing but impressing himself? Patrick, you know that's not true. Why, look at everyone at school, we all do things for others. What about the Mission Week? Or all the other service projects we do during the year to help others?"

"Yeah, I know, but think about it. We take pictures of all that stuff and put in the yearbook . . . to impress ourselves. Or, like when somebody gives up soda for Lent, they always want to talk about it. Don't you see? When a person is doing good . . . deep down he's only doing it to win his own self approval."

"What are you saying?"

"I'm saying . . . maybe it's a sin to be good."

The lunch bell rang.

Father Dunelli snapped the book shut. "This sounds like a lot of rubbish. We do good because we love God, not for ourselves. Maybe you should go eat lunch and relax."

Patrick refused to take the book back. It was time to go all the way. His voice was a bit shaky, but he had to do this. "I wish it were that simple, Father, but when I try to pray, I noticed there's part of me off to the side admiring me for trying. If you stop and think about it . . . if I do *any*thing good for God, deep down I don't love Him at all. I just want to love myself. I'm just trying to save myself from hell."

Father Dunelli frowned and pulled back while shaking his head, the book still in his hand. "Patrick, you're taking all this too seriously. This is just a book by Mark Twain. One man's take on life. It's not the Gospel."

"Yes, Father." This was getting him nowhere. Maybe he should have gone to Father Murphy.

"But . . . I can tell you're sincere, so I'll tell you what I'm going to do."

"Yes?"

"I'll read it for you and tell you why it's wrong."

"You think you can?"

Father Dunelli fidgeted with his track and field whistle. "With God's help, of course."

"Oh, that's great! How soon, Father?"

"I don't know. Sometime this semester."

Patrick stood up. "But Father, I'm afraid that's no good. I mean . . . I have a paper due Monday. Actually, it's more than the paper. I just really want to know what you think, because I always respected you, the way you look, and the way you walk around the hallways looking at the floor."

"Who told you I look at the floor?"

"No one, I just noticed it. Father, can you do it for me? Please? Can you help me out? Before the end of the week?"

Father Dunelli looked over at his wall calendar with all the track meets, then back at Patrick. "Well, it is a thin book, and if it means that much to you. OK, I'll write you a report to answer your concerns by the end of the week."

Patrick leaned over the desk and shook his hand. "Oh, thank you, Father, thank you." He felt better already.

Father Dunelli slotted the book in his brief case, and put the book on abstinence through athletic activities back on the shelf.

Chapter 14

AFTER A QUICK LUNCH, Patrick felt better. Father Dunelli was going to help him, and his paper was as good as written. This called for a smoke. It was time to relax. But his weekend pack of Camel non-filters was gone. No problem. He could bum a cigarette from one of the guys out by the smoking section. He headed to the doorway off the cafeteria that led to the smoking section—a little patch of sidewalk with a sand-filled concrete urn for an ashtray. Half a dozen guys stood around. The view was ugly, just a back parking lot, and the dumpsters, smelling of sour milk and humming with flies. The sidewalk where they stood was flecked with spit like a Jackson Pollack painting.

Smokers at St. Aloysius tended to have lower GPAs, and little athletic involvement. They were the party crowd, the longhairs, the soul searchers, the guys with I-don't-care neckties. Some wore neckties with the backside longer than the front. Others—with the knot loosened around the collar, because they wore the same tie every day and never untied it, only loosened it enough at the end of the day to throw it on a bedpost for tomorrow.

The group stood around, one hand in their pockets, their free hand working their smoke, flicking ashes between drags while they flipped their bangs out of their eyes and shared the sacrament of despair—tobacco. Tony was there, along with Jimmy Purvis. Tony pulled out his Camel pack and rifled one up for Patrick.

"Thanks." Patrick took the cigarette and lit up.

Tony wanted to tell Patrick more about the golden key, but too many guys were around, so he made a tactical decision to wait.

Barney Halady, the guy with the longest hair in the school, was planning a party for the upcoming Saturday night.

"You guys should come; it'll be dee-eee-e-cent."

Patrick took another drag of his cigarette. Here it was only Monday at lunch break, and already the smoking-section crowd was reaching forward to—practically living for— the next weekend. The school week to them was just a technicality to be endured between weekends. Barney's party, complete with beer and a bonfire, was to be at the Haladay family farm. Plus, they had a horse trail with a creek, and a cave and a burial ground with a pile of rocks on a dead Indian girl. His parents would be there, of course, but they were cool. His mom thought boys should get drunk properly, in one spot, and spend the night, so they wouldn't drink and drive. And since the farmhouse had some extra bedrooms, and a barn good enough for sleeping bags, it was the perfect place. Not only that, but the next morning, his mom would make a big breakfast and they could ride horses all Saturday.

"What kind of breakfast?" Jimmy Purvis asked.

"Oh, shit, man, it won't be Cheerios. My mom'll make pancakes and sausage, and biscuits and gravy, and scrambled eggs . . . and rows of bacon as stiff as a diving board, and a big pitcher of orange juice with ice in it. And we'll have cowboy coffee."

"What's cowboy coffee?" Tony asked.

"The best fucking coffee you ever had. None of that instant shit," Haladay said. "You take a bunch of big coffee beans and put 'em in a pot of water sitting on a grate over a campfire and just boil the shit out of 'em, like they do in those John Wayne movies. It's dee-eee-e-cent."

"Damn, that sounds good," Jimmy said.

Almost everybody said they wanted to go and would try to get permission from their parents to spend the night. Patrick just nodded, but didn't say anything. He wasn't interested. He had that paper to write, and, he was damned tired of running around like a fool on the weekend trying to push the red button of life. Tony said it all sounded pretty cool, but Patrick noticed that Tony didn't say he would be there, which later he would understand why. Tony was planning something different. Something better. Something secret that he would share with Patrick. Privately.

The bell rang.

The smokers moaned and took their last drags, and somebody harked up a quid and spit on the sidewalk, which prompted a volley of spitting by everyone else. Which then triggered another match to see who could flip their cigarette butts into the concrete urn ashtray. Some went in, some missed, but nobody bothered to pick up the ones that missed. When Patrick started back, Tony held him back until all the other guys had left. Then, Tony told him the secret.

"Remember that key I showed you?"

"Yeah."

"I'm watching a house for a neighbor going out of town this weekend, you know, to water his plants." Tony flexed his eyebrows and studied Patrick's reaction.

"So?"

"So? Don't you get it?"

"What?"

"We get a couple girls . . . and. . . . Who needs The Love Machine when you've got a Love House?"

Patrick took a breath to say no way, but in that breath he saw it all: Slow dancing to records on the high-fi set, sitting by the fireplace not having to say a word, kissing Virginia again like at the pool, only now, there would be nothing to stop them. Tony and his date holding hands, running upstairs, then Virginia saying they'd better go upstairs, too.

Oh shit. "No way."

"Don't decide yet; just think about Virginia and what you'll say to her when you call her."

"I'm not gonna call her."

"You *have* to call her."

"I don't have to do anything."

Tony grabbed Patrick by the back of his belt, and this time, raised his voice. He was adamant. "We *all* have to do God's will. Look at the facts. You kissed her. She gave you *the look*, and now, God gives you this golden opportunity." He pulled out the key again and flashed it in the sun. "And another thing, for a project like this, we need *public* school girls. That's why you have to call her. Get her to line up a blind date for me . . . just make sure she's from a public school."

"I have to go." Patrick pulled away from Tony. "You're gonna make me late for biology class."

"I'm trying to make you *on time* for biology class. With a real woman, not a book."

Patrick hurried off to biology class. It was the beginning of a long week of suffering.

Chapter 15

AFTER SCHOOL Virginia von Bierhart got on her horse, Applesauce, and rode him down past the elk and buffalo to a spot out of view from the house, in case her mother was watching from the window. Her mother had reminded her when she came home from school that she was grounded for getting in a fight at the party with her brother.

Once Virginia reached the boundary of the property, she dismounted and tied the horse's reins to the white fence. With no one to see her, Virginia climbed the fence, cut through some adjoining yards, past swing sets, and knocked on the back door of a home about three mansions down, where Loretta Sharp lived. Loretta had promised to find out all she could about this Patrick Cantwell guy from the girls she knew at Joyous Days High—and, she promised to keep Virginia's name out of it.

Loretta's mom, very pregnant, opened the back door and let Virginia in.

"Why, Virginia, what are you up to coming in the back door?"

"I'm grounded, so I can only stay a minute. I cut through the back yards."

"What are you grounded for?"

"Oh, I got into a fight with Nelson and knocked him into a swimming pool, but he had it coming. When's the baby due?"

Mrs. Sharp rubbed her belly. "Having a C-section next week. Can't believe we'll have another baby in the house again. You shouldn't fight with your brother. Who knows? Someday he might introduce you to the man you'll marry."

"Is that how you met Mr. Sharp?"

"No, it was a blind date. A blind date, and now, here I am."

"Is Loretta home?"

"Yeah, she's upstairs, pretending to do homework to get out of unloading the dishwasher like I told her. You go say hi and tell her to come down and help."

"OK."

Virginia ran upstairs and knocked on Loretta's door.

"I'm doing homework."

Virginia opened the door and saw Loretta was still in her Joyous Days High uniform, a red jumper skirt with a white, short-sleeve blouse. She sat sprawled out in a stuffed chair with her legs up on the bed. Her legs were unshaven and she wore no makeup. Even with her wild brown hair, Loretta could look pretty if she wanted to, but lately she didn't care. On a side table was a glass of milk and a half-eaten sleeve of Fig Newtons. She was reading a paperback: *How to Be Your Own Best Friend.*

"Doing homework?"

"Shit, no. I thought you were my mom."

Virginia sat down on the chair by Loretta's desk and pushed aside a stack of untouched schoolbooks for elbowroom. "She told me to tell you—"

"I know. She wants me to empty the dishwasher, and get domesticated." Loretta put down the book and noticed Virginia looking at her legs.

"Why should I? What's the point?"

"Why should you what?"

"Shave my legs."

"I didn't say—"

"I saw you looking." Loretta took her legs down off the bed and put some Visine in her eyes. "Man, I've got the munchies. Look, I don't have to look good all the time like you do at Ladue High. There aren't any boys at Joyous Days . . . and even if there were—" She chewed her Fig Newton and smoldered.

"I didn't mean to bring *that* up," Virginia said, "Are you still upset about him?"

Loretta folded her arms across her chest. "The guy who dumped me after we were in a play for six weeks? After making out with me after every rehearsal? After telling me I was 'like no other girl'?"

Virginia nodded.

"Hell, no. I don't think about him. Or *any* guy. Who needs them!" She got off the chair and walked across the room throwing a vase of dead flowers in the trash. "Fuckers. They're all actors. All guys everywhere. Pretending to care. All they really want—" Loretta saw Virginia was looking at the bottom of her skirt. "What are you looking at now?"

"Loretta, why do you have staples in you hem?"

Loretta laughed and grabbed her stapled skirt to brag about it. "This? You wanna know about this? Shit! That's for Sister John Margaret, a real tough old, wrinkled nun bitch. Roams the halls ringing this little hand bell when all the girls are talking." Loretta hunched over and walked around the room ringing an imaginary bell, imitating the old nun with a scratchy voice. "Gells, Gells, no talking in the halls, no talking in the halls."

Virginia clapped at the performance, and Loretta curtsied and plopped down in the chair smiling.

"Yeah, Sister John Margaret. If she catches you with a loose hem, damn, it's a demerit, so we all just staple our skirts to stay out of jug. We don't give a shit how we look. I guess I look like a real cruddy bitch."

"Yeah."

They both laughed and Loretta threw the sleeve of Fig Newtons to Virginia. Virginia got out a cookie, but she only looked at it. Loretta studied her. Virginia glanced up waiting for some news on *the project*.

"Are you still thinking about that guy who kissed you by the pool?"

Virginia nodded.

"You should forget about him. I've been reading this book. Hey, eat your damned Fig Netwon."

Virginia popped one in her mouth, and between chews, she said, "What'd you find out about him?"

Loretta grabbed another Fig Newton and washed it down with milk, then grabbed another and turned it over to admire its floury smoothness.

"Stop stalling. Just tell me already."

"I'll give it to you straight. No bullshit."

Virginia took a breath and held it.

"He's a loser."

Virginia choked on the cookie. Loretta handed her the glass of milk. She took a quick drink and said, "What?"

"Yeah, a total loser. I talked to four different girls. Same story every time. He doesn't play sports; he's not in any plays; not that smart; always talks about quitting smoking but never does; he got into some kind of trouble with the police in grade school, a couple of times, too, a real shit disturber. But then in high school, he got all serious and mysterious and hardly ever goes out."

"Has he got a girlfriend?"

"No."

"Well . . . that's good news."

"No, it isn't. Virginia, no guy is the answer to your life, but especially not *this* guy. Plus, when he does go out, he hangs with this Italian guy—another loser—the guy you played strip poker with."

"Tony Vivamano."

"That's him. He's a crazy man, a make-out machine with bad cologne. He drives his mother's station wagon, for God's sake, like a rocket, too. And they hang with this Hoosier group of girls and guys who meet every weekend night on the steps of their grade school gym. How lame is that? They score some beer and get drunk on the golf course and eat White Castle burgers and probably burp and fart till midnight."

Virginia gagged on the dry Fig Newton. She jumped up and grabbed Loretta's milk. They both started laughing when Virginia burped. Then Virginia sat down and started crying.

"Oh, shit, don't cry. I'm sorry, Virginia, I didn't mean to hurt your feelings." Loretta reached for her box of Kleenex, and Virginia blew her nose.

"I feel like a fool," she blubbered.

"Don't be mad at yourself. You have to like yourself for who you are—without any guy. A guy kisses you and you imagine it's the start of something, but that's bullshit. You need to change your self image, girl."

Virginia grabbed a handful of Fig Newtons and absentmindedly stuck one right after the other into her mouth. Then, talking with her mouth full, she said, "But I still want to talk to him. That's the crazy thing, even if he is a Hoosier. I don't care. Oh, hell, I'm just going to go home and call him and ask what the hell that kiss was all about." Virginia got up and threw the rest of the cookies on Loretta's bed and ran down the steps, ran through the kitchen, ran past Loretta's mom, and out of the house.

She ran all the way to the fence, wanting to cry some more, but nothing would come. All she could feel as she got closer and closer to her horse was the Fig Newtons flouncing in her stomach. She untied the reins, hopped the fence, and jumped in the saddle ready to gallop off. But before she could turn away— she heard Loretta yelling, "Virginia, Virginia, wait!"

Virginia looked and saw Loretta racing across back yards on her little brother's Stingray bike, her wild hair breezing back, her red jumper coming apart at the hem staples while she spun the pedals.

"You can't call him!" Loretta yelled as she skidded to a stop at the fence.

"Why not?"

"Why not? Why not?" She was panting and leaning on the handlebars. Finally, she caught her breath. "Hell, because you're Virginia von Bierhart. One of *the* von Bierhart's."

"Yeah, so?"

"So, as soon as he knows that, he'll act different than if you were just any girl."

"You're right. I hate being me. I wish I were dead."

Virginia reined the horse's head toward her house, but Loretta leaped up on the fence and grabbed his bridle. "Wait! Don't say that. Don't *ever* say that." Then, glancing back toward her house and the waiting dishwasher, Loretta said, "Can two ride on him?"

"Sure, but I thought you had to empty the dishwasher."

"To tell you the truth, I'm not really a dishwasher-type person. But you know, that's OK. You have to like yourself for who you are."

Loretta hopped on the back of Applesauce, and Virginia kicked the horse's haunches. Applesauce sauntered along the creek trail nice and easy. As the horse ambled along beneath the afternoon sun rippling through the trees, Virginia watched the orange leaves drift in the water. And they brainstormed about Patrick and the impossible problem of how to find out why he kissed her.

"Here's an idea. This might work," Loretta said, "What if—"

Virginia listened while Loretta bragged about how being in school plays had helped her become a much better liar. She had learned the art of pretending to be another person.

"But what does that have to do with me?"

"Just listen," Loretta lectured. "What if we pretend we're two different girls, with fake names? We could change your looks somehow, and then accidentally run into this Patrick Cantwell on a weekend night."

"What good'll that do?" Virginia asked.

"Don't you see? You hang around him for just a few hours, and you'll not only get sick of the way he talks and acts, but I'll bet you, he'll try to kiss you again, but he won't know it's you. That's when you'll see what I mean."

"What do you mean?'

"I *mean* . . . what's he doing kissing you, the *pretend* you, when he doesn't know you're *you* . . . you know, the same girl he kissed at the pool?"

"That's right!" Virginia yanked on Applesauce's reins. "Who does he think he is? He shouldn't be kissing me a second time if I look different and he doesn't know I'm the girl by the pool that he kissed the first time. Makes me want to punch him flat."

"Well, you should."

"You're right."

"That's for damn sure. I know I'm right. A girl has to be her own best friend. Guys are trouble. Nothing but."

"All right, let's do it. This weekend."

The girl's shook on it, but then Loretta remembered something. "Oh, shit, I've gotta go on a damned retreat."

"What's that?"

"You know, some of the girls from the school are supposed to go into the woods to do some soul searching."

"Can't you get out of it?"

"I'm afraid the other girls would kill me."

"Why?"

"I'm supposed to bring the pot."

"On retreat?"

"Yeah, well, to hell with them. Damned mooches. I got it! You ask your parents if you can go on retreat with me."

"I don't want to go on retreat."

"I know that. Don't worry, we'll ditch it. That way we'll have the whole weekend to get you over this guy."

"But how do you ditch retreat? Don't they have a list?"

"Hey, I'm in theatre, remember?"

They rode along some more, Loretta coaching Virginia about how to use acting skills to lie to her parents about going on retreat. "If you can get permission, then I'll figure out my end on how to ditch retreat," Loretta said. Virginia gave Applesauce a swift kick and galloped him back to the fence to drop off Loretta. As Loretta climbed over the fence and got on her brother's bike, she said, "Remember, you've gotta be your own best friend."

Virginia watched her and smiled. How good it was to have a clear-thinking friend in a crisis.

Chapter 16

THE BUTLER SERVED dinner promptly at seven o'clock every night at the von Bierhart estate. That gave brewery president and CEO Hugo von Bierhart enough time to get home, change into his dinner jacket and loafers, have a couple of drinks while lounging in his favorite leather chair, and chat over the latest crisis on the home front with his wife. Tonight was lobster again, and small potatoes with green beans al dente, and a Ritz salad. Virginia was upstairs practicing her lines for her scene she was about to perform, while her parents and her brother Nelson waited at the dining room table covered with a red linen table cloth, and the chandelier lights dimmed. Low lights, Mrs. von Bierhart always said, helped soothe everyone's nerves after a long day of industry.

"I'm sorry, but it's not over caution, these sort of things *do* happen all the time," Mr. von Bierhart said. He was lecturing Nelson about how brewery executives, and especially their children, could be kidnapped for a ransom if they aren't careful of their whereabouts. Nelson had just asked his parents if he could go skiing in Vale with some high school buddies. But Mr. von Bierhart was against the idea of having the only male heir to the brewery three states away where anybody could snatch him and demand a ransom.

"Dad, you're being paranoid," Nelson said. "My friends' dads aren't worried about that stuff."

"I suppose you've never heard of the Coors brewery kidnapping, or the Lindbergh baby kidnapping, or what was that other one?" he asked, looking at his wife at the end of the table. "The car dealer's son?"

"Bobby Greenlease."

"That's right, little Bobby Greenlease, killed by kidnappers just because his father owned a Cadillac dealership. They caught them right here in town. It was back in the '50s."

"Well, this is the 1970s. None of that stuff happens now."

"Where is that girl?" Mr. von Bierhart said, glancing over at Virginia's empty chair. "Our dinner's getting cold."

Just then, Virginia came downstairs, looking neat and sharp, the way her father always liked it. She was wearing a dinner jacket over her regular after school clothes and riding boots.

"Virginia, we've been waiting," he said.

"Sorry, Dad, homework."

"Well, let's eat."

They didn't say grace, but all looked up the table at Mrs. von Bierhart, her salad fork, untouched on the table. This was one of the few moments of absolute power she had over the family. So, she moved her right hand *ever so slowly*, grasping her fork and looking around at all her family. She smiled with her eyes and touched the tip of her fork into her salad.

It was as if she had fired a starter pistol.

Mr. von Bierhart and Nelson grabbed their forks and attacked their lobster tails. Virginia was in no hurry. And she wasn't hungry for lobster. That was her father's favorite dish, but even lobster can get old when you have it once a week. She thought about the kiss.

"Father."

"Yes," he said, his mouth full.

"Loretta asked me to go with her this weekend, on a special outing. I'd be away all weekend. Would that be all right?"

Nelson perked up, eager to see her dealt a disappointment.

"Virginia, aren't you still grounded?" her father said, cracking a lobster claw.

"Yes, but I thought since I've been good and wrote Nelson such a nice apology memo, and not one typo, that maybe—."

"It was a nice apology," Mrs. von Bierhart said.

"I didn't think so," Nelson said, "She's a liar and a slut."

The parents looked up at each other, each wanting the other to say something.

"I hate you!" Virginia shouted. She threw an al dente string bean across the table with the fury of a killer and it skipped off Nelson's shoulder like a skier going off a cliff.

"*Vah-gin-Yah!*" her mother yelled, pounding the table. "I want no rioting! You go pick that up."

"Make him pick it up! He called me—"

"Point of order!" Mr. von Bierhart said clanging his water glass with a spoon. "We must have order."

Before anyone could move, the butler ran in, picked up the string bean, and vanished backwards into the kitchen.

"Now, let's all calm down and enjoy our dinner!" Mr. von Bierhart said. "Let's try to act . . . professional."

Everyone started eating again, the only sound the sulking chatter of knives and forks, and the tired ticking of a clock down the hall. Finally, Mr. von Bierhart took charge to keep order in the corporation.

"Even if you weren't grounded," Mr. von Bierhart said, stuffing a small potato in his mouth, "you know I don't believe in sleepovers."

Mrs. von Bierhart sipped some white wine and chimed in. "That's right, dear; sleepovers are for children . . . curfews are for teenagers."

"I know, you're right, Mother. But Father?"

"Yes."

"This is a special kind of sleepover."

"How is it special?"

"It's a retreat."

Everyone at the table stopped eating and looked at her.

"A retreat?" Nelson said. "What? Are you going *Catholic* on us?" He started laughing and looked to see if his dad would laugh, too.

Mr. von Bierhart held his hand up toward Nelson. "Now, son, Catholics are some of our best customers, remember that."

"Yes, sir."

"So, what is this retreat all about, dear? What interests you about this?" Mrs. von Bierhart said, dabbing the corner of her lips with her napkin.

And now . . . it was performance time. The monologue. Loretta had told Virginia earlier in the day how she sometimes practiced her role in a play in her room. "The key," she'd told her was that "you have to set yourself aside and believe you are another person who really *wants* what they want in the play.

"Well, Mother," she said, taking a sip of water like an innocent, "Loretta says it's just girls and they try to do some real thinking about what life is really all about."

Nelson moaned. "Oh, God, this is all lies."

Virginia lowered her head to wait for him to stop and continued meekly. "Loretta says they have this retreat center with a safety fence around it, and no boys are allowed in. There's even a guard at the gate to check everybody's name. And when you get inside, everybody has their own room where they can study and try to find out what life is about."

Mr. von Bierhart took a sip of his wine and put down the glass. "Virginia, may I first say, I forgot to tell you, you look very professional tonight with that dinner jacket on. You look good enough to drop by my office."

"Thank you, Father." She kept her demeanor low key, like somebody who needed to find the meaning of life.

"But you don't need to go out in the woods with a gaggle of teenage girls to find out what life's all about. Just ask me . . . I'll tell you."

Everyone but Virginia started eating again, thinking that had settled it, but Virginia kept at it. "Father, don't you want me to grow up and mature? Don't you want me to find out *for myself*? Can't I ever be my own person?" Her voice cracked a little, and Nelson looked back and forth at his parents to see if they realized what his sister was doing.

"You *are* your own person. More than you know, dear," Mrs. von Bierhart said.

"I wish I were. I wish I were strong like you, Mother, but Father doesn't trust me to leave the house and have a new idea." She threw in a sniff for effect.

Mr. von Bierhart clunked down his fork. "Virginia, please. Don't say that. You know I trust you to have a new idea. I love new ideas. Why, just today, we were looking at ultra-light aluminum cans to save on shipping weight."

Virginia raised her voice. "Father, I'm not talking about cans. I *need* to go on this damn retreat and find myself."

Nelson beat his lobster carcass with a fork and just shook his head.

Mr. von Bierhart looked at his wife for help, but she only shrugged. "Look, Virginia, you talk as though you've been misplaced," her father said. "You don't need to find yourself. You're right here with us, where you belong." He reached over and patted her hand.

This time, Virginia started to cry the way she had always cried for traffic cops. Sometimes it worked; sometimes not.

"Don't let her pretend to cry and get her way," Nelson said. "Out in the woods on retreat, she could get kidnapped. Tell her about Bobby Greenlease."

"He's right! I forgot about that," Mr. von Bierhart said, raising his voice to be heard like he did over his full board of directors. "Virginia, I was telling Nelson before you came down—"

"Wait a minute! Wait one damned minute," Mrs. von Bierhart said.

Everyone looked down the table at the woman whose salad fork was like a queen's scepter with the power that allowed them to start eating. She picked up her salad fork and pointed at all of them. "If Virginia has a heart to try to improve herself and see what life is all about, I say let her go."

"But, Mother," Nelson said.

"And another thing, Hugo. I say if Nelson wants to go break a leg on his damned ski trip, let him go. No one's going to kidnap him. He's too ugly."

They all laughed. Laughed so hard and long that the butler and the cook came in to see what was wrong. Mr. von Bierhart told them that he made a decision. *He* had decided to let his children spread their wings, to find out what life is all about. Mrs. von Bierhart nodded, knowing it was best to let him take credit for things.

For dessert, they ate chocolate cake and ice cream, and it turned out to be one of the nicest family meals they'd had all year.

Chapter 17

TWENTY MEN IN BLACK, the Jesuits of St. Aloysius, filed out of their residence hall and back into the school that night for a special meeting. No one talked as they strode down the hallways to the library, everyone preoccupied with what was coming. Father Woerstbrauth unlocked the library and flipped on the lights, which came on in stages as the men took their seats around a long, rectangular table. Father Woerstbrauth stood at the head.

"Men, Judgment Day is coming, and we are going to be ready."

They all laughed. Father Woerstbrauth was referring to the scheduled Friday arrival of the two top Jesuits from the Vatican, whose official agenda was to "see how things were going." But Father Woerstbrauth knew what that meant. They would open the books. They would want to see revenue and expenditures, enrollment projections, academic rankings, articles on winning sports teams, and most of all— plans for alumni fundraising and the state of the endowment fund. St. Aloysius was a relatively new school, only six years old, a westward expansion into the suburbs of Jesuit education, and it had been relying on the annual seed money from the Vatican. Father Woerstbrauth's fear was that the school was about to be weaned of its milk money.

"Looks like we're all here . . . let's begin."

Just then the door creaked open, and Father Dunelli slinked in carrying his briefcase. He crossed the room looking at the rug, and took his seat at the far end of the table. Once he was seated, everyone turned back to the principal. With no one looking, Father Dunelli reached in his briefcase and pulled out the book, *What is Man?* to do a little speed-reading during what would be a long meeting. The book took the form of a dialogue between two men, one older and cynical, and the other, young and idealistic. The cynical man argued that every man is only interested in one thing: winning his own self-approval, doing whatever it takes to admire himself. The younger one argued that man could be noble and selfless, and Father Dunelli was rooting for the younger man as he flipped through the pages.

"Father Dunelli, what's that you're reading?" Father Woerstbrauth asked. All the Jesuits turned and looked down the table at him.

"Oh, nothing," he said, closing the book with his finger marking the page, "Just a little homework."

"What is it?"

"A book by Mark Twain."

"Well, we're in a crisis. This is no time for Tom Sawyer. Come here."

Father Dunelli rose and walked to the head of the table, all eyes on him as he walked, head down, carrying his book beneath his arm to where his boss stood. "Yes, Father?"

"You speak Italian?"

"Yes, Father."

"Fluently?"

"Yes, Father."

"Good, you will act as our special liaison when our visitors arrive, and you'll need to be conversant in all the many issues facing the school that may come up. Can you do it?"

"Well, Father, I'd be glad to help, but the C-team has an important cross country divisional meet at Shepherds by Night this Wednesday."

All the other priests laughed.

"You're a good coach, but I'm sure the boys can run on momentum for one week without you and do just fine. You've trained them, right?

"Yes, Father."

"Good, now have a seat and take notes on tonight's meeting. And type up two summaries for us—one in English, and one in Italian."

"Yes, Father, but, may I ask when the assignment will be due?"

"How do you say 'tomorrow' in Italian?"

"*Domani.*"

"That's when. Domani."

They all laughed at him again, and he smiled. Father Woerstbrauth slid a yellow legal pad across the table to him, in front of the empty seat next to him. Father Dunelli sat down and covered up the book, *What is Man?* with the legal pad and started taking notes. Father Woerstbrauth turned back to the entire group, his eyes shining with a budgetary glow the priests had seen before.

"Now, let's assume the real reason they're coming is to tell us the seed money is cut off. So, let's show them we can take care of ourselves. Let's get that endowment fund up and running before they even get here. Wouldn't we all feel better about ourselves if we could show Rome we don't need them to save us?"

The Jesuits applauded, everyone except Father Dunelli, who was taking notes like a lost freshman in a lecture hall.

"What do you say men? Shall we do it?"

There was more applause. This time Father Dunelli put down his pen to clap and show solidarity, then quickly picked it up to write down whatever Father Woerstbrauth said next.

"Let's show them what kind of school we're able to make St. Aloysius into—a self-sustaining school we can be proud of."

This time, there was a standing ovation. Father Woerstbrauth wiped his forehead with a handkerchief and signaled for everyone to sit down and get to work. For the next two hours, they discussed plans to spruce up the school, create a flow chart on alumni fundraising goals, and to identify a list of potential wealthy families who might make donations to the endowment fund before Friday. On the list was the grandmother of sophomore, Matt Baimbridge, an average student who had been jugged that day for pretending to trip over an invisible obstacle in Father Ortega's Spanish class. It came to their attention that the grandmother was in declining health and she could use a pastoral visit from the Jesuits to ensure that her legacy will not be forgotten. Father Woerstbrauth decided that he and Father Dunelli would handle the case personally.

Chapter 18

ON TUESDAY MORNING the students arrived in their carpools to find the main lot roped off and all cars diverted onto the upper ballfield for parking. It smelled like tar. Brother Hannigan, superintendent of the grounds, had been working through the night on his tractor to spray a fresh coat of black driveway sealant onto the lot. No one was to set foot on it for a day, to avoid tracking tar into the school. Inside the school, the students could smell the paint. The Jesuits, donned in paint clothes, had worked overnight to touch up the woodwork and trim, removing all the handprints and scuffmarks. Morning announcements updated students on the preparation for the visitors, with a reminder for everyone to get a hair cut. As a special incentive, barbers would visit the school on Thursday, with extra credit offered in any class a student wanted, if he would get a businessman's cut.

The students moaned, but many considered the benefit of getting a haircut to raise their grades. After all, a good grade would last on their semester report card, but a haircut would only last a month or so.

Every homeroom had a big trashcan brought in for the teacher and students to throw out all unnecessary papers, magazines, and obsolete books. Students were all instructed to look under their desktops and remove all gum, whether they put it there or not. Teachers with ratty sofas and easy chairs assigned students to carry them out to the dumpster.

Throughout the day, the grounds crew could be seen from the classroom windows, trimming the fields, cutting away dead limbs from trees, and planting new shrubs and mums, both red and yellow, by the administrative office entrance. During free hour, students were given rags soaked in solvent, so they could scrub kick marks off the metal lockers. All boys in the school choir gathered for extra practice in the gym. And students on Jug that week did all sorts of things to improve the school appearance—replace dead light bulbs, clean toilets, and pull weeds that would grow back later.

The school was shaping up. After lunch Monday, Tony and Patrick went out to the smoking section and found the concrete urn ashtray was gone. In its place was a sign that said: "No Smoking. Any student caught smoking on school grounds will receive a demerit."

So, they wandered off school grounds into the woods to smoke.

"Are you gonna call her today?" Tony asked Patrick.

"No."

The bell rang, and the two boys ran back to school, coughing and spitting.

And the day wore on: Algebra, Chemistry, Western Civilization, Religion, English and gym. Father Dunelli had the boys exercise in the gym, because the grounds crew was going over the football field. He said nothing to Patrick about the book he was supposed to be reading, but when their eyes met, Father Dunelli looked burdened, as if maybe he had been reading it. That's good, thought Patrick.

It was good to know a top Jesuit mind was revving up to solve the problem, like the floor buffer the janitor switched on to polish the gym when the final bell rang.

As Patrick joined the crowd pouring out of school, he relished the thought that Father Dunelli, the most humble of all priests, would be searching his library to find answers. Even though Father Dunelli didn't know the burden Patrick felt from kissing Virginia von Bierhart—*that,* he would have to suffer alone—he *did know* about his *What is Man?* burden. It was good to know a priest with wisdom passed down from the ancients could research a proper answer.

The burden fell freshly on Patrick on the school parking lot. It was colder, and the days were getting shorter. High school was racing along. Life was racing along. They were all supposed to be thinking about eternity in their spare time at St. Aloysius. But that was the one thing Patrick wanted nothing to do with. Eternity was for the dead.

Patrick got in the car, shut the door, and his carpool left school for home. It was good to know that Father Dunelli would be working through the night to find some answers.

Chapter 19

FATHER DUNELLI AND FATHER WOERSTBRAUTH parked outside the nursing home, on their way to see Margaret Baimbridge, the grandmother of sophomore Matt Baimbridge. They got out of the car and walked up a moon-lit, winding path toward the old brick infirmary, surrounded by one-hundred-foot-tall oak trees, dozens of them crowding the hilly grounds. Glancing at his watch, Father Woerstbrauth led the way carrying a brief case with the necessary forms. Father Dunelli, carrying his small, black, leather-bound prayer booklet with its scarlet page marker, followed behind him, his head down. The wind was picking up. Sudden gusts blew leaves across their path, while clouds scudded across the moon above the tree limbs.

"When we meet her, you can address her spiritual needs and I'll finish up and tell her about the school's needs," Father Woerstbrauth said.

"How serious is her condition?" Father Dunelli asked.

"Well, I'm not sure, but—" Before he could finish, they heard a crack behind them and turned to witness a large oak limb slam onto the lawn.

"We'd better hurry," Father Woerstbrauth said.

They entered the front hallway, a dark-paneled room with a black and white checkered floor and a reception desk lit by a green lamp. The nurse behind the desk signed them in.

"This way," Father Woerstbrauth said, leading the way.

As they walked down a dim hallway, they heard piano music. Passing a side den, they glimpsed a white-haired woman in the piano light, plunking out the tune, "Ain't She Sweet," as best she could, while a few bald men in sweaters crooned about her.

"You see, these places aren't all full of dying people," Father Woerstbrauth said. "Maybe we'll find her singing, too."

"You're right."

Just then, a team of paramedics pushing an elderly man on a gurney came running around the corner, barreling straight for the two priests. They threw their bodies into the wall as the bullet train shot past them toward the exit.

"We'd better hurry," Father Woerstbrauth said leading the way.

They speed-walked past rooms with open doors where TV sets with the volume on hi threw light on the blanketed legs of widows in easy chairs. Up ahead, an open and brightly lit nurse's station thronged with patients in wheel chairs lining the walls, passing the time. The patients looked up at the visitors, some reaching out with their hands like the doomed in a leper colony. Some mumbled for help.

One man in a blue plaid bathrobe reached out and grabbed at Father Dunelli. "Don't let 'em take me!"

Father Dunelli stopped to shake his hand. "Hello, friend."

The man repeated his plea. "Oh, Father, don't let 'em take me there!"

"Where?"

"The south wing."

"What's wrong with the south wing?"

"That's where they take you when . . . you aren't coming back."

Father Woerstbrauth turned around and saw Father Dunelli falling behind. He signaled him to catch up.

"May God keep you in the north wing as long as possible," Father Dunelli said, pulling his hand free and making a quick sign of the cross. Other hands reached out, frail and liver-spotted, but Father Dunelli kept pace, nodding at the faces as he passed by.

"She's in here," Father Woerstbrauth said. He knocked on a closed door.

They listened. Nothing. He knocked again.

"Go away."

The two priests looked at each other, then Father Woerstbrauth put on an apostolic face and opened the door. A gray-haired woman laid under the covers, propped up in bed, her profile aglow in the flickers of a color TV. The movie, *They Shoot Horses Don't They?* played. On the screen, pairs of exhausted contestants were dancing to stay alive in a Depression era dance marathon.

She looked over in the dark at the visitors and tried to make them out. "Who are you? What do you want?"

"You must be Matt's grandmother," Father Woerstbrauth said stepping forward to shake her hand.

"Is he in trouble?"

"Why, of course not. He's one of our top students." Father Woerstbrauth introduced himself and Father Dunelli, who was lurking in the shadows, distracted by the dance contest on the TV. The music was picking up pace and some of the dancers were falling down on the floor facing complete elimination. "Father Dunelli! Come say hello."

His head down, Father Dunelli approached the bed and looked up and offered her his most sincere and caring glance, then nodded again and took a step back.

"What's this all about? Am I dying or something?"

"Why no, we have good news," Father Woerstbrauth said speaking up over the TV. "May we please turn off your program for just a short pastoral visit? Father Dunelli and I have a word for you."

She reached around under the covers for the remote control, and pulled out a wad of used Kleenex, a hairbrush, and a *National Enquirer* with Sophia Loren on the cover. Father Woerstbrauth spotted the remote and snatched it. He pressed "OFF" and the room plunged into darkness.

"Are you trying to steal my purse?"

"No, Mrs. Baimbridge, we're Jesuits—"

"I don't like this. Turn on a light. Hurry, hurry! Turn on the lamp, there by the table."

Father Dunelli dove for the lamp and something fell on the floor and shattered.

"What the hell are you throwing around now?" she said.

"Sorry," Father Dunelli said, fumbling for the switch. The lamp came on and the priest jumped back when he saw her scowling at him.

"Now, look what you've done, she said leaning over to see the mess on the floor. "That was my favorite picture of my grandson."

Father Dunelli stooped down to gather up the broken pieces. A few sharp shards of cracked glass forked out over the photograph of her grandson Matt. "My apologies, I'll have it fixed—"

"Leave it broken," she said, "serves him right for not visiting."

She leaned back on the pillow and pulled the covers up to her neck, like a woman who could never quite get warm enough. "Now, what is it you two want? What's your business here with me? Are you here to get money?"

Father Woerstbrauth hid his briefcase with the donation forms on the floor.

"Why, Mrs. Baimbridge, we've come on a pastoral visit. Father Dunelli here will tell you." He pointed to his subordinate with the remote, as if he were clicking on a new program. Father Dunelli smiled and took a step forward toward the bed. As always, he was looking at the floor.

She sat up a bit straighter in her bed and cocked her head sideways to see his face. "What's bothering you? You don't look right. Stand up straight and look at me . . . you're worse than my grandson. I always know something's not right when he won't look me in the eye."

Father Dunelli raised his chin and looked at her, his Italian eyes filled with the endurance of a cross-country runner.

"Well, say something. State your business."

"Mrs. Baimbridge . . . we just came to find out how you're doing, and offer any prayers we could for your recovery."

"Ha! Lotta good that'll do. I've had Masses said by the top priest down at the New Cathedral. Look at me. I'm still here. It's no use." The woman sighed.

Just then, there was a knock at the door and the nurse came in. "Mrs. Baimbridge, it's time for your ointment."

"Ointment today, embalming fluid tomorrow," she said yanking the cover off her leg and plopping it atop the blanket.

"Gentlmen, if you don't mind . . ."

"Ah, let 'em stay. We were having a . . . what'd you call it? A 'pastoral visit!' Ha!" She laughed at them and then winced at her leg pain.

Father Dunelli recoiled when the nurse removed the bandage. An open wound along her shin oozed with puss. The nurse cleaned it with a warm washcloth and dabbed on the ointment.

Mrs. Baimbridge saw Father Dunelli looking queasy, so she raised her leg up off the bed to give him a better view. "Men used to lust after these legs," she said with a chuckle. She dropped her leg back down with a gasp, the way the boys sighed doing burpies. "Now, this nurse here still has good legs. What do you think of her legs, men?"

The two priests avoided looking at the nurse. Father Dunelli had already covered his eyes with his hand.

"Have you taken your pills?" the nurse, asked feeling Mrs. Bainbridge's forehead.

"What pills?"

"The antibiotics, the pills I left for you." The nurse searched the bedside table for the medicine cup.

"Oh, I don't know. I lose track. So many damn pills." She raised up and pretended to look for them.

"Mrs. Baimbridge, if you don't get better, they'll have to move you to Urgent Care on the south wing."

Father Dunelli gulped. The south wing! The land of no return.

Mrs. Baimbridge raised her covers and peered beneath them. "Oh, here they are . . . How did they get there? Give me some water. I'll take your fool pills." The nurse handed her a glass of water and Mrs. Baimbridge swallowed her pills like a captured Nazi spy taking cyanide.

"That's better," the nurse said, fluffing Mrs. Baimbridge's pillows. "Visiting hours are over in five minutes, and Mrs. Baimbridge needs—"

"Five minutes? We just got here," Father Woerstbrauth said. He bent down and picked up his briefcase.

"Hmmph. Well, you've been here long enough, boys," Mrs. Bainbridge said. She turned to the nurse and added, "They're after my money for that school of theirs."

"Five minutes, please," the nurse said, nodding to the priests as she turned and walked out.

"Where's my remote? My movie . . . they were having this dance contest."

Father Woerstbrauth held the remote control behind his back, and took a breath to consider the graveness of the situation. "Mrs. Baimbridge, because the time is short, I must come to the point."

"Well, it's about time."

"We at St. Aloysius are building a school dedicated to helping boys like your grandson Matt prepare for the future . . . to be new men for Christ."

"New men for Christ? What's that fancy talk supposed to mean? You think my grandson ever comes by to spend time with me? I could hardly ever get him to rake my yard right without going out in the cold and doing half the job myself. He left enough leaves under the bushes to build a wigwam! I think he was swooshing 'em under there to avoid having to bag them up. Lazy kid. . . . But it's not all his fault. His father was the same way. Now, he's got such a big shot job, he's always outta town on big business trips. Comes by on weekends just long enough to please himself that he came by, to check me off his list, and half the time he falls asleep in that chair over there. So, don't tell me about new man for Christ! I know better."

She snatched a Kleenex from beneath the covers and wiped her eyes.

Poor woman, Father Dunelli thought as he looked down at the floor, trying to block out the image in his mind of her pussed-up leg. Once the pretty girl whose legs men lusted after, and now lying alone in a nursing home with rotting flesh, and missing her family. And here they were, two priests lurking like vultures on a high wire, ready to swoop down on her money. He was ashamed of himself. If only he could heal her like a real apostle. But who was he? Just a C-team cross-country coach. She rooted under her covers for more Kleenex.

Father Woerstbrauth jabbed Father Dunelli with his elbow to do something.

Without moving or looking up, Father Dunelli said, "Mrs. Baimbridge, don't give up on God. Don't give up on yourself! Please let me pray for your leg."

"Oh, good grief. If it'll get the two of you to leave, all right, but hurry up."

Father Dunelli rushed forward, but tripped on Father Woerstbrauth's foot. Dunelli's hands flailed like a man falling from a cliff. He grabbed onto the first thing he could to break his fall—Mrs. Baimbridge's puss-filled leg.

Down by the nurse's station they were counting pills when they heard a sudden shrieking and cursing. They dropped their pills and ran. As the nurses stormed into her room, they saw Mrs. Baimbridge writhing on the bed.

"Somebody shoot me! Just get it over with! Shoot me. Shoot me now!"

Father Dunelli backed away and offered a quick sign of the cross. Father Woerstbrauth grabbed his briefcase and they hurried down the hall, two Jesuits slinking away into the night. Visiting hours were over.

Chapter 18

POPE PAUL VI sat in a bedroom chair with a sheet around he neck, while his personal barber gave him a haircut. He liked to stay sharp.

There was a knock at the door.

"Come in."

Two of his top Jesuit aides, dressed in black, walked in carrying suitcases packed for the trip to America. They bowed.

"Your Holiness."

"Yes, what is it? Can't you see I'm having my hair cut?"

"Please forgive the interruption, but have you any message for the school, for the boys at St. Aloysius?"

"Hmm . . . let me think." The pope reached out his hand. "Give me an envelope."

One of the men opened his luggage for an envelope while the Pope watched. A pair of black Jesuit brand tube socks fell out and rolled beneath the gold-leafed legs of a sixteenth-century dresser.

"Hurry up, man!" Retrieving the socks, the Jesuit put them back in the suitcase and handed the pontiff a piece of paper, an envelope, and pen.

The pope wrote a personal message to the school and—on a whim—picked up some hair clippings off his lap and put them in the envelope. The Jesuits looked at one another and nodded in approval at this personal honor the Pope was bestowing upon the school. Not only a hand written letter, but also hair clippings.

The pontiff licked the envelope and sealed it, then put it on his lap to address it in his own hand:

To the young men of St. Aloysius
from
Your Friend, Pope Paul VI

The two Jesuits took the letter and bowed. The Pope gave them his blessing and they were off, striding through the marble hallways of the Vatican with their baggage, and a personal message for the school.

Chapter 20

ON WEDNESDAY MORNING the barbers arrived at St. Aloysius—twelve of them in all—to administer mass haircuts to the students willing to participate in what the boys all referred to now as "The Sacrament of Extra Credit." Hundreds lined up, including Patrick and Tony and Jimmy Purvis and Matt Baimbridge, along with most every guy with long hair and mediocre grades. They stood stoic as they signed the form entitled: "Proof of Extra Credit," checking off the class they wanted to apply the extra credit toward before taking their place in one of the barber chairs.

But not everyone lined up. Many of the straight A students already had short hair. They complained the extra credit for the long hairs was unfair. There were a few holdouts with long hair, too. One of them, the guy with the longest hair at school—Barney Haladay—sat in the principal's office on the leather sofa, while Father Woerstbrauth paced behind his desk.

"Look, be reasonable, the pope's men are coming. We can't have you looking like Jesus."

Barney Haladay picked at his fingernails. What he really wanted was a smoke. But the smoking section was still closed, so that was out. But what he really, *really* wanted was for the weekend to get here. He tuned out Father Woerstbrauth and concentrated on how *dee eee-cent* the weekend beer party would be at his farm. Good times, good tunes, no homework.

"Now, pay attention," Father Woerstbrauth continued. "I want to make a deal with you. What would it take to get you cut your hair?"

"How short?"

"Not too short . . . but, as short as everyone else."

Barney Haladay let out a little gasp of disbelief at the thought of cutting his hair. He flipped his hair around with his hands. "You're asking an awful lot, Father."

"I know, I know. But what would it take? Let's discuss this like men. What have you always wanted?"

"Well . . . it would mean an awful lot to my mom if—"

"Your mom? You're not asking for yourself? You want something for your mom?"

Barney swallowed. "Yes, Father."

"Barney you're a man for others. What do you want for your mother?"

"Good grades."

The principal sat down behind his desk ready to do business. "OK, let's make a deal. What do you have in mind?"

"I don't mean just good grades in one class." Haladay watched for any resistance from the priest. "In *a-l-l-l* my classes."

"How good?"

Wow, that was easy Barney thought. So he gave it his best thinking effort. He didn't want straight A's; he knew there was no way he would be able to maintain them. And his mother would be more disappointed in him later. But he didn't want just a C average, either.

"I'm not greedy, Father."

"Just name it. What's your price?"

"I want all B's on my semester report card."

Father Woerstbrauth leaned back and smiled. "All B's, huh?"

"Yeah."

"So, if we agree you'll get all B's, you'll get your haircut?"

"No."

Father Woerstbrauth shot forward and raised his voice. "What?! I thought—"

"Hear me out, man . . . I mean, Father. Please. I know you don't want anybody to see my long hair on Friday. Right?" Father Woerstbrauth nodded slowly. "OK, so, if you agree to give me all B's, I'll have a cold on Friday and not come to school." Haladay cracked his knuckles and looked at the principal. "That's the same thing for you, isn't it?"

This time, Father Woerstbrauth nodded with newfound respect for Barney Haladay. "Mr. Haladay, you have made a proposal that we can both be happy with. And I must say, you've taught me a lesson."

"I have?"

"Yes. You've taught me not to think less of boys in the long hair community. I doubt some of our straight A students with crew cuts could have done as good a job as you . . . negotiating. Tell me, what do you want out of life?"

"I don't know. I'm just trying to keep on keeping on."

"Well, young man, don't settle for that. You have a fine future ahead of you. God has blessed you with shrewdness . . . intelligence . . . and determination."

"You think so?"

"Oh, I *know so*. I only hope someday when you've made your fortune, you'll remember your old school through charitable donations to help the next generation do as well as you have."

"Can I go now?'

"Yes, yes. But wait, one thing, and I must have your handshake on this. Please do not tell *any*one, not even your mother or your best friends about our arrangement. This will be our solemn secret, OK?"

"OK."

They both rose and shook on it.

"And Mr. Haladay, think of this as a new beginning. The grades you'll be getting . . . try to build on them to show the world just how smart you really are."

"We'll see."

Barney Haladay walked out of the meeting with his long hair intact, but a new burden—to impress himself with better grades in the future.

Patrick and Tony sat in the barber chairs down the hall. Their hair fell on the floor as the barbers sawed through their shoulder-length identities to transform them into new men.

Chapter 20

VIRGINIA VON BIERHART gripped the chrome armrests on the salon chair as she sat down to change her appearance. She had never been to this salon before, and no one there knew her. It was Friday morning. An older crowd of housewives engaged in a Thirty Years War against gray roots sat getting trims and perms and dyes. They noticed the newcomer, but didn't recognize her as the brewery heiress they had read about in the gossip columns. It was a dimly lit salon with yellow vinyl chairs and plastic leaded glass-style ceiling lamps over each workstation. A radio tuned to "The Music of Your Life" station was playing the Patsy Cline song "Crazy." Virginia took a deep breath and looked at her watch. It was almost time to make a phone call to get Loretta out of school—so they could ditch retreat. Virginia had practiced her lines all morning, had gone to the bank for cash, and to the store for casual clothes, some that she wouldn't have ordinarily picked out. When she left home earlier with her suitcase, her father had given her a final word of caution. "Virginia, I'm letting you go on retreat, just don't come back a different person."

A stylist came behind Virginia and gathered up her shiny black hair that hung down to her waist. She looked up in the mirror to see a man in his thirties, a quick, thin man in nylon slacks and a paisley shirt. His hair had that Dry Look spray style, with stiff bangs jutting out above his forehead.

"Such pretty hair, just a little trim today?" the man asked with a sniff.

An industrial strength impulse to flee came over Virginia. I changed my mind; forget it, she thought, coiling to get up. Don't go through with this. Just get up and go back to school. The whole idea—changing your appearance to find out who he really is—what a stupid idea! Get over him. Just tell the stylist you made a mistake and leave. Get up now.

The stylist waited, tapping his foot.

She thought of the kiss by the pool again.

"Cut it to here," she said, holding her hand like a machete against her neck.

"Oh, no, no, no. That's too much. Your hair is beautiful; you look like a princess."

"That's what I want. And then I want it dyed red."

The lady customers on either side of Virginia overheard what she said and looked at the girl.

"Oh, no, honey," one of the women said. The other agreed.

"I know what I want," Virginia said looking at the stylist in the mirror.

The stylist shrugged. "It's your hair."

"Thank you. And another thing—"

"Yes, miss?"

"May I please use your phone while you work? I'm in a hurry. I have to be somewhere soon."

"Sure. I think it'll reach." The stylist stepped over to the front counter and brought the banana yellow princess phone with a long wiggly cord over to Virginia. She thanked him and put it in her lap.

"Go ahead and cut. You won't bother me."

The stylist grabbed a hunk of Virginia's hair and whacked it off. Long black strands fell onto the floor. Virginia didn't even look up. Instead, she took out a piece of paper from her purse and dialed the number to Joyous Days High. The school receptionist answered the phone.

Virginia lowered her voice as deep as she could, and then let out a low, lingering moan. "Hello . . . is this Joyous Days High?"

Everyone in the salon stopped talking.

The receptionist at Joyous Days put aside her *Good Housekeeping* magazine and asked what was wrong.

Virginia began to squirm in her chair, pretending she was Loretta's mother going into labor. "The baby's coming early! Oh mercy . . ." Virginia groaned again. "O-o-o-h-h-h, I'm having another . . . con . . . traction. . . ."

When she fanned her legs open and shut under the apron, the stylist took a step back and looked around the chair to study her stomach. It was flat. She didn't *look* pregnant. But obviously something was happening. Some of the other stylists rushed over, their mouths and scissors open wide. All of the customers swiveled their chairs around, a few lighting cigarettes nervously. Virginia didn't notice. She was in character.

"This is Mrs. Sharp . . . Loretta's mother." Then, as if she was between contractions, she started talking faster and panting. "Sorry to call at the last minute, but I need my Loretta right away . . . to help with the new baby coming. Please don't tell anyone but Loretta. I'm so embarrassed!" Virginia spread her legs apart again and slid down in the chair with a gurgling gasp while the receptionist talked on the other end.

"If there's no time, I helped deliver puppies once," a woman getting a highlight yelled.

Virginia nodded and kept talking on the phone. "That's right, please go tell Loretta the good news, and I'm sorry she can't go on retreat. Tell her to come home now. It's a miracle about to happen!" She belted out a long moan to wrap up the call and hung up with a sigh. She handed the phone back to the stylist calmly. "Thank you."

"You want us to call an ambulance?" one of the ladies shouted.

"No, thanks, I'm better now." She sat up straight and looked in the mirror. She hardly recognized herself with short, very short hair.

The commotion now over, the other stylists frowned at each other and went back to their customers, everyone murmuring about what it could mean. What was wrong with this strange girl? Was she on drugs?

Virignia's stylist, a little winded, and his Dry Look shelf bangs shaken loose, took back the phone, "You still want it dyed red, or do you have to go see a doctor?"

"I'm OK. I was just practicing for a play I'm in. It was nothing."

He slapped the phone down on the counter by the mirror and raised his voice. "A play? You mean to tell me this was all for a damned play?"

Everyone stopped what they were doing and whipped their heads around to catch the finale.

Virginia nodded meekly.

The stylist grabbed a tube of red dye and stomped around her. "I almost need a drink. My God, girl . . . my armpits are wet. What the hell's this play about?"

Virginia answered softly, gazing at her new identity in the mirror. "It's a love story, about a girl who thinks she's in love, but finds out she's really her own best friend."

"Well, honey," the stylist shook the dye tube at Virginia, "from now on, don't come in here practicing your plays and upsetting all the customers. Life isn't a play."

"Yes, sir, I'm sorry. It won't happen again."

The salon grew quiet. And then a lady with perm rods lined up on her head laughed, and then everyone laughed. Virginia laughed the hardest, and her stylist dyed her hair red.

An old nun in a black habit ringing a hand held bell ran outside Joyous Days High to a line of girls getting on the van leaving for the retreat. "Gells, Gells . . . Loretta . . . Loretta Sharp!" she called out.

Loretta stepped outside the van acting surprised. "Yes, Sister?"

"Your mother called," the nun said, panting for breath.

"Is she OK?"

"Shhhhh!" The nun grabbed her by the arm and pulled her aside. "She told us not to tell the others, but she's having the baby and you need to get home right away. You need a ride?"

"Oh! No thanks, I've got a car."

"OK, but drive slowly. And pray. We'll be praying for you and your family, too."

"Thank you, Sister."

The other girls on the van watched with envy as Loretta walked away, wondering how in the world she had managed to get out of retreat.

Chapter 21

EARLIER THAT MORNING, Patrick paced and waited. He was alone, deliciously alone, in the gloom of the administrative foyer. It was a red-carpeted area with pictures of dead priests on the walls. There were so many of them. Their eyes watched him pace. He was waiting to meet Father Dunelli.

This was it, he told himself. He was finally going to get answers to the *What is Man?* crisis. But where the hell was Father Dunelli? The hallway from the priests' side was empty. Patrick looked to the other side of the foyer into the school hallway. It was empty, too, only lockers and padlocks stretching into infinity.

Patrick looked out the window at the football field. It was also empty. Sunlit, but empty. Empty and waiting. Waiting for the Vatican visitors to arrive. Waiting for the special bell to go off, so everyone would run out to greet them. Patrick didn't care about the Vatican visitors. He only wanted to see Father Dunelli. It had all been arranged the day before. "Meet me in the administrative hallway at nine o'clock," Dunelli had told him.

But that was yesterday. Now it was five minutes after nine and no Dunelli.

Father Dunelli was still in his room at the Jesuit residence hall typing the final lines of his report. He had overslept. The night before had been exhausting. Father Woerstbrauth had called all the Jesuits over to the library again for "an urgent announcement." Some of the older Jesuits, including Father Ortega, had already been in bed. When they all dragged into the library and took their seats around the table, Father Woerstbrauth announced the news:

"Wonderful, wonderful news. Late this afternoon, someone—a very, very,

very generous donor—has made a $500,000 contribution to the school endowment fund." There was wild applause, but Father Woerstbrauth silenced them and turned to Father Dunelli, who was seated beside him taking notes.

"Put down that pen and stand up, man," the principal said.

Dunelli stood up and looked at the carpet.

"And don't look at the carpet. How do you say 'congratulations' in Italian?"

"Congratulazioni!"

"Sounds like a pasta dish, but that's what I'm here to tell you . . . We owe it all to you, Father Dunelli. Congratulazioni!"

More applause. Father Dunelli looked stunned as he shook hands with his boss.

The principal silenced the crowd with a wave of his hand and explained. "His prayer and pastoral touch worked. The money comes from Mrs. Baimbridge . . . She's the grandmother *what's-his-name*, that sophomore that's always late."

"Matt," Father Dunelli whispered

"That's right, Matt, a promising student," the principal said.

Out in the crowd, the Spanish teacher, Father Ortega, shook his head.

"Because of Father Dunelli, her infection is healing," Father Woerstbrauth said.

Father Dunelli was thunderstruck. He'd only uttered a half-finished prayer. Had God answered? Or was it just the antibiotics?

"I can't take credit—" But before he could finish, all the Jesuits rushed forward to pat him on the back. The endowment fund was secure and they had met their goal before the Vatican visitors would arrive. Several hearty Jesuits hoisted Father Dunelli on their shoulders and everyone started singing, "For He's a Jolly Good Fellow." They carried him around the table, between the book stacks, and past the empty slot where Patrick had removed the book, *What is Man?*

Cold beer was brought in, and sandwiches and cake. The twenty proud Jesuits drank and smoked and celebrated until midnight. When Father Dunelli finally got back to his room, he remembered his appointment with Patrick the next morning. He had not even read the whole book yet. So, he splashed some water on his face and sat down with pen and paper in his easy chair to finish the book and take notes. But his eyes were heavy and he fell sound asleep. When he awoke, it was 8:20. He had less than an hour to shower, shave, get dressed for the special visitors, and type up Patrick's paper.

The bell rang. It was 9:15.

Patrick looked up and down the hallway. Still no Father Dunelli. Young men with fresh haircuts, ironed shirts, and evenly tied neckties flooded out of the classrooms and headed toward the football field. Patrick turned to the window. Should he wait? Then he looked up. A helicopter hovered into view just above the tree line.

Father Dunelli sprinted with his briefcase down the long corridor connecting the residence hall with the administrative foyer where Patrick was waiting. He was out of breath.

"Mr. Cantwell."

Patrick jerked around. "Father! You're here."

"Sorry, I'm late." He reached into his briefcase and pulled out an envelope containing his report. "We've had quite a week. I hope these thoughts I put together answer your concerns."

Patrick took the envelope. "Thanks, Father. I can't wait to read what you dug up."

The helicopter hovered over the football field. *Womp, womp, womp, womp.* Cheering students could be heard from within the building. The band started to play the school theme song: "Be a New Man."

Father Dunelli looked out the window and snapped his briefcase shut. "They're here! We need to take our places on the field." The priest hurried off and rushed out the door as the helicopter slowly descended toward the center of the football field.

"I'll be right out," Patrick said as he watched Dunelli disappear.

For a minute, Patrick stood still looking at the envelope. The gallery of dead priests on the walls watched him. Finally, he opened it. It contained a single sheet of white paper with a short, concise report:

Patrick,

Samuel Clemens began his career as a humorist, penning the classics *Tom Sawyer* and *The Adventures of Huckleberry Finn.* Later in life, after experiencing the death of a son and daughter, and many personal financial setbacks, he became embittered. His later works, including the one you referenced, may have been overshadowed by negative thoughts that we all suffer from time to time, thoughts that we must strive to overcome.

Sincerely,

Father Dunelli

Source: *World Book Encyclopedia*

"*What the hell*? Is that it?" Patrick turned the letter over. The back was blank. He glanced back at the window. The helicopter had landed. Two Jesuits in black got out. He looked back down at the letter again, and then one thing struck him: *World Book Encyclopedia*? How could a report based on the *World Book Encyclopedia* be any good? Not only had Father Dunelli turned in his paper fifteen minutes late, his report was based on only one source—the *World Book Encyclopedia*. Hell, even freshman knew that was against school policy. Patrick crumpled the paper in his hands as the hundreds of cheering students and the band continued to play to impress the visitors. Did anybody out there understand? Had *anybody* figured it out? Was everybody from every generation just fooling themselves? Working to be good only to impress themselves?

Patrick ran his fingers through his cropped-off hair and wished it were still long. He wished it was the weekend already. He wished he was getting drunk on ice cold beer. Most of all, he wished he had taken Tony's advice and called Virginia. Maybe there was still time. Besides, if the ancient questions have no answers, then man should stop asking them. What is Man? Who gives a shit. Give man a woman. Yeah, maybe that's all there is.

Patrick threw the wadded-up paper into the mums as he walked out the doors and felt the wind from the helicopter blades, still whirling.

In center field, the pope's entourage of two Jesuits handed the envelope from the pope to Father Dunelli. Father Woerstbrauth grabbed it, thinking it contained a check. He opened it on the spot. The pope's hair clippings blew away in the helicopter wind. Father Woerstbrauth read the letter:

To the Boys of St. Aloysius.
Keep striving and go to class. Someday we'll all understand.
Pope Paul VI

Chapter 22

AT NIGHTFALL Patrick left the house to get drunk, his undone homework dumped on the desk, the lamp off, the room dark. He sulked down the sidewalk in the shadows, hands in the pockets of his jeans. He wore a dark windbreaker, and a cruddy ball cap from a failed little league team to hide his haircut. The night air was cool, flickering the candlelit grins of pumpkins on porches watching him pass by. Above him—tall trees shedding their dead leaves one by one, leaves twirling down toward their own moonlit shadows on the lawns, until the leaves and the shadows met and that was the end of them.

This was a night for a new start. No more St. Aloysius, no more Carl Jung and Mark Twain. They were all dead. The only person he really wanted to see was Virginia von Bierhart. She was a living goddess of love and beauty, the answer to all his questions. But seeing her tonight was impossible. He had looked up her number in the phone book after school, but it was unlisted. All the better, he thought. Anyone not in the phone book wasn't real anyway, and he was ready to forget her.

Yes, he was over her now. And to prove it, he imagined her up ahead on the sidewalk coming toward him. She was looking at him intently as they got closer, inviting him to embrace her. But he was going to show her. He would just walk on by and go on with his life. And to prove there was nothing between them, he'd kiss her once more, just a little peck, very detached and clinical. Then they would both realize it this time—that it was only a fluke—that first kiss by the pool. Then in his mind, he grabbed her when she reached him, and she grabbed him back, and they made out and fell over onto the ground, rolling over and over and over in a neighbor's pile of oak leaves. Oh, Virginia, Virginia, Virginia . . .

Patrick was jolted back into reality when a man clanking the lid on a metal trashcan startled him. He took a few breaths and blew them out hard, and kept walking, more briskly now, toward Tony's house. That's what he needed. There, he could fall back into some of the old routines—go out partying with the gang up on the gym steps, drink some cold beer and forget all the false promises of love, and the deep questions of the ancients. This night was going to be like a retreat, for getting back on center, back to the old Patrick, the person he really was—the old man. What he really needed was a Camel non-filter. Tony, he knew, would have some. Like always, he walked in Tony's back door without knocking.

Tony's mom in curlers kissed him, and his dad in his business suit shook his hand and gave him a bowl of spumoni—Italian ice cream. They hit him with the usual questions: How are things? How are your folks? How's is your lovely mother and all those babies?

Fine, fine, fine, he'd answered, just like always. "Where's Tony?"

"He's upstairs," Tony's mom said, "not acting himself. Says a paper's due . . . He was a reading a book."

"A book? On a Friday night?" Tony's dad said.

Patrick acted like Tony, to cheer them up. "Aaahhh, don't worry, Mrs. Vivamano," Patrick told her, "he's probably just a little introspective from all those deep questions the Jesuits throw at us. What he needs is some fresh air. I'll take him out. I'll rescue him."

And so, Patrick bounded up the steps, with his bowl of spumoni and a spoon, eating as he climbed. Such pleasure in good spumoni, he thought.

He knocked on the bathroom door with his spoon like a hammer.

"Who is it?"

"What are you doing in there, playing with yourself?"

Patrick swung open the door. Tony looked up at him, under a tub of suds, holding a paperback of *Jonathon Livingston Seagull*.

"What the hell are you reading?"

"It's for the paper due Monday; something about this bird."

"Let's go."

Tony took a deep breath and looked at the book. "Shit. All right; gimme a minute here." He tossed the book to Patrick, and Patrick went into Tony's bedroom to wait.

"Can I bum a smoke?"

"They're on my dresser," Tony called back.

Tony's bedroom was a mess—the bed unmade, a plate of dried spaghetti on his desk, the dresser cluttered with cologne bottles, and that wonderful poster of Sophia Loren looking down on it all. What a caring bosom she had. She understood.

Patrick found the smokes and lit up, flopping in a chair to read the bird book. It was something about a seagull flying around looking for the meaning of it all. He tossed the book on the bed, and Tony, wrapped in a towel, walked in, the golden key on the string still around his neck.

"I've decided I'm not going out tonight." Tony said. He was pissed. He looked in the mirror and started combing his hair, but, like Patrick's hair, there was little left to comb after the Jesuit haircut day. Patrick decided to apologize.

"I know, I know, your pissed about the house."

Tony pulled some underwear out of his dresser and pulled them on under his towel, then let the towel fall on the floor.

"That's part of it. Honestly, that's most of it. Hell, that's *all of it*. We should've been working together all week to get dates for that house. But *no*, you weren't interested." Tony turned around and pointed his comb at Patrick. "And now, at the last minute, you show up wanting to go out, and we haven't got a shit chance of ending up there tonight with two girls."

"I know, I know. I'm sorry. I've been thinking about other things."

"What other things?"

"It doesn't matter now. I'm through thinking."

Tony nodded and put on some cologne. "Now, you're talking sense. We might swing by that mixer at Holy Footsteps and meet some girls."

"Whatever you want."

Tony put on a black shirt with wide collars and pearlescent buttons. "Hell, that's no good. Those Holy Footsteps girls are daughters of the Industrial Revolution. We need some public school girls from the Middle Ages."

"Let's just go up to the gym and hang out with the gang and get some beer."

Tony put on some more cologne and grabbed a pair of socks. "Shit man, there's defeat in the air before we even begin."

"I know."

"I don't think you *do* know how it could have been. Let me tell you."

Patrick flicked his ashes in the trashcan and smoked and listened.

"This house . . . this test of our manhood, which, by the way, we are failing, offered us the perfect arrangement. It was quiet, nice couches, a good hi-fi set for dancing."

"Dancing?"

"Yes, dancing! There must always first be dancing. Slow dancing. You know, to get the juices flowing."

"This old man . . . what's his name?"

"Old man Henley?"

"Old man Henley, what kind of records did he have for slow dancing? Lawrence Welk?"

"No, it would've been the Chairman of the Board, Mr. Frank Sinatra. You and me and our dates with the lamps down low, slowing dancing to "Strangers in the Night, "and then, the girls taking sips of wine, practically falling asleep in our arms. Damn, I can feel her body heat now."

"Who?"

"I don't know her name. The girl I'm dancing with. And your date would've been just as warm and glad to be with you. And right there beside the dance floor, we'd look over and there it would be."

"What?"

"The staircase . . . can't you see it?" Tony gestured toward the Sophia Loren poster, as if she were waiting for him atop the stairs. "The most beautiful staircase in the history of our lives on earth. Just ten steps our dates would gladly climb to finally show us what it's all about."

"This book you've been reading about this bird has gotten to you."

Tony slipped on his shiny black dress loafers and selected another bottle of cologne. "Don't make fun of our plight."

"Plight? Another new vocabulary word? These Jesuits have made a new man out of you."

Tony walked over to Patrick with a gangster face like he was ready to pull out a gun and shoot him. Instead, he sprayed him with cologne. A lot of it. Patrick tackled him onto he floor and wrestled him for the bottle. A chair fell over. Mrs. Vivamano, who was in the upstairs hallway with laundry, heard it. She opened the door and stood there, curlers in her hair, holding the laundry basket.

"Boys! No wrestling in the house."

They stopped wrestling and stood still. Heads down. Trying to look contrite. Trying not to laugh. Smoke rose from a cigarette on the rug.

"And no smoking in the house. I've told you that forever, Tony Vivamano!"

"I know, sorry, Mom."

Patrick picked the butt up.

"It was mine."

"Don't cover for him, Patrick. A lie is like bad cologne. God can smell you." She started gagging and put down the laundry basket to run and open a window and fan the air. "Now promise me one thing."

"What?"

She was coughing so much Tony rushed over to pat her on the back, but his over-powering cologne got her gagging again, so she pushed him back. "That house your watching," she said pointing dead between his eyes—"you don't set foot in there except to water those plants. I don't want any trouble."

"Mom! I know that. Give me some credit. Look at my haircut." He smiled.

She took a step over and kissed Tony on the cheek. "Make your bed before you go, and straighten up this mess."

"OK, Mom. Love you."

After she walked out, Tony threw his towel on the bed and blew a kiss to Sophia Loren. He stole the ball cap off Patrick's head, threw it on the desk, and flipped off the lights. "Let's go."

They left the house on foot.

When they walked in front of the house that Tony was watching for the weekend, they stopped. There it was—a quiet, Cape Cod style home with matching shrubs on either side of the front door, and a detached garage out back. A single lamp glowed in the living room to make it look like somebody was home. Tony touched his chest to check for the key.

"Now, whatever you do," he whispered, looking around right and left, "don't tell anybody about this. We don't want two hundred people showing up."

"Got it."

Chapter 23

ON THE GYM STEPS outside the school, the whole sophomore gang sat around in the dark with nothing to do. Bobby Jones, Kim Springer, Jimmy Purvis with his extra-credit haircut, Cindy Matthews, JoAnn Greggerman, Buck Wilson, Peggy Nolan, Bryce Nix, Martha O'Connor, Tom Baker, Diane Otto, Jim Bruntz, Lynn Perry, Steve Bicks, Barbara Dogelsdorf, Emily Carlton, Mike Barry, Jiggs Sullivan, John Doyle, Mary Beth Fletcher and Jane Sullenbrook. Everyone was there, except Jane's boyfriend Nate. He was working again at the pizza parlor. Everyone else was talking at once, joking and flirting, boasting, and smoking—taking the latest version of their personalities for a test flight, hoping for a Kitty Hawk moment.

The plan was to go to East St. Louis and get some beer, but it was too chilly to drink outside anymore, and they didn't have a house. A car came around by the gym steps and stopped. It was a yellow Trans Am with two girls inside. Loretta was driving, and Virginia was sitting next to her. They all stopped talking and coveted the sports car. Loretta cut the engine and they got out.

"Hi," Loretta said.

The group gave a collective "Hi" back. The girls studied Loretta and Virginia's hair, makeup, and clothes; the boys studied the important stuff—their bodies and faces, in that order. Loretta wore blue jeans with a khaki windbreaker over a tight pullover top, and sneakers. Her brunette hair, ordinarily wild, was pulled into pigtails. To look even less sexy, she added a pair of fake wireframe eyeglasses to her ensemble. Virginia also wore fake eyeglasses. They were props the girls had borrowed from the theatre department at Joyous Days High. Virginia had chosen reddish plastic frames to match her cropped red hair, and she wore a baggy, yellow windbreaker to hide her figure, along with baggy jeans. Her feet were covered with old, blue Keds. The girls stepped away from the car and walked to within a few feet in front of the group eyeing them.

"I'm Patty, and this is my friend, Pam," Loretta said.

"Where you go to high school?" Kim Springer asked.

Everyone listened up. Their answer would reveal everything—what kind of girls they were, their religion, family income, intelligence, and ranking in the sports community.

Loretta had anticipated this question, and decided on a school far away, so no one would ask if they knew so-and-so from any local schools.

"We go to public high school in Kansas City."

"What are you doing here?"

"We're here for a wedding."

"Who's getting married?"

Now it was Virginia's turn to fool them. She had practiced this part in the car.

"Our uncle. Patty and I are cousins, and our uncle . . . he's already been married once, but his first wife died and now he wants to get married again."

"What'd his first wife die of?" Kim Springer asked.

"Cancer," Loretta said.

"What kind of cancer?"

"Cancer of the toes," Virginia said. She made that part up on the spot and wished she had thought of a better kind of cancer.

"I don't understand. Why didn't they just chop off her toes and save her?" Jimmy Purvis asked.

"Oh, it spread so fast, didn't it, Patty?" Virginia said.

"Yes, I hate to think about it. That's why we came out tonight. We thought maybe we'd find some new friends and party."

"You guys *do* party here in St. Louis, don't you?" Virginia asked.

The whole group on the steps *whooped*, and a few girls got up to pat the new girls on the back and welcome them to the party.

"First thing we need is beer, two bucks a six-pack," Bobby Jones said. "One of us'll go get it while the rest wait. Takes about a half hour, but then—"

"What we really need is a place to drink it, someplace warm," Kim Springer said.

"Hey, where you girls staying?" Buck Wilson asked. "You got a house we can party at?"

"No, we're staying at our uncle's house," Loretta said fake-laughing, "There's no way he'd let us party there, right Pam?"

"You're right, he wouldn't," Virginia said, while she scanned the boy's faces for Patrick. Where was he? "Is everyone here who's coming tonight? I mean . . . maybe somebody else will show up and let us use their house?"

"No, I don't think so," Bobby Jones said. "It's getting late."

Virginia looked at Loretta. The whole show was for nothing. Patrick wasn't even there tonight.

"Wait, look," Jane said, pointing down toward the playground.

Patrick and Tony, about a hundred yards away, were walking toward them.

Virginia and Loretta looked. They didn't recognize the boys with their haircuts.

"Is that Patrick Cantwell and Tony Vivamano?" Kim asked.

Virginia's heart jumped.

"They got the same buzz job I did," Jimmy Purvis said.

"Maybe we can party at one of their houses," Virginia said.

"No, their parents are always home," Bobby Jones said."

"Maybe we can party at one of their girlfriend's houses. Have they got girlfriends?" Loretta asked.

The girls all laughed.

"Tony has lots of *attempts* at girlfriends," Barbara Dogelsdorf said, the girl he had made out with the night before on the bluffs. "That's about as far as it goes."

"What about the other guy; what's his name?" Virginia said.

"Patrick? Well, I'll tell you," Jane said, "just last week he told me a secret."

All the girls leaned in, Virginia leaning in real close.

"I shouldn't tell."

The girls all pinched her and jostled her around.

"OK, stop! I'll tell, but don't tell him I said it. He told me last week that he does like a girl."

"Who?!" all the girls said at once.

"*Shhhhh!* He'll know we're talking about him. I don't know *who* he likes. He wouldn't say, but, he told me, she's some girl he only just met."

The girls sighed and studied Patrick with fresh regard. So, he had a secret love.

Virginia looked at Loretta, but Loretta shook her head. "That could be any girl. I mean, we can't count on getting a party house out of something flimsy like that."

The Congress of girls agreed it was something they'd have to try to find out more about, but it didn't get them a warm house on a cold night.

Tony and Patrick walked up to the group. Virginia put her head down and listened, standing off to the side by Loretta. She clenched her right hand into a fist. If Patrick recognized Virginia, the plan was to attack him right away, and not wait for him to try to kiss her later. Loretta had convinced her in the car that was the only way. If the disguise was no good, she'd have to cuss him out in front of whoever's watching and knock him flat. "I owe you this!" she would say, and sucker punch him right in the nose, harder than she'd hit her brother.

"Hey, guys," Patrick and Tony said.

"Where's The Love Machine?" Jimmy Purvis asked.

"No wheels tonight; on foot," Tony said. He looked around and noticed two new girls. His eyes lit on the brunette. Sophia Loren was a brunette.

"We have some visitors tonight," Kim Springer said, "Patrick and Tony, this is Patty and Pam."

Patrick looked at their faces. Virginia tightened her fist, and flexed her toes inside her Keds, ready to leap forward and strike him down. But all he did was nod and say hello. He didn't recognize her.

Tony's eyes fixed on Loretta. "So, where you girls go to high school?"

"They're from Kansas City. In town for a wedding," Kim Springer said. "They go to public school."

Those three syllables—public school—made Tony's blood warm the house key resting on his chest. "Public school? Kansas City? Welcome to St. Louis." He stepped forward to shake their hands. His cologne was overpowering. Loretta took a step back. Virginia loosened her fist and shook his hand. She looked over at Patrick to see if he would shake hands, but he was looking around at the grade school, the dumpster, the statue of Mary on the Church roof, and the stars.

"OK, let's get the beer first and figure out where to drink it later," Bobby Jones said. "Who wants to make a beer run?"

"We'll go, Pam and me," Loretta said, "if a couple guys will come along."

"We'll go!" Tony almost shouted, "Me and Patrick here. We know the place."

The girls in the group cut their eyes around at one another. They knew something was odd about these two visitors, but no one could explain it yet. Everyone gave Patrick the money and he got in the back seat. Virginia climbed in next to him. Loretta sat behind the wheel, and Tony got in next to her.

"If you don't hear from us in a half hour, call the police," Tony called out the window. "We've been kidnapped by two girls from Kansas City."

Everyone laughed, and the yellow Trans Am screeched down the parking lot, zipping between the school and the church into the night.

Chapter 24

STAGE FRIGHT STRUCK VIRGINIA as she sat in the dark backseat, pretending to be a girl from Kansas City. It was her first big play and she didn't know all her lines, because there was no script. Just act shy, she told herself, and don't say too much, wait for him to try to kiss you, and then kill him.

"If he tries to kiss you in the car," Loretta had said, "we'll beat the shit out of both of them and leave them by the side of the road somewhere."

Virginia's hands were ice cold. "Turn up the heater; it's freezing back here," Virginia said.

"Why don't you cuddle?" Loretta said laughing. Tony laughed, too, and looked back at Patrick to see if he would put his arm around her. But Patrick was huddled in his corner, his arms folded.

Loretta wished Patrick would hurry up and make a move becasue she couldn't take the smell of Tony's cologne much longer. Virginia wished Patrick would do something, too—anything—because her stage fright was getting worse: jittery hands, shaky legs, and a hot face. To hide her fear, she turned to Patrick and blurted out the first thing that came to mind.

"What are your thoughts on premarital sex?"

Patrick choked on his spit and coughed. His mind raced with scenes from the gym film on men whose penises caught fire after premarital sex.

Tony reeled around. "Who me?"

Loretta backhanded him hard on the forearm. "No, not you . . . She's talking to him in the back seat."

Tony rubbed his sore arm and looked at Loretta. "Sorry, I just thought—"

"Let him answer the question."

"OK, but would you like to know my personal feelings on that?"

"No, and what's that cologne you're wearing? Smells like you rode your bike behind a mosquito truck."

"To tell you the truth, we had a little accident back at the house with after shave." Tony laughed at himself, knowing a man's laugh can open doors later.

Virginia looked over at Patrick. His eyes were down on his blue jean knees. Then he looked over at her.

"I don't know."

Virginia considered his reply. This could just be a line. Maybe next he'd lean over and ask if she was available. She tightened her fist again, ready to break his nose. But he dropped it. Patrick didn't know what to say. He looked over at the strange girl next to him and nodded, then looked out the window. He concentrated on the downtown skyline and the Arch. The smell of hops and malts from the brewery drifted in car. "Midnight at the Oasis" was playing on the radio.

Tony turned up the volume and put his hand on the house key around his neck and looked over at Loretta. She gave him her stage smile. My God, she *does* look a little like Sophia Loren, he thought. The car crossed over the river.

Patrick listened to the song, thinking of how he had tried to call Virginia. If only her number were listed. If only she had picked up. He imagined the phone call as the car rolled along.

"Hello, is this Virginia?"

"Yes, who's this?"

"Well, you don't know me, but I'm calling to say *I'm sorry*—"

"Sorry for what? Who *is* this? Is it . . . *you*?"

"Yeah, it's me. Are you mad?"

There was a long pause.

"I'm not mad. I'm afraid."

"Me too. I was wondering—"

"Did something happen to us?"

"I wanted to ask you the same thing."

"What *did* happen?"

"I don't know. I feel like . . . like part of you has been with me all week."

"I feel the same way. It's weird. I feel like I know you."

"I feel like I know you, too."

"But you don't. We don't know a thing about each other, do we?"

Patrick was smiling blankly in the back seat of the car when Virginia reached over and jabbed his knee, and pointed toward the front seat. Tony was asking him a question.

"How much money you got?"

Patrick got out his Knucklehead Smith wallet and started counting the beer money everyone had given him. They were coming into East St. Louis, and the town was jumping. It was Friday night—neon lights, shiny cars, and men standing on corners smoking outside bars.

"Thirty-two dollars."

"Get us something," Virginia said as she dug a ten-dollar bill from her purse and handed it to Patrick.

"You want a six pack of von Bierhart?"

"No, anything but that," she said. "Get us some wine."

"OK, what kind?"

"I don't know. I'll go in with you."

They pulled onto the gravel parking lot of the liquor store. The girls saw the graffiti, the Kool cigarette sign, the burglar bars, and a couple of rusty cars parked in the lot.

"Where the hell did you take us?" Loretta said to Tony. "Is this place safe?"

"Safe? East St. Louis is like a dream vacation; everyone is nice here."

Patrick and Virginia got out.

"I'll keep the engine running," Loretta said.

Virginia walked toward the liquor store door, a few steps ahead of Patrick. Tony turned to Loretta to compliment her on something, anything he could think of. "You know, Patty, you have a nice calm way about you, very relaxing."

She screamed.

Tony looked over at what made her scream. There was a man on the parking lot with a gun rushing toward Virginia.

He pointed the pistol at her chest. She stopped, too shocked to scream.

Without thinking, Patrick jumped in front of Virginia. The gunman raised the barrel toward Patrick's face, two feet away. Time stopped. His mind raced. This is it, boy. This is really it. This is what death looks like, the shiny metal circle around that dark hole on the tip of the gun. He couldn't take his eyes off the circle, waiting for the flash, waiting for the bullet, waiting for his brain to yell, "Lights Out!" Waiting . . . and waiting . . . and waiting . . .

"Hurry up, motherfucker . . . your wallet."

Patrick blinked. He reached in his pocket and tossed the man his wallet.

The gunman glanced at the leather etching on the front of the wallet, the strange image of Knucklehead Smith, a ventriloquist dummy from a childhood TV show. "What the hell kinda wallet is this?"

"It's Knucklehead Smith from the Winchell Mahoney hour . . . we used to watch it before grade school. What a great show! There was this one episode—"

"Shut up, fool!" The gunman stuffed the wallet in his pocket. And just then, the cowbell over the liquor store door jangled. All heads turned. The door swung open.

Another man with a gun ran out, yelling at the first gunman.

"You dice-cheatin' son of a bitch! I told you if I ever seen you again—"

The robber pointed at his old rival and the two men opened fire. Everyone running and ducking. Bullets flying across the parking lot. Two shots hitting the Kool cigarette sign.

Patrick and Virginia ran for the Trans Am and jumped in the back seat. Loretta floored it in reverse. Dust and gravel sprayed the parking lot. The car skipped the curb and swerved out onto Route Three, narrowly missing a family of singing evangelists headed for the New Life Temple in a shiny Dodge Polara.

"Shit!" Loretta yelled. She dropped the Trans Am in low gear and raced down the road like East St. Louis was a nightmare she was trying to wake up from. A blur of neon, buildings, and cars rushed by.

Tony tried to soothe her, knowing this would make her trust him more later—when she was in his arms. "You know, Patty, if you could slow down just a little, East St. Louis is really a beautiful little town."

"Shut up, you idiot. Are you all right, Vir— ?" she said looking in the rearview mirror.

Virginia nodded and looked over at Patrick. Virginia realized she was holding his hand. And her hand was on top of his, so it must've been her idea. She snatched her hand back and folded her arms.

"What we need is a drink," Tony said.

"I got something even better," Loretta said.

"What?"

"Quick! Open the glove compartment." The Trans Am hurtled down Route Three.

Tony opened the glove box and found a plastic baggie of pot with a joint already rolled. It was a big one. Practically a Havana. He lit it up and handed it to Loretta.

"Here you go babe; this'll settle you down."

"Shut up." She grabbed the joint from him, stuck it between her lips, and inhaled deeply. The speedometer needle on the Trans Am curved down to the thirty-miles-per-hour mark. Her mood calmed. She exhaled with a sigh.

"You see," Tony said. "Look around . . . East St. Louis is really quite beautiful."

Just then, gunshots flashed as two speeding cars passed them on either side. It was the robber and the other gunman. They both were leaning out their windows, shouting and shooting each other.

Loretta screamed and stepped on the gas pedal to get away. But the Trans Am only lurched forward into the firing line.

Two shots punched holes in the rear quarter panel of the Trans Am. They all felt it.

Patrick pushed Virginia down on the seat and flopped on top of her.

"We've been hit!" Loretta yelled, as the Trans Am surged between the two racing gunmen. "God, is anyone shot?"

Patrick and Virginia sat up, checking themselves for blood.

"We're OK," Patrick shouted.

"Just get us the hell outta here!" Virginia yelled.

It had been a calm night at the East St. Louis Waffle House, where a patrol car was idling on the side of the building watching for speeders. When the rolling gun battle raced by, the officer was taking his first bite of an egg sandwich with catsup, lightly salted. He cursed and chewed, tossing the sandwich on the passenger seat, dropping the car in gear. The patrol car shot out into traffic, with lights flashing, siren wailing, and roared up behind the three speeding cars.

"Cops! Slow down! Let 'im pass!" Tony yelled.

Loretta took her foot off the gas, and the police car eased up behind them. He saw the Missouri plates and swung alongside and looked at the four frightened occupants. Loretta pointed to the two cars speeding away. Then the cop floored his car and gave chase after the two cars still trading shots. Loretta wanted to pull over and look at the damage.

"Oh, God . . . my car's been shot," Loretta said, near to tears. "What am I gonna tell my dad?"

"Don't worry, babe, it'll probably buff out," Tony said.

Tony convinced her to keep driving, to get out of East St. Louis before another cop came along. So, they drove back across the river toward the Arch. None of them said anything. They just passed the joint around in shock. It was no small thing to be shot at, even by accident. Had anyone spoken right away, it would have all come out:

Who they really were. What they were really doing with each other. What fools they were.

But the pot calmed them, and in the darkness of the car, they began to cooly calculate their own agendas.

Loretta wanted only one thing—to get away from Tony. She wanted to drop Tony and Patrick off at the state line and ditch them, maybe pull over, and ask them to check the bullet holes, and then speed off.

Tony wanted only one thing—to end up with Loretta at the Love House later on. He could sense that this Kansas City version of Sophia Loren was deeply attracted to him, but needed a little more time to admit it to herself.

Virginia wanted only one thing— to kiss Patrick right now, just tell him who she really was, and pour it on in the back seat. He had risked his own life to shield her during the robbery. What a guy! But wait a minute. Maybe he only did that so he could make out with the girl from Kansas City later on. What a fake. Loretta was right. Everything with guys is a big act. You can't trust them ever. She studied Patrick out of the corner of her eye. What was he thinking over there so quietly? She knew he was probably thinking about only one thing—sex, sex, sex.

Patrick could tell no one his true feelings. He was mourning the loss of an old friend—his Knucklehead Smith wallet.

Chapter 25

LORETTA SHARP'S MOTHER went into labor. No need anymore for that Monday C-section. It was Friday night and the baby was coming. Her husband had run out the front door empty-handed to warm up the car, while she dragged her heavy suitcase down the steps . . . *kah-thump, kah-thump, kah-thump* . . .

Halfway down, between contractions, Mrs. Sharp thought of Loretta. Poor Loretta, away on retreat, praying and soul searching—she would miss out on the miracle. At the bottom of the steps, she grabbed the hallway wall phone and dialed the retreat center long distance.

"Hello, this is Loretta Sharp's mom. Please tell her I'm having the baby early."

The head nun held the phone in one hand—and a butterfly net in the other—chasing a parakeet that had escaped its cage and was flying around the administrative office. Swinging at the bird darting about the ceiling, the nun told Mrs. Sharp that Loretta wasn't there.

"Not there? Are you sure?"

"That's right. She never came. She left the school around noon, when they got your first call about going into labor." The bird flitted from atop a bookcase, to a lampshade, to the head of a statue of St. Francis of Assisi.

"*First* call? This is my first call."

"Well, I'm sorry, she's not here," the nun insisted as the bird swooped to the floor and flew up the nun's habit.

"What are you talking about? Put her friend Virginia on."

"We have no Virginia here," the nun insisted, dancing wildly. She dropped the phone, lifted her the skirt of her habit, and ran around the sofa screaming. The parakeet darted from beneath her skirt and through a crack in door, escaping down the hallway.

Hugo von Bierhart and his wife Joy were enjoying a quiet Friday night at their estate, sitting in the paneled den after dinner. Tiffany reading lights down low, drinks in hand, and a Tony Bennett record on the hi-fi playing softly in the background.

"Oh, the good life," Tony Bennett sang. Such a soothing voice. So relaxing to the nerves after a long day at the brewery, Mr. von Bierhart mused.

"It sure is peaceful this evening," he said to his wife, sipping and savoring a scotch. "You were right to suggest we let the kids do their own things."

"Yes, they're certainly maturing," Mrs. von Bierhart said, glancing up from her paperback.

"What's that you're reading, dear?"

"Oh, nothing you would like," she said as she laid the book in her lap, hiding the title from him: *Helter Skelter: The True Story of the Manson Murders.*

The phone rang and the butler answered it. There was a pause and then the butler rushed into the room. "Sir, it's Mrs. Sharp. I'm afraid there's an emergency."

Mr. von Bierhart shot a glance at the butler, and then back at his wife. "Emergency? Hmmph . . . probably homesick. Well, she'll just have to stay. I'm not about to drive out there and get her because she changed her mind. Maybe you should take it, dear."

Mrs. von Bierhart closed the book around her index finger and stood up to take the phone call from Mrs. Sharp.

"Hello? No, Loretta's not here. She and Virginia went on retreat. Right?" Mrs. von Bierhart clutched *Helter Skelter* to her chest. "What?! Are you sure? Did you call out there? What do you mean they're missing?" The paperback slipped from her grip and fell on the floor. Mr. von Bierhart saw the title. He saw the demon eyes of mass murderer Charles Manson on the cover staring at him. His wife turned to him.

"Hugo! Our baby Virginia is missing!"

"My God, I warned you of this," he mumbled, leaping from his chair, knocking over his scotch in the panic.

"This is Hugo von Bierhart," he said grabbing the phone, "What's going on here? Where's Virginia? Just tell me who's taken her."

Just then, Mrs. Sharp felt a deep, stabbing contraction and groaned into the phone. "Oh, the pain, I cannot be-*lieeeeve* the pain!" She let out a molar-grinding scream.

He didn't know she was having a baby. "Mrs. Sharp, is someone hurting you? Where are the girls? Who's behind this?"

Mr. von Bierhart heard a horn honk in the background. Unaware of the crisis, Mr. Sharp was in the driveway getting the heater going while he enjoyed a Blues and Blackhawks hockey game on the radio. The score was tied and there was a lot of tough corner checking.

"I want answers!" Mr. von Bierhart yelled into the phone, pounding a side table. "Tell me exactly what you know."

Mrs. Sharp leaned against the breakfront and started panting and perspiring. She knocked over a Delft windmill plate from Holland, and in a broken whisper told Mr. von Bierhart to call the police. She told him Loretta drives a yellow Trans Am. She tried to give him the plate number before another contraction hit her.

"Hold on, I'm not a dicta-phone! I need a pen!" The butler ran into the room and shoved a pen and paper at him. Virginia's father wrote down the information and then he heard a dial tone. Virginia's parents looked at each other. Dead silence enveloped the mansion. The Tony Bennett record had run out. Something horrible was happening. The family was under attack. He called the head of security at the brewery and told him to notify the police. "Find Virginia! Find my daughter! And my God . . . I almost forgot . . . Get Nelson, too!"

At Lambert International Airport a Trans World Airlines 727 passenger jet taxied along the runway to prepare for takeoff. Nelson von Bierhart and his two buddies sat on the plane, laughing as they looked at a Penthouse magazine hidden inside a travel magazine. Nelson was almost free. The plane swung around with its nose facing west toward Colorado. The moment had arrived. Everything good lay ahead: girls, drinking, skiing. The pilot revved the engines and the plane picked up speed. Nelson looked out the window so he wouldn't miss the takeoff. His favorite part of flying was when the wheels left the ground. He wanted to see the airport and the city where his father ruled over him get smaller and smaller and disappear. The pavement started rushing by. The plane was really moving.

"Colorado, here we come!" one of Nelson's friends said.

Nelson smiled at his friends. They smiled back. He looked down at the *Penthouse* magazine in his friend's lap. The naked woman in the magazine smiled up at him. Her whole body was trembling with the plane. Who knows? Maybe she'd be at the ski lodge.

But then the engines eased back, and the pavement outside the window slowed down, and the captain came over the loud speaker. "Attention passengers, we have been instructed to return to the terminal. Our flight will continue after a short delay."

All the passengers moaned. Nelson the loudest. His friend closed the magazine. Nelson looked out the window. As the plane got closer to the terminal, his stomach tightened. Somehow, he knew his father was behind this, and the root cause of it all had to be his sister, Virginia. What the hell had she done this time?

Chapter 26

LORETTA HAD TO PEE, so she when she got off the highway in Webster Groves, she turned toward the bright lights of civilization—the skating rink. As they drove up, they could see stadium lights shining down on the outdoor rink crowded with skaters. After she parked and saw the bullet holes for the first time, she laughed and cussed like a maniac. Then she started to cry. Tony tried to put his arm around her to comfort her, but she turned away and hugged Virginia instead.

"Don't feel bad," Tony said with his fingertips feeling the house key through his shirt. "It's not so bad. It's not like when Bonnie and Clyde's car got shot up with holes. At least yours is drivable." He told her all she had to do was hide the bullet holes from her parents for a few weeks and park the car facing the other way so they won't see the damage. Then act surprised when they're discovered. Blame it on squirrel hunters in Kansas City, he told her.

Loretta shook her head at Tony. "Pam and I need to pee." The girls started to walk off toward the pavilion.

"You want to go skating?" Tony called out. "We've been through a shock and skating will do us—"

Loretta whipped her head around and called back. "Hell, no, not with you."

Patrick and Tony leaned against the car and watched the crowd skating around the oval. "What do you think of them?" Tony asked Patrick.

"We need to get back and tell everybody what happened. They're waiting for their beer."

"I know, but what do you think? If we play our cards right, the four of us could be back at the Love House later tonight."

"I can't."

"Why not?"

"I'm still involved."

"Involved? What are you talking about? With what, your paper?"

"No, not my damned paper. With Virginia! Virginia von Bierhart. *We're a couple.* There, I said it. Now, don't tell anyone."

"Virginia?" Tony laughed. "You're not involved with her. She's out on the town with some rich guys dancing. You think she's thinking about you?"

"Maybe."

"Forget about her. Better yet, pretend Pam is Virginia. Please, man, do it for my sake. Just tonight . . . We have to stick together on this project. These are *public* school girls."

"We have to get back to the others and tell them there's no beer. They're waiting."

"OK, but go with the flow, and don't ruin a good thing."

Loretta and Virginia came out on the parking lot. Loretta had told Virginia in the restroom that it was time to wrap up the act, to bring it to a showdown, and Loretta had decided the finale would come out on the ice. "We want to go skating," Loretta said. She undid her ponytails and shook her hair out wild and attractive.

"I love a good skate," Tony said.

"What about the others? They're waiting for their beer. We need to tell them what happened," Patrick said.

"They can wait," Loretta said, taking Tony's arm. "Besides, we've been through a shock, and skating will do us all some good." She reached down and slipped her hand into Tony's and led him in. Tony turned and raised his eyebrows at Patrick.

Patrick stuck his hands in his pockets and walked in with Virginia. She was quiet. Loretta had told Virginia in the bathroom that skating would make the boys feel romantic. They'll hold hands with them and hear the music, and then the boys will try to kiss them. That's when Virginia could cuss out Patrick and punch him out cold on the ice. The girls could drive away and leave the boys stranded at the rink.

"What do you think about this skating idea?" Patrick asked his date from Kansas City.

"I hope nobody gets hurt." Virginia said, afraid her remark had shown she didn't really want to have to punch him.

"Don't worry, I'll catch you." Patrick thought she was afraid of falling. He was blind to the danger of her fists.

Loretta paid for the skates and they laced up and took to the ice, the four of them. They glided out onto a rink crowded with middle school kids, boys and girls holding hands. The intercom system was playing a Carol King song, "It's Too Late."

Tony was a great skater and he soon discovered that Loretta could skate well, too. They began to outpace Patrick and Virginia, circling the rink, skating backwards, stopping short like hockey players, and spinning like Olympic medalists. For the first time that night, Loretta began to tolerate Tony. Watching his sure athletic legs weave between slower skaters, she started to pretend that she really was a girl from Kansas City in town for a wedding, and that Tony and she were attracted to each other. Loretta thought, too, that maybe if Patrick saw that she and Tony were getting romantic, that it will embolden him to make a pass at Virginia, and then Virginia could punch him in the face. Loretta and Tony skated in front of Patrick and Virginia. Loretta took Tony's hand. Tony smiled at her. He had a fine smile, she thought.

"So, tell me about yourself," Patrick said to his date.

Virginia remembered to keep her words few, and keep it shy. But Patrick kept asking her follow-up questions. She told him that she was from a poor family in Kansas City and that her father was a schoolteacher, a fifth-grade teacher, and he loved kids.

"He must help you a lot with your homework."

"Yeah, he does, and he spends a lot of time with me."

"Doing what?"

"Oh, playing catch in the yard, or teaching me how to shoot baskets. He gets off work early being a schoolteacher, so he never misses any of my games. We're very close, very close."

Tony and Loretta skated by, arm-in-arm, crosscutting in unison, and Virginia pointed at them to change the subject.

"They skate very well together, don't you think?" Virginia said.

"Yeah, they do. So, what else do you do in Kansas City?"

Virginia cringed. She couldn't think of anything except her horse. "I've got a pet goldfish named Applesauce."

"Applesauce? Why do you call him that? Does he look that color?"

"No, he's orange, but he likes to eat applesauce." She winced at how stupid that sounded.

"You put applesauce in your fish tank? Won't he get fat? Doesn't it make the water cloudy?"

"Oh, not much. We have a good filter, and I give him plenty of exercise."

"How can you exercise a goldfish?"

Virginia paused to think of something. They skated around a slow boy with a straw in his mouth.

"Oh, I just take a straw and swish the water around to get him to ride—I mean—*swim* around. But mostly I just spend time with him and talk to him."

"You talk to your fish?" Patrick looked over at her as they skated along. "What can a person say to a gold fish?"

"Oh, anything really. Just, you know, just talk to him about your day and what's on your heart, so he won't get lonely."

"Do goldfish get lonely?"

"Oh, very."

"Do you think Applesauce understands you?"

"He's the only one."

Two middle-school boys having a race sliced right in front of them. Patrick lost his balance and Virginia grabbed his arm to steady him.

"Thanks."

Tony and Loretta passed by again, still holding hands, talking.

Virginia saw Tony and Loretta's hands knit together and slid her hand down Patrick's arm, and held his hand. Loretta had told her to do it, to tempt him to kiss her. Their fingers tingled together with warmth, like high voltage wires finally reconnected after a storm. The electricity was flowing. He looked over into her eyes, puzzled. They stopped skating. She could tell it was coming. He was going to kiss her. So he was going to kiss the girl from Kansas City just like that! She knew he didn't really care about the girl he kissed last week by the pool. She was nobody. He was probably roaming about kissing a new girl every week. Who the hell do you think you are, buddy? She made a fist with her right hand and heard her knuckles crack.

Just then Loretta stopped with Tony—so that Patrick and Virginia could see them. To egg Patrick on, Loretta kissed Tony. Tony kissed her back. Patrick and Virginia saw them. They turned and looked at each other. He's about to do it, Virginia thought. He's really going to do it. She drew a deep breath to get ready to punch him.

A raw egg hit Virginia on the forehead. *Blam*!

"Webster eats shit!" someone yelled.

Patrick and Virginia looked up. On the road overlooking the rink, a carload of boys from Kirkwood High School was hurling eggs at the crowd. From what they were yelling, Patrick guessed it had something to do with rival football teams, and the impulses of nationalism acted out between neighboring zip codes.

Egg yoke and white eggshell bits oozed down Virginia's glasses. She took them off, laughing and smearing the egg down her nose. Tony and Loretta skated up and slid sideways into a quick hockey stop.

"Are you all right?" Tony said.

Virginia slung the yoke off her face onto the white ice and laughed even harder.

"What's wrong with you? What's so damned funny?" Loretta said.

Virginia smiled at the three of them. "Don't you get it? I've got egg on my face."

They all shrugged and skated off the ice and put their shoes on to leave. It was time to go back and tell the others about the robbery and no beer.

But first Loretta wanted to go somewhere to eat, "I've got the munchies bad."

They all did.

Chapter 27

THEY ENDED UP at a spot nearby on Route 66—True Love Pizza. Tony had suggested it to Loretta in the car. She liked the sound of it, thinking it might have romantic booths that would tempt Patrick to kiss Virginia so they could get to the violence. Maybe Virginia could throw her soda in his face, then pound his nose with her fist while his eyes were closed.

They sat in a booth of red, cushioned vinyl under a plastic Pepsi-Cola leaded glass lamp in a cozy corner. The waitress brought them bread sticks and a pitcher of Pepsi, which Loretta noticed would be perfect for dousing Patrick with after he kissed Virginia. Tony ordered a pepperoni pizza, and Patrick poured out the Pepsi into everybody's glasses.

"This is great," Tony said looking at Loretta.

"It's so romantic," Loretta said biting off the end of a bread stick. She was using her acting skills to create an aura of romance.

Virginia dipped her napkin in her Pepsi and took off her eyeglasses to wipe off the egg yoke film.

"What are you, near sighted or far sighted?" Patrick asked.

Virginia stopped to think. With perfect vision, she wasn't sure which was which. "I don't know. I just have trouble seeing things the way they are, I guess." She put her fake glasses back on and grabbed a bread stick.

"Well, me and Patrick are sure glad we got to see you two tonight, aren't we Patrick?" Tony widened his eyes on Patrick to remind him of the house key, the house key, the house key . . .

Patrick nodded and looked at Loretta. "I'm sorry about your car, Patty."

"Oh, that sort of thing happens all the time. Don't mention it."

"I hope you don't get in too much trouble. I got grounded for a year from driving when I had an accident," Patrick said.

"Were you hurt?" Virginia asked betraying a hint of concern for him.

"No, he wasn't hurt, but the car was," Tony said.

"What happened?" Loretta said faking interest.

"Well, I was fifteen, almost sixteen, and I took my mom's station wagon out for a spin. Tony was with me."

"You mean you didn't have a license?" Virginia asked.

"No, but I had sneaked the car out before, so I knew how to drive a little."

"I was with him," Tony said, "He was driving up Sherwood, the flattest, widest, safest street in town, no traffic, driving only about twenty-five miles an hour."

"What happened?" Virginia said.

"Have you ever seen that TV show *Mannix*?" Patrick said.

Everybody had seen *Mannix*.

"Well, I was humming the theme song to *Mannix* and I began to think that maybe I *was* Mannix. I always liked the way he palmed the wheel with one hand to make quick turns in a chase scene."

Tony cut in with a mouth full of bread stick. "He was only going about four-miles-an-hour, backing out of a driveway to turn around and he palmed the wheel too far and clipped the front side of the car against a telephone pole. After that he stopped humming *Mannix* and we had to go tell his mom."

"Did she go ape shit?" Loretta asked laughing.

"A little. She slapped me in the face."

Loretta looked at Virginia, reminding her that she, too, would soon know the pleasure of slapping Patrick. Virginia looked at Patrick.

"I guess your dad hit you, too," Virginia said.

"No, he was real calm. He just said I was still part of the family, but my punishment is I can't drive until I'm seventeen."

"Well, that was nice of him," Virginia said. "At least he didn't hit you. It's just *awww-ful* when a dad hits you . . . I've heard."

Patrick and Tony were quiet. Patrick wondered if Virginia's dad hit her. But Patrick didn't think so, because he knew her dad was a schoolteacher who played catch with her in the yard and went to all her games. They were very close. Tony broke the silence with a laugh to keep things light.

"I wish his dad *had* hit him, instead of grounding him for a year. I ended up driving most of the time. Cheap bastard . . ." They all pretended to laugh and a young man in uniform walked up carrying their pizza. He put it on the table.

"Hi, guys."

It was Nate Algers, the boyfriend of Jane Sullenbrook, the girl who had tried to kiss Patrick last weekend because Nate was always working overtime and she missed him. But Nate didn't know about that; he was so busy with work and school.

"Nate, how are you?" Tony asked.

"Lots of hours." He looked tired. He made eye contact with everyone at the table, and noticed their bloodshot eyes, and the smell of marijuana. But he welcomed them to True Love Pizza with a smile, the way the manager had trained him. Then he turned to Patrick. "Jane called to see when I'm off. Told me they're looking for you guys . . . said you left with their beer money."

"Nate, it's not our fault," Patrick said. "You wouldn't believe what we've been through." He wanted to tell Nate about the robbery.

But just then, Loretta bit down on the end of a breadstick and aimed the other end at Tony's lips. Tony and Loretta started nibbling away until the bread was gone and they were kissing. And they kept on kissing, on and on and on. Tony got so excited some of the bread in his mouth spewed out on Loretta's chin, so she gagged and spit all her bread out into a napkin.

Nate straightened his assistant manager's apron and pretended not to notice. "Jane said they gave up on you, and went to buy some Coors out of a guy's trunk. So much partying." Nate sighed. "Man, I just wish Jane would get a job."

"Where are they?" Patrick asked.

"They're at a mixer. That's where the guy had the Coors in his trunk on the parking lot. Lots of loud music on the phone. She called me from the gym. Wants me to go dancing. But I can't leave work to go dancing."

"You're a hard worker," Tony said.

"Where's the mixer?" Loretta asked, slurping her soda.

"Holy Footsteps," Nate said. "If you see her, tell her I'm working, and I'll try catch up later after we close."

"OK."

Nate told them to enjoy their meal, just like the actor on the training film had, and walked away. They all watched him, but didn't know what to say. Nate was like an adult in a teenaged body. He was responsible and saving for the future. They were all blowing money, and getting robbed and shot at, getting high, and engaging in romantic subterfuge.

"He's a good man," Tony said.

"I feel sorry for his girlfriend," Virginia said.

"She should break up with him and dance with somebody new, don't you think?" Loretta asked, looking at Patrick.

"I don't know. Nate and Jane, they're a couple."

"A couple? What's that supposed to mean?" Loretta said.

"Well, she told me that they got married in a field in the sixth grade."

"Married in a field?" Loretta laughed.

"Yeah, it was just kid stuff, but ever since then, they've been a couple. They don't date anybody else, and Jane misses him all the time."

"She's a fool," Loretta said, "She should learn to be her own best friend and forget him. What do you think, Pam?"

They all looked at Virginia who was sucking soda through her straw. She came up for air and sighed. "I think it's beautiful that they got married, but I wonder."

"What?" Patrick said.

"What was she wearing?"

Patrick shrugged. "I don't know . . . we weren't there."

"I just wondered if she had a wedding dress."

"What a romantic night it's been," Tony said, putting his arm around Loretta, studying her lips. He was eager to finish eating and get back to business. He knew there would come the right time to tell the girls about the house key, but he wasn't sure when it would be. He just had to believe it would happen and move in that direction. Loretta could see the lust in his eyes from her peripheral vision and felt annoyed. Why wasn't Patrick looking at Virginia like that? Loretta gave Tony a quick peck on the lips to jump-start Patrick into kissing Virginia. But then an elderly couple with white hair sat down across from them and ordered a mini-pizza and a salad. The woman with gray hair kept looking at them like she was thinking of when she was young. She was. There was no way they could make out now.

Virginia chewed on her straw, and Patrick started chewing on ice cubes. He was thinking about the girl he'd kissed by the swimming pool. Where was she tonight? Who was she with right now? What was she thinking?

"Hell, let's get outta here," Loretta said. "Let's go to that damned mixer."

Chapter 28

THE PARKING LOT behind Holy Footsteps Academy was full of cars, and many more parked on the grass in the soccer field. This was the biggest mixer of the fall. When they got out of the car, they felt the base notes of the rock music shaking their faces from the gym up ahead. There was a light by the back door where couples were coming and going holding hands. This was sophomore year, Patrick thought. How did life get to be such a burden? Here he was in the midst of a moral collapse, in love with a girl whose phone number he didn't know, and stuck on a double date with a girl who talked to her goldfish. The night smelled of Halloween, and reminded him of Halloweens gone by when he was happy. But he was too old now to smash pumpkins and go trick or treating. He was a sophomore.

Loretta slotted her arm into Tony's and leaned into him as they walked toward the gym in front of Patrick and Virginia.

"I hope they have a slow dance, so we can all just hold each other," Loretta said, loud enough so Patrick would hear.

Patrick kept his hands behind his back, looking up at the stars and around the parking lot for any sign of the others. His plan was to get inside the gym and drift away from this shy girl from Kansas City, just let the flow of the crowd take her, so he could go on with his night. He wanted no part in Tony's big plan to take the girls back to the Love Nest. That scheme, he hoped, would fall apart on its own without him arguing about it. All he had to do was get inside the gym and let the music and the darkness pull them apart. They got to the gym door and something good happened.

"I'm sorry, but the dance is closed," the nun with the cash box said.

"It can't be closed. There's still music," Tony said.

"We're not letting anyone else in. It's over in two minutes."

Patrick was relieved. Now he wouldn't have to go in and dance with this girl. Soon everyone would be streaming out and they could get on with the evening. But Loretta wanted to get Virginia and Patrick out on the dance floor.

"Oh, Sister, can't we please go in? We came all this way and had a flat tire, so we're late."

Tony piled on. "Yeah, Sister, we just want to dance the last dance after all the homework we did this week."

"Well, I don't know. Where do you go to high school?"

"St. Aloysius, me and my friend."

"Me and my friend? What are those Jesuits teaching you? That's not proper grammar. You should say 'my friend and I.'"

"Right . . . my friend and I."

"OK, I'll take a chance on you. Go ahead, no charge."

Patrick cringed and walked in with Virginia. The waxed hallway floor was bright with fluorescent lights, but then they entered the dark gym, lit only by the sparkling crystal ball hanging over center court.

The lead singer of the live band who had hair almost as long as Barney Haladay was announcing the last song. "Thank you all very much. Holy Footsteps, you've been great. And now for our last song . . ."—Patrick hoped it would be a high-tempo number for dancing apart—"we want to do a number for all of you in love, called, "Colour My World."

The crowd clapped and the keyboard player started in on the slow, romantic intro.

Patrick sighed. Couples on the sidelines flooded the floor. Loretta saw Patrick was just standing there, so she took charge. Loretta took Patrick's hand and led him out the dance floor, wagging her head to Tony to get Virginia. Patrick started dancing with Loretta, like a store mannequin with a woman of flesh and blood.

"You're pretty good," she told him.

"Thanks."

Tony danced with Virginia, with his engine revving, but his transmission in neutral. He didn't know why Loretta had switched all of a sudden. He could go with the flow and dance with Virginia, but he had already kissed Loretta a few times and didn't want to have to start over with a new girl. It was like playing the Chutes and Ladders game and ending up back at the start.

"So, what do you think of Patrick?" Tony asked Virginia as they slow danced.

"He's a little shy."

"Oh, he likes you, I can tell."

"I thought he already had a girlfriend."

"Who, Patrick? No, he wishes he did, but he hasn't even kissed a girl in years. Maybe you can help bring him out of it."

Virginia nodded, looking over at Patrick with renewed scorn. Hasn't kissed a girl in years? Bullshit, she thought. You liar. What about that girl last week at the pool?

Loretta had her arms around Patrick, whispering lies to get him to feel romantic toward Virginia. Patrick was listening, but keeping an eye on Tony and Virginia as they turned his way.

"Pam likes you, I can tell," Loretta said.

"But I don't feel that way about her."

"I know, but don't be selfish with your feelings. If you don't dance with her, she'll go back to Kansas City feeling lonely like nobody likes her. She needs just this one kindness from you to build up her confidence."

"I don't know how to build up my own confidence, let alone hers."

"Sure you do. Just go over there and dance with her, and when the song ends do one little thing to make her happy."

"What?"

"Kiss her."

"But I—"

"Don't be selfish. Think of her. Show her that even though you just met her, even though she's just a random girl, she's good enough for you to pay her the compliment of kissing her on the lips and meaning it."

"Well, I don't know—"

"You can do it. Hurry up now, let's switch."

Midway through the song, the flute solo spoke of loneliness worse than a goldfish circling a fishbowl. Loretta let go of Patrick and cut in on Tony. Virginia looked over at Patrick and he took a step toward her.

"Hello," she said. The last time she had said that to him at the pool it was sarcastic, and he grabbed her in his arms and kissed her. But this time it was with fake shyness hiding her anger. She knew Loretta had been tempting him in someway to kiss her, as though she were just any girl. She knew a kiss was coming and she was supposed to deck him. Patrick took her hand and put his arm around her back. The muscles on her back were tight. His hand felt warm, and the electricity was flowing again between them. Her back muscles relaxed. This was bad. She was starting to enjoy dancing with him, starting to dread the idea of punching him. What a lousy play Loretta had gotten her into. The stage fright was returning. She was in and out of character. She concentrated and had to think of some motivation to just get through the scene. She decided to pretend that Patrick was her brother. That would make it easy to punch him. Forget who Patrick might be, or who she hoped he might be, just think of this as another fight about to erupt with Nelson. Nelson had it coming. That damned Nelson. She was ready now. She was ready.

Patrick was thinking about what Loretta had said, how Pam needed building up. He searched his mind for something he could say to encourage her.

"Pam?"

"Yeah?"

"I never thought it could be so nice."

"What?"

"Dancing with a non-Catholic. You're pretty good."

"Thanks."

They moved around slowly to the music, their cheeks in each other's hair, their foreheads touching.

Tony held Loretta in his arms and closed his eyes. He thought of Sophia Loren, and the house key, and the exceeding delicacy of the moment, the need to choose just the right words to move things along.

"Patty, dear?"

"Yeah?"

"Dancing with you makes me want to move to Kansas City."

"I wish you would. I really do."

Tony took that as a signal, and opened his eyes to kiss her on the lips. Loretta saw it coming and gave him her cheek. She didn't want to waste a kiss that would be unseen by Patrick. She jostled Tony over a little into view of Patrick, and turned her face directly in front of Tony's. Tony kissed her. His blood surged, the blood that had been flowing through his fertile family for generations going back to the foothills of Italy during his favorite epoch, the Middle Ages.

"You know, Patty, the Italians are a gifted people in many ways."

"Oh, please, no gifts. Not tonight."

Loretta peeked over Tony's shoulder and waited for the turnaround to see

Virginia and Patrick. The song was on the home stretch and she wanted a good view of the bloodshed. Obviously Patrick hadn't kissed her yet, Loretta thought, or Patrick would already be splayed out on the floor. Loretta watched Patrick's lips, waiting for him to swing them from the side of Virginia's head to the front of her face. C'mon, Patrick, don't be selfish, do it for that shy Kansas City girl who needs some confidence. Don't send her home lonely. Just move your lips onto hers and kiss her like you mean. You can do it.

Patrick held her tight. He wanted to at least tell her how much fun she was—that lots of guys would love to be her boyfriend. He wanted to tell her that even though he just met her that *he too* felt attracted to her, but he was already spoken for. He knew how stupid that would all sound. So he didn't say anything. Maybe he should just kiss her once to build up her confidence. He looked at her lips. There they were, in range. Kissing her would be as easy as putting a plate in the dishwasher that wasn't his mess. But he couldn't do it.

He was too selfish. As the last cord played, he held onto her, but thought only of his own feelings. He wasn't kind enough to help the Kansas City girl. He was only interested in himself. He was wondering where Virginia was. She had to be somewhere out there in the night. If only she were dancing with him right now. What all he wanted to tell her.

The song was over and Patrick and Virginia let go of each other.

They avoided each other's eyes and looked over at Tony and Loretta.

Tony was still slow dancing. He would not let go. He was dancing without music, like a sailor refusing to go back to the submarine. The lights came on and couples left the floor, but Tony was still humming and dancing with Loretta, until the janitor came by with his push broom and asked to cut in.

"OK, we'll leave," Tony said.

Chapter 28

LORETTA HUDDLED with Virginia in the parking lot, while Tony bought Coors from a guy's trunk, enough beer to make up for what they were supposed to get in East St. Louis. The whole gang was there, conspiring on where to go now to drink it. Loretta asked Virginia where things stood.

"I want to tell him the truth," Virginia said. That's when Loretta went directorial—lecturing Virginia like an actress who was losing interest in her role.

"No way in hell . . . you can't break character in the middle of a play. Besides, for all we know *he knows* who you are and is only pretending to be a gentleman to fool you into liking him. You have to stay in your role; make *him* break character."

"But how?"

Loretta looked around at the guys to make sure they weren't within earshot, then whispered her plan. "If he knows who you are and is just faking ignorance, give him a chance to talk alone with his friends, and if he tells one, the word will spread like wildfire. Someone will slip up and tell us. Some girl will say something."

"Then what?"

"Then, in front of the whole group you can show him who you really are, that you don't need him or any guy to feel complete. You can punch the shit out of him, and we can ditch this bunch of losers, maybe go to Steak 'n Shake and get some ice cream."

"All right, if you think that's the way, but—"

"It's the only way. You can't tell him the truth now about who you are and find out later he knew all along. Then he'll be boasting behind your back that he tricked you twice."

"I guess you're right. We can't let him trick us. He's a crafty one, him and that damned Tony."

"Oh, God, I only wish *Tony* had kissed you by the pool and not Patrick, because I don't know how much more of him I can take."

"Is it bad?"

"Well, he is a good dancer and skater, and a great kisser, and he has bedroom eyes. But he's wearing me down."

"You be careful, Loretta, I don't want you to forget it's just a play."

"I'll try, but God, I do love it."

"What?"

"Acting. This whole thing is better than any play we ever put on at school."

They all piled into the yellow Trans Am and followed two other carloads down Sherwood Drive, a long, dark residential street, and parked by the Frisco tracks and Highway 44. Hoisting the coolers like Teamsters bound for a Labor Day picnic, they walked up a gravel path through a tunnel of overarching bushes between the last house on Sherwood and the train tracks. The path sloped up to a dead end street that connected to a pedestrian walk bridge over the highway. Traffic was zooming by, east and west, cars of people on dates, and lonely truckers hauling freight across country.

The gang slid down the embankment under the bridge to a dirt clearing surrounded by bushes. There was a rusty fifty-gallon drum there they used for fires. Some of the guys started gathering sticks, while everyone grabbed a Coors. Soon the fire was crackling orange and hot, and everyone was divided up in little groups socializing, mostly the guys on one side and the girls on the other. The talk among the guys turned to the two girls from Kansas City.

"So, how far have you gotten?" Bobby Jones asked Patrick and Tony. All the guys listened.

Tony lit a Camel non-filter and looked around to make sure the girls couldn't hear. "Well, I'll tell you . . . so far, this has been the best night of my life, a lot of kissing, and slow dancing with her breasts right against mine, and it's not over yet." He took a drag of his cigarette and was about to blurt out the secret of the house key, but somebody butted in.

"What about you, Patrick? Have you made out with yours yet?" Buck Wilson asked.

"What can I say?"

"You haven't done shit. You can say that," Steve Bicks said. That got a laugh from all the guys. Tony didn't want any of the guys thinking Patrick's date was available and spoil the whole architecture of the evening, so he told them Patrick was right up there with him on the project.

"He's doing fine. We've been skating and dancing and even bought them some pizza."

"That's not what we're asking," Jimmy Purvis said. "We want to know *how far* have you gotten."

"Ask us tomorrow," Tony said with a chuckle. "Just ask us tomorrow."

"You better have something good to tell us," Bobby Jones said, "'cuz when we saw you two get in the car with them, we could only think you better not waste this chance."

Meanwhile, the girls were circled around the fire, trying to get some information out of Loretta and Virginia.

"I hope you didn't let them go too far," Kim Springer said. "Or my Bobby and all the guys will hear about it and—."

"Nothing happened," Loretta said. "All we did was go skating and dancing and let them buy us some pizza."

"Where'd you go for pizza?" Jane Sullenbrook asked. "Was it True Love Pizza?"

"Yeah, I think so," Loretta said.

"Did you see my Nate there? Did you talk to Nate?"

"Oh, yeah, I forgot. We met him."

"What'd you think? Did he mention me?"

"Yeah, he said to tell you he missed you and wished he could be with you sooner, but he was saving up for the future."

Jane smiled and looked at all the girls. "You see, that's my Nate all right."

Virginia felt sorry for Jane, the way Loretta was lying to her. Nate hadn't said he missed Jane. All he really said was he wished Jane would get a job. "Did you really marry him in a field?" Virginia asked.

"OH, GOD!" several of the girls moaned. "Don't ask her to talk about that again," Jiggs Sullivan said. "It's all we've heard about since sixth grade."

"Well, I think it's beautiful," Virginia said.

All the girls took a silent swig and looked at her. Who the hell was this Kansas City girl to come around telling them what was beautiful?

"What about you and Patrick Cantwell?" Peggy Nolan mocked. "Are you gonna marry him in a field? Is he *the one*?"

They all laughed at her and she laughed along.

"She's not ever getting married. She's her own best friend," Loretta said. "She just means it's beautiful for Jane, if that's how Jane feels about it."

The girls let up, and then opened some more beers. Gradually the guys and the girls drifted back together. Loretta walked around from person to person, eavesdropping on anything the girls might have heard that would prove Patrick was pretending he didn't know his date's real identity. But the report she hoped to overhear never came. More beers got pulled from the coolers, and a freight train barreled by on the Frisco tracks at the bottom of the embankment. There was diesel smoke and oily train smells and the metallic clatter of the Industrial Age in the breeze. After the train passed, the party fell quiet again, except for the zoom-zoom of traffic on Highway 44 beyond the tracks.

The stars were out, but they only came into view at the very end of a beer, when necks were craned all the way back. Soon, everyone was drunk, and those who had them, lit joints, which got passed around. No one talked of homework, or grades, or the future. No one knew how good they had it, with free beds and refrigerators full of food awaiting them at home, with years and years of life ahead like real money in their wallets they could spend. It was just one beer at a time, one joke after another, stories and laughing, twenty overlapping voices of high school guys and girls hiding in the bushes from the future.

"What are you finding out?" Virginia asked Loretta.

"Nothing."

"Look, he hasn't tried to kiss me, and he doesn't know who I am. I want to just tell him the truth."

"Not yet. I feel we're very close to a breakthrough."

Before Virginia could answer back, a passing truck driver down on the highway blasted his horn. All the boys hooted and the girls shrieked with laughter. They were pointing up on the pedestrian walk bridge. One of the girls, Martha O'Connor, had pulled down her pants above the highway and mooned the traffic. This was something altogether new. The entire party erupted in applause as Martha pulled up her pants and left the bridge.

JoAnn Greggerman stumbled up the path onto the bridge and walked out above the traffic. The boys went wild, cracking open more beers, and jostling for better views.

"Make'm honk!" Jimmy Purvis yelled.

Loretta and Virginia watched. JoAnn pulled down her pants and mooned traffic. Several cars and trucks laid on their horns. Lynn Perry and Jiggs Sullivan got in line.

"I've got it," Loretta said.

"No way."

"No listen, maybe he hasn't kissed you because there was no beer before. He wanted to kiss you all night, but he was just barely able to hold back because he was sober. You go up there now and flash your gorgeous white ass, and I guarantee you he'll make a move."

"No."

Emily Carleton and Diane Otto ran up on the bridge.

"Virginia, when you're on the stage, you gotta play the part all the way. You can't hold something back from your performance."

There was more buttocks flashing, horn honking, and applause.

"Ha! Then *you* go up there and do it!"

Loretta looked over at Tony who was watching the show with his hand over his mouth. "Are you crazy? I don't want to get him stirred up."

"And I don't want to get Patrick stirred up."

"That's what I'm trying to tell you. He's been stirred up all night! He's just been hiding it."

"I'm sorry, I can't. I won't go up on that bridge."

Loretta finished her beer and threw it as hard as she could down on the tracks. "Shit, all right. Let's go. We'll do it together."

"Together?"

"If that's what it takes."

"You'd do that for me?"

"Let's go."

"All right."

Loretta and Virginia walked up the path toward the bridge. The guys all saw them climbing up and got excited.

"I can't believe it!" Buck Wilson said showing his buckteeth, "We're partying with two Kansas City girls who are about to show us their asses."

Tony and Patrick stood next to each other. Tony had to pee, but he could not miss this. No way. He was biting his knuckle watching. Patrick watched, too. The whole show had been unbelievable—grade school girls he used to stand in line with during Holy Week for confession were now mooning traffic. Was he feeling it? Of course he was feeling it. Every guy there was. But he was

150

also wondering what it meant. Why were they doing this? What brought it out? Maybe Tony was right about the Middle Ages. It was still there below the surface. Flash a little buttocks from the Middle Ages to a truck driver down below strapped into a big rig from the Industrial Age and he goes wild, honking his horn, wishing he could take the exit ramp to a more primitive time, but he has to keep on rolling forward into the future.

Loretta turned her back to traffic and pulled down her pants. The cars and trucks honked and everyone on the hillside cheered at the splendor of her naked behind.

"And God created woman," Tony said.

Loretta pulled up her pants with a savage yank, and then waved Virginia to come out on the bridge.

"Why is all this happening?" Patrick said.

"Don't question why water is wet when you're thirsty. Just drink it."

"But what about—"

"I have to go pee," Tony said running off. "Keep me posted." He darted down the path, trying to unzip before he wet his pants.

Patrick looked up at the bridge. Loretta walked off and Virginia walked on. His shy dance partner from Kansas City was about to lose her shyness without any help from him. Virginia stood above the traffic lanes. She turned her back to traffic and reached for her belt buckle. Everyone watched. There was some hesitation. Was she chickening out? They could see Virginia looking to the side over toward her friend Loretta. Something was wrong. Loretta ran back onto the bridge and grabbed Virginia by the arm and they ran off the bridge. That's when somebody yelled it.

"Cops!"

A police car with its headlights off was creeping up the dead end street toward the entrance to the footbridge.

"Run!"

Everyone scattered, grabbing the coolers, thrashing through bushes, hopping fences, and stumbling down the gravel path back toward the cars. A lone police officer walked calmly along the ridge of the hill, pointing his flash light down on the bushes. Tony was crouched in the thicket, having been caught in the middle of an unstoppable pee when everyone ran. The officer's shoes crunched along the gravel. His walkie-talkie crackled with an update from a female dispatcher.

"Base to Sergeant Kurtz, do you copy?"

"Sergeant Kurtz, I copy."

Tony's veins filled with adrenalin. Sergeant Kurtz. He was the cop who interrogated Patrick and Tony in eighth grade, when somebody put a snow globe in the hand of Mary on the church roof. That one didn't go well for Kurtz, and he had warned Tony, "Don't ever let me catch you when you're older, out on the street." Tony wanted to run, but he held still and listened.

"Be advised, we have the Missouri plates on that yellow Trans Am wanted for the shooting in East St. Louis."

"Go ahead—"

Tony listened as Kurtz walked back up the path toward his car. When he heard a car door shut, Tony ran as fast as he could down the path to the yellow Trans Am parked on Sherwood. Patrick, Virginia, and Loretta were already inside waiting. He got in, slammed the door, and sat there panting out of breath.

"What took you so long?" Loretta said.

Everyone listened. But he was still breathing hard—and thinking. Thinking deep tactical thoughts. Thoughts about what he should say, and shouldn't say. He knew he better not tell Patrick about Kurtz. That might scare Patrick sober and ruin things to come with the girls. He had to say something. It came to him instantly, that the time had arrived—the time to reveal to her the golden key. He looked in Loretta's brown eyes, but thought only of her buttocks on the bridge. Yes, it was the perfect time.

"We've got a situation with the police. We need to lay low. But I know this house with a garage."

Chapter 29

THEY PARKED THE TRANS AM in the garage out back behind the house and shut the door. Then Tony pointed toward the empty house.

"Let's go inside for a few minutes and discuss the situation."

So, they all followed him as he opened the kitchen door. The only light in the kitchen was a dim oven hood light. Tony bolted the back door and drew the shades.

"Wish I could offer you a drink, but the guy I'm watching the house for, he doesn't drink. I already checked."

The girls kicked off their shoes. Virginia sat down at the kitchen table and Loretta swung open the refrigerator. The refrigerator light was harsh and made everyone squint. There was nothing good to eat, so she grabbed an apple and bit into with a big crunch.

"So what's the situation?" Loretta said. She picked up the wall phone and flicked the hook. "Hey, the phone's dead."

Tony checked. No dial tone. He hung it up. "Maybe it's just the kitchen phone. You want to come upstairs with me? We can check the upstairs phone."

"No thanks, we'll stay on the first floor. Now what's the situation, you know, with the police?"

Tony nodded, knowing he had to come up with something, but he wanted to think it out, knowing too much police talk can spoil romance, so he ran some water in the kitchen sink and began to wash his hands and face. Everyone watched the production. He was practically scrubbing for open-heart surgery.

Then he wiped his face off with a dishtowel that had a rooster on it and hung it back up on the oven door.

"Nothing like feeling *fresh*," he said with a sigh. He took off his jacket and hung it on a chair, his muscular arms now free. "This is a nice place. You guys want a glass of ice water?"

"Sure," Loretta said, "but what's the situation?"

"Well, I'll tell you," he said getting out four glasses. He put them on the countertop and opened the freezer door for some ice. Then he started humming a Sinatra song as he put ice cubes in the glasses. He shut the freezer door, filled the first glass, and gave it right away to Loretta. He wanted her drinking water, so she wouldn't have her mouth free to ask a lot of questions.

"Patrick, why don't you fill up these other glasses, and I'll go put on a record."

"A record?" Loretta said. "We can't stay that long."

"I know, I know. But maybe we better keep that yellow car off the street for a while. It's too easy to spot."

Loretta looked at Virginia and she shrugged.

Patrick filled up a glass of water for Virginia, while Tony put on a Sinatra record in the living room, right off the kitchen. There was a couch in there and a coffee table.

Sinatra started singing "Strangers in the Night," but not too loud; just right.

"Hey, Patty, come on in and we'll . . . talk."

Loretta rolled her eyes at Virginia and walked into the living room with her glass of water and her apple. Tony was already sitting on the couch. He patted the open spot right next to him for Loretta. She got to the couch and set her glass down on the coffee table. She took another bite of the apple and thought about the play. The play had already had many scenes: the shootout in East St. Louis, the dance at Holy Footsteps, the mooning party by the bridge. Everything had been building up to make Patrick want to kiss the girl he had only just met from Kansas City so that Virginia could punch him. Things had been going well until the cop interrupted, but now, maybe this was the final scene of the play. Maybe with Sinatra playing, and if Patrick saw Loretta and Tony making out in the living room—maybe Patrick finally would make a move on Virginia, and this damn play could end.

Loretta got back into character. "Well, this looks cozy," she said setting her apple down on the coffee table.

Patrick gave Virginia her water and she took a little sip, keeping her eye on him. He backed away and leaned on the counter across from her chair. They didn't say anything, but both heard a rustling sound and looked over to see Tony and Virginia kissing on the couch.

"We'll only stay here a little while," Patrick told Virginia. "And don't worry. I won't try to kiss you."

Virginia looked up at him. "Why not?" She drank some more of her water and studied him.

"Well, I don't know what to say."

"Try."

He cleared his throat and coughed into his hand.

"You need some water?"

"No, I'm fine."

"Here." She held out her glass, but he hesitated to take it, so she stood up and gave it to him.

"Thanks." He drank some of her water, and sighed and put the glass down on the counter. She was standing right in front of him looking in his eyes. What sad blue eyes she had. "What did you want to tell me?"

"Well, let's see . . . you're a lot of fun to be with, and a good dancer and all—"

Loretta was kissing Tony with her eyes open watching from the couch, wishing they would hurry up in the kitchen and wrap up the play.

"Why don't you dance with her?" Loretta called out.

Patrick and Virginia looked over at the writhing couch then back at each other. He took Virginia's hand and put his arm around her back, but very businesslike, so he could get on with his presentation.

Sinatra started singing another song, "Summer Wind," and Patrick tried to tell her what he could. "The first thing is, there's not a thing wrong with you."

"Oh?"

"That's right. I like your personality and your looks. You're very good looking, and I especially like that you take time to talk to your goldfish, Apple pie."

"Applesauce."

"Applesauce, sorry. But I can't be your boyfriend."

"Why not?"

Tony kicked off his shoes to take a better command of the couch. He got his legs up on the upholstery like Loretta was a Volkswagen Beetle and he was going to remove her engine. Loretta sighed a bit for effect, but kept one eye open toward the kitchen.

Patrick and Virginia slow danced, avoiding eye contact like strangers on an elevator. "Well, I don't want to hurt your feelings, but just last week I met someone."

Virginia held him tighter and hid her face over his shoulder. "Who?"

"Oh, somebody. You wouldn't know her."

"She must have a name."

"Everybody has a name."

"What is it?"

Meanwhile, on the living room couch, Tony's lips began to repel in smooching leaps down Loretta's throat toward her blouse.

"I shouldn't say."

"Please. I know this sounds strange, but I have to know her name. I won't tell anyone." She rested her chin on his shoulder and waited.

Patrick thought of Virginia by the pool and wondered if he would ever see her again. "Her name is . . ."

"Yes?"

"Virginia."

Before Patrick could say her last name she kissed him.

Patrick pulled back from her. Her lips. He remembered her lips, and his eyes were opened.

"Virginia?" It was Virginia. The girl from Kansas City was Virginia von Bierhart! Her blue eyes teared up. They kissed again, cautiously at first, then all out, wrapping their arms around each other, tighter and tighter. It was just like at the pool. Only better. They could both feel it. As if, somehow, their spirits swept into each other and sat down and shared their whole life stories without words. They were naked together and not ashamed. They were a couple in a strange dream from which they never wanted to wake up. Loretta saw all this from the couch. She waited and waited for it to come to blows. But they just kept on kissing, and Tony kept up his southern campaign moving past Loretta's collarbone toward the V of her blouse. Loretta groped on the coffee table for her ice water and poured it on Tony's back.

"Oh, shit, I'm sorry," Loretta said, "I was thirsty."

"That's OK, babe. I'll get a towel."

"No, wait, don't move."

Loretta and Tony looked into the kitchen and watched Patrick and Virginia slow dancing. "They seemed to have finally hit it off," Tony said.

"I hope she knows what she's doing."

"She made the right choice, and so did we." He flexed his eyebrows and moved toward her again, but she leaned back.

"Cut it out. We need to discuss the situation. Gimme a cigarette."

"We're not supposed to smoke in the house, but OK, just this once."

So they smoked and put their legs on the coffee table and watched the floor show. Virginia and Patrick slow dancing and whispering in each other's ears until the record ran out. When it was over Patrick whispered something in Virginia's ear, and she laughed and they walked into the living room holding hands. She motioned for Patrick to sit on a reading chair, and she sat on his lap.

"Well, well," Loretta said.

"We have something to say," Virginia said. She took off her fake glasses and looked at Tony.

Tony sat up straight, feet on the floor, flicking his cigarette ashes into a potted plant, and listening carefully. Loretta leaned back with her legs on the coffee table. Virginia told Tony who she really was.

"NO SHIT?" he said, covering his mouth with his hand, "But what happened to your hair?"

"She dyed it for a theater project," Loretta said.

Tony grinned and laughed and lit another cigarette. "This is incredible. I can't believe it." He had two cigarettes going at once. He put the old one in the pot of a houseplant. Then Tony turned to Loretta. "But Patty, how do you know Virginia all the way in Kansas City?"

"You dumb shit, my name isn't Patty. I live here, down the street from Virginia."

"Damn! So what's your real name?"

"I don't know if I want to tell you. You're the most *hands-on* date I ever had."

"Oh, go ahead tell him," Virginia said. "I know you've had a good time with Tony. He's a good guy."

Loretta patted Tony on his hand and told him her real name.

Tony sighed and practiced her name. "Loretta? That's a beautiful name. I like it even better than Patty."

"I knew you would."

"Well, now that we're all properly introduced, maybe I should put on the other side of the record." Tony leaped up and jostled with the record player. There was a water stain on the back of his shirt the size of a continent. The record was stuck on the metal post notch and he was so eager to wriggle it loose he almost broke the record. But he got it going again on Side Two, and sat back down. Sinatra started singing "On a Clear Day." He sat back down next to Loretta and put his arm around her.

"We still need to talk about the situation," Loretta said.

Virginia cut in. "First Tony and I need to talk about something else."

Tony looked at her. "What?"

"The night you and I were playing poker."

Tony started laughing and slapping his thigh with his free hand, cigarette in mouth making his eyes wince with smoke. "Heh, Heh, Heh, that's right. Shit, what a night."

"I believe I was holding a straight flush and you had four of a kind," Virginia said, "You owe me something."

"What? An apology?"

"No, something more."

"Oh, that." Tony took his cigarette out of his mouth. "I never paid up, did I?" He looked at Virginia. She was staring at him poker faced. Could she really mean it? He looked at Patrick and Loretta. They were all straight faced. Could this be happening? Did Virginia want him to pay up right now? Take off his clothes? Would Loretta take off her clothes? And Patrick and Virginia? Would they all fly up the steps to the bedrooms to find out what it means for a man and a woman to be fully alive on Earth, his favorite planet?

Virginia smiled and the three of them all started laughing at Tony. It was a joke.

"Shit, for a minute I thought—"

"OK, Sinatra, let's talk about the situation," Loretta said, "and can you *please* get me some more ice water?"

"Sure, babe."

Chapter 30

LORETTA AND VIRGINIA KNEW THE SITUATION WAS THIS: The cops knew the plates on Loretta's car. That meant they knew her parents' names and address. That meant they had probably contacted Loretta's parents telling them about the chase. That meant Loretta's parents called the retreat center and found out she wasn't there. That meant Virginia's parents were also aware they were missing. It all meant only one thing. The girls had to call their parents and tell them they were all right and go home.

"You go first," Virginia said to Loretta. "I don't want to face it all yet."

"Fine."

"You want me to show you where the upstairs phone is?" Tony said.

"I can find it." Loretta got off the couch and went upstairs.

Sinatra was singing "My Baby Just Cares for Me." Virginia was staring at the rug, thinking and fingering Patrick's hair behind his ear. Just as Tony got up and started pacing the floor, Loretta came down and told them the upstairs phone was dead, too. Tony clapped his hands together. "I got it. Here's what we should do. Now, sit down and hear me out."

Loretta sat down and Tony paced some more. Then he started in on how life was hard in the Industrial Age and they were all under a tremendous strain. He talked about parents expectations, homework, after-school jobs, getting up early to go to school Monday through Friday. "And what for? So we can have a little slice of freedom called the weekend. Now I say to you, why turn yourself in on a Friday night, when you know you're gonna get grounded for about two weeks at least, maybe longer. Why not turn yourself in on a Sunday and get the same punishment? The only wise thing to do is stick together."

"We're not gonna stay here and have sex with you. Is that what you're thinking?" Loretta said.

"Of course not. I'm not thinking that."

"Well then, what are you thinking?" Loretta said.

Tony took a deep breath, patted his ribs, and riled up his shoulders to get some ideas going. "I got it. How about this—"

His plan was for the girls to spend the night at the house alone, then in the morning Tony and Patrick could come pick them up in The Love Machine. They could drive out into the country to Barney Haladay's farm for the big party. Virginia and Loretta looked at each other, undecided.

"I like the part about going to sleep," Loretta said, "I'm exhausted. But I don't know about going out to some farm. What do you think, Virginia?"

"Do they have horses?"

Tony had no idea. "Of course, it's a farm. You can ride horses, go on walks. It'll be a beautiful October day, all the fall colors. Probably a barbecue, cold beer, a last reprieve before you turn yourself in."

"Well, let us think about it. Let's say goodnight," Loretta said.

Tony kissed her before she could step aside, a restrained, understated kiss to show it would be safe with him tomorrow. That's when he could really win her over. Patrick and Virginia got off the chair and hugged goodnight.

"Will you be here in the morning?" he asked.

"I will."

Tony and Patrick left the house and Loretta bolted the kitchen door behind them. They walked along in the dark, wondering what to say about such a night. Then Tony broke the silence.

"I can't believe it."

"What?"

"Our lives are finally going so well for a change. Tomorrow's gonna be great."

Chapter 30

ON SATURDAY MORNING, Tony's mother agreed to let him use The Love Machine for the day—under one condition: that he swing by Grandpa Vivamano's house and pick up a stool sample for the clinic.

"It's extremely important they start the lab work today, or else he might need surgery. Now don't disappoint me."

"I won't," Tony promised. And so he ran into his Grandpa's house, visited about winemaking, World War I, and tomato gardening—until finally he got the stool sample, wrapped up in a napkin, and could leave. Tony hurried out the door, thinking of Loretta, her lips, her buttocks on the bridge, the mystery of her unseen breasts. He was thinking more and more of her as Sophia Loren by the minute. Digging in his pockets for his keys, he put the stool sample on the roof of the car and forgot about it. Only halfway to the clinic did he look over on the seat to check and remembered where it was. By then Grandpa Vivamano's stool sample belonged to the ages and would never be seen again.

Tony showed up at the Love House with a mournful face and found Patrick and Virginia at the kitchen table with coffee. The sunlight was on them and they looked sober. Maybe too sober. Tony could sense there was trouble in the air, but he had troubles of his own. He sat down brooding.

"What's wrong?" Patrick asked.

Tony told them, and said he even tried to go Number-Two himself at a Shell station, but had already gone at the house and had nothing. He looked at Patrick.

"Don't look at me. I went, too."

"Me too," Virginia said.

"Where's Loretta?"

She was still asleep, the only person in the house who might be able to help.

"I got it," Tony said. "Breakfast in bed. We make her a big breakfast and then tell her about it—when she has to go."

So they went to work, opening the refrigerator, scrambling eggs, making toast, cooking a can of campfire beans, and pouring her a glass of orange juice and a cup of hot coffee.

"This should get her going," Tony said. They all three brought a tray with her breakfast up to her room, which was still dark with the blinds shut, and got into bed with her—all three of them. Loretta stirred.

"What the hell? What are you guys doing?"

"Good morning," Tony said. "We just thought you might like a good breakfast to help you get moving."

She sat up and propped a pillow behind her. "What time is it?"

"After ten," Virginia said. "We want to get going to the farm, but first—"

"You have to eat first," Tony said.

"Well, all right, as long as you *all* stay here." She looked at Tony. "It's a good thing you didn't come up here alone with this to try to get something out of me." She took a bite of her toast slathered with strawberry preserves. The three conspirators were silent, smiling at Loretta as she ate.

"Something's up, I can tell. What are you guys trying to get out of me?"

"We're not trying to get *anything* out of you," Tony said.

"What's with the beans? For breakfast?"

"That's what cowboys eat, and today we're going to be cowboys out on the farm."

"Hmmph! Don't know if I wanna be a cowboy after last night." She drank some orange juice and wolfed down her eggs and started feeling better. She was well enough to begin a list of complaints—all the trouble they were in because of Tony and Patrick, pausing just long enough for another bite of toast, and she scolded Virginia for being too dependent on a boyfriend, instead of being her own best friend.

"I know. You've given a lot to me this weekend already," Virginia said.

"Well, don't expect me to give anything more. Not one damn thing."

"Drink your coffee, babe, that'll get you going."

Virginia picked up the fork and fed Loretta the rest of her beans and petted

Loretta's hair. Tony rubbed her feet, which she objected to at first, but then admitted she liked it.

"That feels pretty good." But then she grew suspicious and stopped chewing. "Why are you guys being so nice to me? What do you want?"

Tony kissed her on the one cheek, and Virginia on the other, and Patrick patted her shoulder. Nobody knew how to say it.

Loretta tightened her face. "What? Oh, God,I can tell it's going to be bad. What is it?"

Virginia cleared her throat and looked at the boys. "You'd better let me tell her in my own way."

Tony and Patrick closed the door and tiptoed downstairs. Through the floor boards, they could hear Loretta shouting.

"No! Damn! Way!"

So, they did the dishes, Tony washing and Patrick drying. Patrick didn't tell Tony what was bothering him—that maybe last night was a foolish dream. And Tony didn't tell Patrick what was bothering him—that their old enemy Sgt. Kurtz was on the case. Virginia came down and helped them finish. She didn't tell them what she had told Loretta—that she needed to go to the farm with Patrick in the sunlight to see if last night was real. A tense quiet fell over the house. They sat around the living room flipping through magazines and watching the staircase for Loretta's feet to appear.

"I don't know if she'll do it," Virginia said, "She didn't promise me anything."

"She'll do it," Tony said, "Just watch. After the way we danced last night and kissed, when she comes down the staircase, you'll see how she feels about me. She'll be holding a turd."

Finally, they heard footsteps. Loretta came down the staircase slowly. They looked at her hands. They were empty.

Tony stood up. "What? Can't you go?"

"Don't talk to me. Don't even look at me. It's upstairs."

"Thanks, babe."

Tony tried to kiss her on the lips as he breezed by her, but she turned her cheek to him and winced. He ran upstairs and found what he was looking for. They locked up the house and got in The Love Machine with the stool sample wrapped in a napkin in the far back seat of the station wagon. When they got to the clinic, Tony hurried inside, past a waiting room of older men. He wanted to leave the sample with the receptionist, but the doctor came out, a bald man in a white coat and glasses.

"You're a good grandson," the doctor said, "It's a selfless thing for you to drop this off."

"I try to help out."

"You're a man for others. Tell me, if I might ask, what are your plans?"

"Well, sir, some friends and me are going out to a farm."

"No, I don't mean today, I mean what are your plans for the future?"

"The future? I don't know."

"The future is approaching. You won't always be young living with your parents. Have you ever considered a career in medicine?"

"No, sir."

"It's a great way to help others." The doctor pulled back the napkin and gave off a hum of approval. "Looks like he's taking that fiber we discussed."

"Can I go now?"

"In a minute, I can tell you're curious. Would you like for me to show you how to read a stool?"

"Oh, I forgot my reading glasses."

"Here, you can borrow mine," he said taking them off.

"No, thanks, really, sir, I've gotta go . . . busy times."

"OK, well, thanks for your help. I'm sure your grandpa will be relieved when you tell him the good news."

"I'm relieved myself."

"We'll get this off to the lab right away. Please tell him he's looking good."

"Yes, sir, I will."

Tony ran out of the clinic, jumped in The Love Machine, and started the engine. They had the whole day ahead of them and the sun was shining.

Chapter 31

THE FARM BOASTED eighty acres of rolling fields, a bluff overlooking a
freshwater creek, a cave, a red barn with horses, and a white frame house with
a wrap-around porch and gingerbread trim. The Love Machine rumbled up
the gravel driveway, swirling dust and yellow leaves in its wake. They parked
by the barn, near a row of half a dozen other cars and got out. Barney Haladay
walked over to greet them in bellbottom jeans, a blue denim shirt, and hair
halfway down his back like a rock star on an album cover. Barney gave Tony
and Patrick a Woodstock handshake, and said hey to the girls. They introduced
the girls as "Patty and Pam," because Loretta had said in the car they needed
to "stay in character." Neither Patrick nor Virginia objected. Neither was ready
to declare to the world they were a couple. Were they a couple? Was it real? It
was a probationary day of keeping up the act. That made it easy to avoid a lot
of questions from the others. Jane Sullenbrook and Jimmy Purvis, and Bobby
Jones and Kim Springer were there—including most of the people who had
mooned truckers last night.

Jane asked the girls from Kansas City why they weren't at the wedding
they had talked about. Loretta lied. She told them it got cancelled because
the bride had second thoughts about the groom. "Yeah, sometimes two people
think they're in love, but they're not really."

"Well, that's sad," Jane said. "I hope she finds somebody someday like I
found my Nate."

"Where is this Nate?" Loretta asked.

"He's working."

"Sounds like he works a lot."

"Saving up for his future!" everyone chimed in.

"He does work a lot." she admitted, "but I'm picking him up later. He let me borrow his car."

"You dudes want a beer?" Barney asked the newcomers.

"Not yet," Virginia said. "What we'd really like is to see your horses."

"You ride?"

She nodded yes, and Tony and Patrick pretended they knew how to ride, too. Loretta said she didn't like horses, that they were big and smelly. But they talked her into it to keep the four of them together. They mounted up and Barney told them to stick to the trail, because the horses knew the route down to creek, up to the bluff, and back to the barn. It was a routine they were used to.

The foursome started off slowly, letting the horses nibble at scrub grass along the fence line. Then Virginia's horse, a painted quarter horse, took the lead and got up to a gentle gallop. The other three horses took off after him as the trail stitched down a hill, cutting through breezy grass, toward a fallen tree, which all four horses jumped over. Loretta closed her eyes and shrieked as her horse cleared the obstacle with no problem. Once on the other side of the hill, the horses slowed to mincing steps through thick woods that sloped down toward the creek. The woods smelled of decaying leaves and earth warming in the sun. When they got to the creek, they dismounted and let the horses drink. Just to their right was a cave entrance, so they tied up the horses and scrambled up a rock path to have a peek inside.

The cave entrance was five foot tall and ten foot across. Just inside, the floor was hard-packed mud, and the smooth limestone walls were scrawled with graffiti. Tony led the way into the cool breath of the earth, armed with his cigarette lighter, holding a flame to the clammy walls to read the writing:

"Len and Renee –1954"

"George Haladay –1936"

"Muggs was here –1914."

It was clear many others had come before them on different days and nights to this same spot. Tony wanted to write his and Loretta's name on the wall, but Loretta told him it was against the law to go marking up a cave. "Besides, there could be wild men in there," she said glaring at Tony. "Let's stick to the trail."

Virginia held Patrick's hand and they walked back down to the horses. Alongside her horse, where Loretta couldn't see them, Virginia kissed Patrick. It was the first time they had kissed since last night.

"Are you glad you came?" he asked.

"Yes, I'm having a good time."

"Me, too."

She smiled and got on her horse and they mounted up. Patrick began to think maybe things would work out. Virginia began to think so, too. The horses sloshed at a slow trot along the edge of the creek, and the riders all started talking about last night and laughing. Everyone was in a better mood because Virginia and Patrick had kissed and there was easiness in the air again. Even Loretta laughed when Tony complimented her on her stool sample. Loretta hated to admit it, but Tony had a way about him. He could dance, skate, ride horses, make out, and he was handsome. Just look at him. He rode that horse with his powerful thighs gripping the horse's ribs like a man from another age. They got to the top of the bluff and dismounted in good spirits. Tony kissed Loretta and she let him. They tied up the horses and stood by the bluff to take in the view. Down below, they could see the creek glittering over rocks, and beyond that, woods singing with red, orange, and yellow leaves.

"Now is when a man needs a cold beer," Tony said. "We should've brought some."

"I've got something better," Loretta said.

She pulled a joint from her bra and they all sat down on a flat rock to smoke. Everyone was quiet in the postcard of the moment. Blue skies, a warm October sun, a trickling creek, horses lined up, waiting to be ridden. Tony looked at the horses, then over at Virginia.

"So, Virginia, you mind if I ask you a personal question?"

"I don't mind."

"Did you really ride a horse naked down Ladue Road at two in the morning?"

"Butt naked."

Tony coughed out his smoke, laughing. "Weren't you afraid somebody would see you?"

Virginia shrugged. "I didn't care. Sometimes you just wanna feel naked, you know, free."

Tony felt a stirring in his loins, and began to think of the Middle Ages again. Just maybe, he hoped, after they smoked their joint, they could all take off their clothes and ride around. But first he had to convince Loretta. "That's beautiful what she said, Loretta, don't you think so? You ever wish you could feel free? Free of these things we call clothes?"

"Me? Hell no. I love clothes," she said blowing out smoke. "I wish I was clothes shopping right now."

"What do you think Patrick?" Tony asked.

They all looked at Patrick and laughed. But he wasn't laughing. He was staring off to the side. The marijuana had gotten to him. He was looking at a big pile of rocks down the ridge. Patrick figured out what it was. It was the Indian burial ground Barney Haladay had talked about at school. Barney had said there was an Indian girl buried on his farm. And there she was—under a ten-foot-tall mound of fieldstones. Patrick could picture the whole tribe carrying rocks in the rain on the day of her burial, one by one, the drums beating, warm hands placing cold rocks over the grave, while the Indian father and mother cried off to the side. It wasn't all sunshine and happiness and kissing in the woods. Then he remembered his paper due Monday. Oh, God, Monday was coming! The paper was in ruins. He had no answers to all the questions he had posed in the first six pages. All he knew was Eternity was for the dead, but if a young Indian girl wasn't safe, then death was coming for all of them—Patrick, Tony, Loretta, and even Virginia. They were naked. Poor, blind, miserable, and naked. And what were they doing? Riding horses around the Garden of Eden, laughing, getting high, pretending Monday wouldn't come. But, Monday was coming. Monday was coming.

"What's wrong, Patrick?" Virginia said, touching his shoulder.

He rubbed his forehead and blinked. "I'm sorry. I was just thinking about this paper due Monday."

They all laughed at him. "I got a paper due myself," Tony said.

"What's it about?" Virginia asked.

"Well, lemme tell you . . . it's about this bird who decides he's tired of being like all the other birds, so he flies higher and higher." Tony got up with his arms out and ran around the group. "And he goes so high that something happens." Tony plopped back down winded next to Loretta. "Hi."

"What happens to your bird?"

"I dunno. I haven't finished the book. I'll whip it together on Sunday."

Everyone laughed, but Patrick was looking again at the rock pile.

"Hey, cheer up, Patrick," Virginia said. "All you have to worry about is a paper. Look at Loretta and me."

He looked at them.

"That's right, Patrick, we're in shit worse than that stool sample I laid today. We'll be grounded for a month."

"Yeah, let's forget about Monday," Tony said standing up. "Never let the future ruin today. I say we get on those horses and ride back to the party and get stinking drunk, drunker than we've ever been, and dance, and eat barbecue, and enjoy today while it lasts."

The girls stood up and Virginia held out her hand to Patrick. "What do you say my true love? Shall we forget about Monday and enjoy the day?"

Patrick reached up and took her hand.

Chapter 32

THE PARTY GOT GOING. Big time. Wash buckets brimming with ice cubes and cold beer cans. Shotguns blasting old paint cans off fence posts. A player piano in the attic of the barn pumping out songs, while some tipsy explorers tried on old hats and antique clothing in storage up there from the Haladay family. There was a softball game in one field, and a band near the barn playing Marshall Tucker songs blasting from speakers. Barbecue smoke drifted from a grill with fat dripping off hamburgers onto the charcoal. The menu included hot dogs branded with black grill stripes, big bags of Lays potato chips, and cherry pies that Barney's mom had made. The eating demanded more drinking, and that's what everyone did, all afternoon long. Drink, drink, drink, drink—until every joke was funny and every story was interesting and everyone was pleased with themselves and life in general. Anyone in love was more sure of that love than any Hallmark card could ever capture, and in the distance, church bells played an old song that welcomed the sunset—an orange purple sunset smeared across the fields like a balm.

"It sure is pretty," Jane said as she watched Patrick and Virginia and Tony and Loretta—and some of the other couples sitting on straw bales by the barn—kissing, "Wish Nate were here."

Everyone kept on kissing and didn't answer her.

"If Nate was here, he'd kiss me now."

"To Nate!" Tony said, raising his beer.

And a dozen others raised their beers. "To Nate!"

"How long you been married?" Virginia asked Jane.

"Coming up on four years."

"Are you happy?"

Jane wrapped her arms around herself and looked at the sunset. "It's not always easy, but it's worth it."

"Are you sure? How is it worth it?" Loretta said.

Jane looked at the fields and sighed. "It's a feeling that no matter what happens, no matter what—you're part of someone else." She leaned on the barn and fell through a rotted board out of sight.

"Hey, what happened to Jane?" Tony said.

Patrick and Virginia looked up from kissing.

Loretta pointed to the hole in the barn, spitting out beer. "I think—"

But before anyone could rescue her, Jane emerged from the hole, brushing off hay, continuing her reveries. "It's a feeling that you're part of him and he's part of you, and even though there are rough spots, and you're apart, you know you're a couple."

"You *know you're a couple?*" Loretta scoffed. "Jane, are you all right? Did you hit your head? Because that sounds like bullshit."

Virginia shushed Loretta. "*Loretta!* Let her explain it."

"I can't explain it. If you were married, you'd know what I mean."

"That's a lie. That's what men want us to believe, so we'll get married and unload the dishwasher," Loretta said.

"Don't listen to her, Jane, I think it's beautiful," Virginia said. "I'm very happy for you and Nate."

Jane thanked Virginia and went over to the wash bucket to get another beer.

"You shouldn't talk to her like that," Virginia told Loretta. "She's in love."

"Ha! Next thing I guess you'll tell us you're in love and gonna marry Patrick in a field."

Tony perked up, thinking of the house key around his neck and going back there later on. "That sounds like a great idea, guys. Hey, why don't we make it a double wedding? What do you say, Loretta?"

"Tony, some people need to live together before they get married."

"I can see that."

"But with you and me . . . I think we'd need to live apart for several decades. And I'm sure that goes for Virginia and Patrick, too."

Virginia stood up and threw her beer can in the field. And it wasn't even empty. It sloshed her face, which was dripping mad when she turned on Loretta.

"You've been cutting down Patrick all weekend. I'm tired of your shit. You hear me? The trouble is, some people just don't believe in love. You only love yourself. You're your own best friend. Ha! Well, don't think I *wouldn't* marry Patrick, if he'd ask me." She looked at Patrick.

Tony elbowed him.

"What?" He was drowsy and not paying strict attention.

"She wants you to ask her to marry her," Tony whispered.

Patrick stood up, brushed the hay from his pants, and composed himself. His head was tight and swirly and reality seemed like a black and white movie. "Virginia, would you—"

"Yes." She stumbled over to him and they embraced.

"Damn, this is great!" Tony said, "If only there was a priest here."

Loretta stood up, pushing what she thought was a joke even further. "OK, I'm tired of your shit, too. You think you're really in love? Who needs a priest when you've got Jesus himself," she said. "Look—" She pointed across the way at Barney Haladay, who was standing by the grill turning hot dogs, his long hair fluttering in the breeze.

"I'll go get him," Tony said bolting across the barnyard.

"I can't wait to see this," Loretta said to Virginia. "How are you gonna get out of this one?"

Virginia and Patrick were necking again, not caring about anything.

Tony walked up with Barney, who was holding hot dog tongs and a beer. "Hey, guys, you really want me to marry you?"

Virginia and Patrick looked over at him, then at each other.

"Well, we *do* want to get married," Virginia said, "but not today. I could never get married without a wedding dress."

Barney started laughing. "Wow, this is great. I've got great news for you. Up in the barn attic, there *is* a wedding dress. It was my grandmother's."

Loretta laughed and slapped her own butt in delight. "Ha! Ha! You've got no excuse to back out now, Virginia, unless . . . you don't believe in love."

Patrick looked at Virginia. "You don't have to get married now if you don't want to."

"I want to. Don't you? You're not trying to get out of it, are you?"

"No, no. I mean, I haven't got a ring."

"We can use a beer tab pull," Tony said, wrenching one of his can. "I'll be the best man."

Virginia looked at the beer tab pull from a Miller beer can. Wouldn't her father just shit. She put her father out of her mind and looked at Patrick. He had been true to her all Friday night and didn't try to kiss her when he thought she was a girl from Kansas City. He had protected her during the holdup in East St. Louis, standing between her and the gunman. He was a good dancer and could ride a horse. Maybe Jane was right. Some things you just can't explain. It's a feeling. When you're a couple, you know it.

"OK, lemme see that damned dress," Virginia said, shooting a hot glance at Loretta. Barney took her in the barn, and in a few minutes, the whole party was gathered in the field in the pinkish, purple twilight. Nothing like this had happened since Jane married Nate in the sixth grade. Everyone was eager to see the bride and find out who she was.

"She's a public school girl from Kansas City," Jane told a guy in a cowboy hat. "They fell in love fast, but sometimes, you just know." The cowboy nodded and turned aside to vomit.

Barney came out of the barn ringing a cowbell to get everyone's attention. For style, he had thrown on his great grandfather's fraternal order uniform, a long gold robe with a pyramid on the chest that made him look like a pharaoh. "OK, we haven't got an organ, so if you guys can sing, 'Here Comes the Bride,' we'll get started."

A guitar player with no shirt and a red bandana around his long curly hair played the bridal procession like Jimmy Hendrix. Everyone looked toward the barn.

And there she was. Dressed in white, Virginia von Bierhart came wobbling out into the open, and the gold robed Barney took her arm to lead her to the front of the crowd and to Patrick, who was swaying a bit himself. They stood facing each other with Tony and Loretta off to the side.

"We're gathered here today for the wedding of Patrick Cantwell and . . . hey, I'm sorry, I don't know the bride's name."

There was a moment of silence. Virginia wondered which name to give. If she married him as Pam, she could make it all seem like part of the play. But if she gave her real name everyone would know the truth about how she felt. She looked at Patrick and then at the crowd. "My name is Virginia . . . Virginia von Bierhart."

Everyone started buzzing. What? Did I hear that right? Who did she say she is? I thought her name was Pam. From Kansas City. Holy crap! Virginia von Bierhart—her dad owns the brewery! She's the one who rode naked on the horse, and zips around town in that black Corvette with the VVB license plate.

She's royalty. This was a princess wedding. This was *totally* dee-ee-cent, man.

"Do you take this man to be your husband?"

"I do."

"And do you take this woman to be your wife?"

"I do."

"All right then, where's the ring?"

Tony rushed forward, tripping on a tangle of weeds, got up and gave Patrick the beer tab pull. Patrick took it and put it on her finger. It wouldn't fit her wedding ring finger, so he put it on her pinky.

"Patrick and Virginia, we all hope you'll have a long happy life together and never forget how decent this day was, and that all you need is love. You may now kiss the bride."

They kissed and the crowd cheered, and Loretta cried. Tony hurried over and put his arm on Loretta's shoulder. "You OK, babe?"

"Yeah, I'm just so damned mad at her, but so happy." She blew her nose, then handed the used napkin to Tony and went over to Virginia to hug her. Both girls cried and the band played Marshal Tucker songs and everyone danced, and some guys over by the grill fired off shotguns. Barney's mom came out to tell them no more shooting after dark and found out what happened and made Barney tell Virginia to give the dress back, because it was "a family heirloom." Virginia changed back into her clothes, and darkness fell over the farm. A chilly wind blew, but Tony felt the warm key around his neck and began to think tactical thoughts.

"We should go back to the house where it's warm," he told Loretta. "It's been a long day."

"OK, but don't get any ideas."

They hugged Barney and thanked him for the wedding, and then waved goodbye to everyone. As they were leaving, Jane asked Tony where they were going. He looked left and right, then whispered the secret to her about the Love House

"Whatever you do, don't tell this crowd."

"You can trust me. I won't blab it around."

Jane kept her word and only told one close friend— Kim Springer, who told Bobby Jones, who told Jimmy Purvis, who told Cindy Matthews, who told JoAnn Greggerman, who told Buck Wilson, who shouted the good news to the rest of the parish gang, "Party house!"

So, by the time The Love Machine was pulling away, several carloads of revelers decided to retreat to a warm house where they could all celebrate the wedding all night long.

Chapter 33

ON THE HIGHWAY back to civilization, Tony noticed the caravan behind them, so he tried to lose them. The Love Machine shot past trucks going 90 miles an hour, but their friends kept up with him. So, as he shared a joint with Loretta, he buried the speedometer at nearly 100.

"What's the hurry, Tony? Slow down," she said. The newlyweds were passed out in the back seat, Virginia's head on Patrick's shoulder. When he zipped off the ramp at Webster Groves and came to a stoplight, Bobby Jones's Cougar pulled up right behind him, followed by Jimmy Purvis in his Nova, and Jane Sullenbrook in Nate's Ford Pinto, all of them revving their engines.

"What the hell?" Tony said. "How'd they all know to follow us?"

"The more the merrier," Loretta said. She rolled down her window and leaned out and yelled, "Follow us!"

All the partiers pulled up in front of the house and everyone got out—everyone except Jane.

"I'm going to get Nate. I want him to celebrate the wedding, too," she yelled out the window, and then took off.

"Shhh!" Tony scolded the crowd to keep quiet as Jane drove off. "OK, listen," he told them in a stern whisper, "everybody has to be real careful not to wreck anything, and no smoking in the house. And take off your shoes."

"You don't want me to take off my shoes," Jimmy Purvis said.

"That's for sure," Cindy Matthews said.

"Why can't we smoke?" Buck Wilson asked.

"OK, you can smoke out back, but don't let the neighbors hear you talking or they'll get wise and call the cops."

Everyone agreed. So, they all followed Tony up the front walk. When he opened the door, he blocked the entry with his arm. "Honeymooners first," he told the crowd. A gauntlet of well-wishers lined the winding brick walkway as Patrick and Virginia staggered along toward the door. Up the steps, onto the front porch they went, and then Tony backslapped Patrick and told him to carry her across the threshold.

Patrick picked up his warm bundle of a bride donned in blue jeans and an old windbreaker, and carried her into the living room and plopped her down on the couch. The crowd cheered.

"Shhh . . ." Tony tapped his finger on his lips and waved them in.

Amid the whispers and giggles, the invaders carried in three coolers full of beer and clunked them down in the kitchen. Tony locked the front door, and made the rounds to all the first floor windows and drew all the shades. He didn't want the neighbors to see the possible bedlam in the house, which was supposed to be empty. Then he turned on a few lights and everyone drank some beer.

The party began like any other: a few couples playing spades at the kitchen table, a couple others necking in dark corners of the living room, guys without dates arguing over sports, smokers coming and going out the back door. But the couple everyone had come to help celebrate their nuptials had fallen asleep together on the living room couch.

As they all settled into the party, they began to ask questions about the newlyweds: How'd they meet? How long had they been going together? Why the fake names? What did they see in each other? What was the attraction? Is there really love at first sight? Or are they just fooling themselves?

Tony and Loretta fielded the questions, sometimes giving different answers.

"Do they really love each other?" Kim Springer asked.

"Of, course just look at them over there," Tony said.

"That's not love, that's exhaustion," Loretta said. "Two actors who've been in a play together, which they both thought was real, and after the play, they fell asleep back stage."

"Let's wake them up and see if they're still in love," Kim said.

Tony put a record on—the theme song to *The Honeymooners*. "I love Jackie Gleason," he said.

"He's a fat slob," Loretta said.

Then Tony walked over and nudged Patrick with his foot. "Oh, guys," Tony said, "wake up. Everyone wants to see your first dance."

Virginia and Patrick sat there dazed for a minute, but then got up in slow motion and stood in the center of the rug. The lush, melancholy love song poured out of the hi-fi speakers. The newlyweds held each other and started to move to the music. Everyone gathered around the sofa and chairs and sat on the edges of the living room to watch.

Tony slipped his arm around Loretta's waist. "Look at them . . . Patrick and Virginia, true love."

The twosome danced like a couple in a marathon dance contest, drowsing on each other's shoulders, dreaming together as the audience cheered them on. But Jimmy Purvis got tired of Jackie Gleason, so he switched the hi-fi set to KSHE-95, Real Rock Radio. Led Zeppelin's "Stairway to Heaven" blared, and everyone cheered and clapped.

The gang watched the newlyweds slow dancing and looked over at the stairway. Of course . . . the stairway! They all began to wonder the same thing and Tony whispered it to Loretta.

"Do you think they'll go upstairs?"

Loretta was also hearing the lyrics and looking at the stairway. "She better not, but after this weekend, I don't know."

The crowd was transfixed.

Jimmy Purvis whispered to Bobby Jones. "If they go up that staircase, you know what that means for you and Kim, for me and Cindy?"

"I know, I know," Bobby said. "I hope they go."

"I just wish I had a girlfriend," Buck Wilson whispered.

The girls watched Patrick dancing with awe and dread.

"It sure would be nice to be *that much* in love," Kim Springer whispered to Cindy Matthews.

"I know," Cindy whispered, "but this was just a fake wedding, right?"

"Damn right," Jiggs Sullivan whispered to them, "You can't get married in a field and start having sex. They need a priest and a marriage license. If they climb those steps—"

"All our boyfriends will want the same," JoAnn Greggerman whispered.

"And we can't let'm," Peggy Nolan whispered, "they still need college degrees and jobs."

"Not only that," Diane Otto whispered, "tomorrow's Sunday. Patrick has to go to Mass. I don't know about her."

"I think she's *public* school," Lynn Perry whispered.

The girls all shook their heads.

"I should never have mooned those truckers first on the bridge," Martha O'Conner whispered. "I got this whole thing started."

"Somebody should stop this," Kim whispered to the girls, loud enough for the boys to hear. But the boys shushed her. And nobody tried to stop it. They couldn't take their eyes off them. They were such a lovely couple.

Virginia whispered in Patrick's ear. "I'm so tired."

"Me too," he whispered back.

"Wouldn't it be nice if it were true?"

"What?"

"If I really was your bride tonight."

"Yeah."

"What would you do?"

"Well, I wouldn't have to wait years and years anymore."

"Years and years?"

"I would take you right up stairs."

"Then what?"

"I don't know, everything, I guess."

"Everything?" She held him tighter.

"Yeah."

"I'm so tired right now. I can't keep dancing for years and years."

"Maybe you should sit down."

"I don't want to sit down. I'm tired of sitting down. I want to go upstairs. Will you take me?"

Holding onto Virginia's waist, Patrick stepped back and studied her. Without answering, he turned and Virginia slipped her arm into his, and they moved toward the staircase.

Everyone watched. The crowd was so breathless and quiet, when Buck Wilson opened another beer, it sounded like a shotgun blast. A few girls flinched.

Patrick didn't know what he was going to do. Maybe he would just say goodnight at the bedroom door, and then come back down and simply go home, make curfew, and go to Mass with his parents, brothers, and sisters in the morning. Or, maybe the pull from the master bed would be unstoppable. Maybe he would just let it take him. He didn't know yet. He didn't know how it would end.

Their feet took the first step. The girls watching from the living room gulped. The guys twisted the fabric on the couch pillows and wrenched their toes, wishing it were their feet on that first step with her. Virginia paused and turned to the crowd. It looked as though she was going to make a speech, but she just hiccupped and blew the crowd a kiss. The guys erupted in hurray's and wild applause.

Patrick looked over at Tony. Tony, his arms wrapped around Loretta from behind, stared back and shook his head in disbelief. "I never thought he'd go first."

Loretta squeezed Tony's hands. "I never thought Virginia would go up first, either." Loretta turned around and faced Tony. "You know what?"

"What?"

"If we hurry, we can at least tie them."

Heat coursed through Tony. "You mean it?"

"Sure, why not? Let's go." She poked her finger in his chest, "But don't think this means we're going steady."

Tony and Loretta crossed the living room, arm in arm, toward the staircase. They, too, took the first step.

The entire party went tribal, yelling and clapping, banging beer cans on the coffee table. This was the beginning of a new era, the dawn of a new Middle Ages in the parish, and Patrick and Tony were leading the way. It was a group initiation. Even the girls felt it.

"There they go," Jimmy Purvis said.

Patrick and Virginia's legs disappeared above the line of the ceiling and they were out of view into the dark privacy of the upstairs hallway. Tony turned to the group and leaned on the railing, like a Senator talking to voters, and smiled. Then in a whisper, he said "I just want to say. I love you all . . . and make yourself at home, please. But don't wreck the place while I'm busy upstairs. And remember, no smoking in the house. And when it comes to love—"

Patrick ran back into view at the top of the stairs. "Tony! Quick!" he yelled.

"Can't you see I'm making a speech? What is it?"

"The garage! The garage is on fire!"

The crowd leaped up all at once and ran for the windows. Tony ran upstairs to look out the window. He could see out behind the house, fifty feet back, at the end of the driveway, the garage was burning like a Godzilla movie. Big yellow flames belched from the windows. Apparently, one of the smokers had flicked a live cigarette that caught the dry oak leaves and up she went. The garage was fully involved. Patrick, Tony, Virginia, and Loretta ran downstairs.

"Shit," Tony said. "Call the fire department!"

They ran for the kitchen phone. But Buck Wilson was already on it, tapping the hang up button. "It's not working," Buck said.

"Shit! That's right," Loretta yelled. "Remember, the phone is dead."

"Let's get out of here!" someone yelled.

With that—the entire house emptied out, everyone grabbing jackets, shoes, purses, coolers, and unfinished beers. In the stampede, the coffee table and a living room lamp got knocked over. Only Patrick, Tony, Virginia, and Loretta were left— in a house strewn with empty beer cans, and playing cards thrown across the kitchen floor. They stood in the kitchen and watched the fire from the back windows. Hungry, orange flames licked along the soffit line and up the slope of the garage roof.

"Oh, shit! My car!" Loretta said. "I've got to get it out!"

Tony held her back. "We can't, babe. It's too late."

Loretta sobbed. "My parents are going to kill me."

Tony patted her on the shoulder, searching his mind for some sincere way to comfort her. "Don't cry, dear. At least now you won't have to worry about fixing those bullet holes."

Loretta whipped around and slapped him in the face. Then she turned and ran into the living room. She plunged onto the couch crying on a pillow. Virginia ran after her and they hugged each other, both sobbing.

Tony rubbed his cheek and gave Patrick a shrug. Then they both turned to look out the back window again, their eyes aglow from the blazing garage. Their faces were blank. It had been a long weekend and they were both spent. Besides, they both still had a paper due Monday. The calm of utter ruin rested on them. They spoke to each other with nothing but blankness left in their voices.

"We're dead" Tony said. "We are both dead."

"When you're dead, you understand everything, but it's too late to do anything about it, because you're already dead."

"Is that from your paper?"

"No, I just heard it once, at a wake."

"You mind if I use that for mine?"

"Sure, you can have it. I don't care."

"Thanks." Tony patted Patrick on the shoulder.

"You're welcome."

The fire engine and police arrived. Detective Sergeant Kirk Kurtz knocked on the front door and Tony let him in.

"Thanks for coming," Tony said.

"Are you the homeowner?"

"No, he's on a trip. I'm guarding the house for him."

"How old are you?"

"Sixteen."

"You've been drinking."

Tony shrugged. "Only a toast. There was a wedding."

Detective Kurtz shined a flashlight in the dark living room. The beam hit Virginia, Loretta, and Patrick on the couch. Beer cans were all over the floor. He shined the light back in Patrick's face, and then again in Tony's.

"Don't I know you guys?"

They both said nothing.

"You're under arrest. You, too, ladies. Come with me."

They walked outside, smelling the smoke, stepping over fire hoses in the flashng lights from the fire trucks. A pump and ladder truck was backed into the driveway, shooting down water on the garage. Neighbhors stood on lawns across the street watching the conflagration. As Detective Kurtz was putting them all in the patrol car, Jane and Nate pulled up behind the fire trucks in Nate's Pinto and got out. It was the first time Nate had made any of the parties. Jane and Nate rushed over to the police car. She pointed at Patrick and Virginia.

"They're the ones, Nate. They got married, just like us." She waved to Patrick and Virginia, and they waved back from inside the police car.

Detective Kurtz shut the door of the car and turned to the two newcomers. "You two been drinking, too?" He pointed at the burning garage, "You part of this?"

"No, sir," Nate said, soberly showing him his True Love Pizza assistant manager badge. "I just got off work. We only came by to wish them well,"

"Wish them well?" Detective Kurtz said.

"Don't you know? Haven't you heard the good news?" Jane beamed. "They're a couple!"

Detective Kurtz watched, hands on hip, as Jane leaned down blowing a kiss to Virginia and Patrick in the back of the squad car. Then she called out, "You guys are gonna have a great marriage, I know. Some parts are bad, but always keep loving each other."

"Get her the hell out of her!" Detective Kurtz snapped.

Nate pulled Jane back toward the Pinto and they drove away. It was a long, tense ride home for Jane. Nate lectured her about how she needed to think about her future, how she needed to take life more seriously, and start preparing for the years and years ahead, and drop all these drunk friends and get her grades up, because the ACT test was coming, and society only rewarded people with skills and patience, people who live for tomorrow and not for today. All this made Jane cry. But when he opened the door for her, she turned around and hugged him, and asked him to forgive her. "Oh, Nate . . . I'm going to try to be less like me, and more like you," she said.

"All right, good night."

As he closed the door, Jane added, "then we can afford a store-bought white dress and flowers, and you can give me a diamond ring, and—."

Nate put the car in gear and slowly drove away.

Chapter 34

THE FORCES OF the Industrial Age overtook Patrick and Virginia. Napping in the back of the patrol car with their heads leaning against each other, holding hands, they had no idea how quickly and finally it would end. When the patrol car pulled into the back lot of the police station and they got out, Detective Kurtz told them to move it along toward the back door, a dented up metal door with a single bulb light above it.

Patrick and Virginia walked in holding hands. Tony tried to hold Loretta's hand.

"Don't touch me!" She snatched her hand away from him and buried her hands in her pockets.

Once inside, the glare of the fluorescent lights made them squint. This was a sober world of polished red floors and burnt coffee, and badges and guns. Detective Kurtz told them all to line up against the wall. Tony and Loretta put their backs to the wall; Loretta moved away from him and crossed her arms in front of her and then whimpered. Patrick and Virgina leaned against the wall, too, still holding hands. Then the detective took his baton and gently lowered it like a butter knife to separate Patrick and Virginia's hands.

"OK, kids, I'm going to need parent's names and phone numbers."

Loretta sobbed. A female officer came over and gave her a Kleenex.

"OK, ladies, this officer will escort you to one room; the men here will come with me," Detective Kurtz said. And just like that, Patrick and Virginia were separated. She smiled at him once more as she turned to go her way, and he smiled back, as if this was just a temporary inconvenience. But soon they would realize their wedding night was over. Soon, all their parents would be arriving to haul them to their separate homes, and there was no telling when they might see each other again, or even talk. Yes, the honeymoon was over.

Once the boys were in an interrogation room with the detective, his face flared red and his bristly, gray crew cut seemed to stand taller. He got right to the point. "OK, who set the garage on fire?"

Patrick shrugged.

Tony spoke up. "Well, sir, we were wondering that ourselves. You see, we were inside, minding our own business, when Patrick looked out the window and saw it. We have no idea."

Detective Kurtz pulled out a metal chair that squeaked on the floor, and sat down across a flat table from the boys. He got out a stick of Dentyne cinnamon chewing gum and put it in his mouth. The boys watched him chew. He could tell they both wanted a piece, but he didn't offer them one. He drummed his fingernails on the table and thought of the lies these same boys had told him before, back when he had asked them who put the snow globe in the hand of Mary on the church roof. At the time, Tony had invented an elaborate lie about how maybe the mob did it.

"Mr. Vivamano, I'm disappointed in you. You were a much better liar in grade school. I thought you were going to tell me the mafia burned down the garage."

Tony thought back and chuckled a little. "Oh, that, hey, I hope there's no hard feelings about that little situation. But honestly, detective, we have no idea what happened."

He turned to Patrick. "Did you boys use an accelerant?"

"A what?"

"Gasoline! Did you pour gasoline on the garage to get it to burn up so fast? And don't lie—we have ways of knowing how it started, even after a fire."

Patrick looked him in the eye. "I swear, all I know is we were dancing to "Stairway to Heaven—"

"And then all hell broke loose," Tony said.

"Well, what did you steal?"

Tony was offended. "Steal? What do you mean?"

"I mean, tell me what you stole from the house. TVs, jewelry, cash? It'll go a lot easier on you later if you admit to what you stole now before the homeowner tells us."

"We didn't steal anything. We have morals," Tony sat up straight in his chair.

"Morals?"

"We go to St. Aloysius," Patrick said.

Detective Kurtz laughed. "Bullshit. Don't try to convince me you're just a bunch of *good Catholic boys*. I know you guys. You're criminals, just criminals who haven't been convicted yet."

Tony and Patrick looked at each other. He was right. The things the gang had done all their life and gotten away with—drunk driving, speeding, smoking pot, mooning truckers, hopping trains, throwing rocks at brand new cars on passing trains, setting off fire hydrants, riding borrowed golf carts around wild, smashing mailboxes, stealing prized garden tomatoes just to throw at buses, pool hopping naked. It was a long list of undocumented sins that would surely add up to prison time, if the truth came out all at once.

"Look, sir, we may be a little wild, but over the years we've also done a lot of soul searching," Tony told him.

"Soul searching?"

"Yeah, we're both writing papers about what life is all about. Mine's about this bird who flies around to find the truth and stuff like that." Tony elbowed Patrick. "Tell 'em what yours is about, Patrick."

Patrick opened his mouth, but before he could speak—

"I don't want to hear about your damned soul-searching," Detective Kurtz said. "All I know is that when this homeowner gets home, he'll swear out a complaint, and you can tell the judge your bird story. You guys are in the *real* shit now. You burned down a garage! Somebody could've gotten killed! You are both finally gonna know what it feels like to get caught, and get punished. No more lying your way out of it."

Detective Kurtz got up and looked down on the two boys as he twirled his chewing gum with his tongue and front teeth. "Yep, you boys are like wild little Nazis headed for Nuremberg this time." On his way out the door, he said, "I'll let you know when your parents get here."

The door closed and they were alone.

"I need a priest," Tony said.

"This isn't death row. They don't have priests."

"I know, I mean, I feel I finally have enough sins built up to make a good confession. Hey, look—"

Through the wire glass window, they spied a couple walking in with a new-born baby. The female officer with the Kleenex box brought Loretta into view and the couple hugged Loretta. It was her parents. Her father signed some papers. Both parents looked grim. The mom had been crying, her mascara all runny.

"Poor Loretta," Tony said.

"Yeah, she lost a car."

"Well, at least there's a new baby around. Maybe they'll go easier on her."

Loretta and her family started to walk away toward the door.

"There she goes," Tony said, waving to her, even though she didn't see him. "I always loved you, Sophia." He studied her body as she walked away. He wanted to always remember her. "I'll never forget her performance."

"You mean pretending to be a girl from Kansas City?"

"That, too, but I meant her performance on the bridge. Mmmm."

Next, they watched Virginia's parents and brother come in, along with an attorney from the brewery. The female officer brought Virginia to them, and Patrick ran his eyes down her arm to her hand.

"She's still wearing the wedding ring," Patrick said.

"That's a good sign," Tony said.

Virginia's father stopped a foot in front of her to make sure it was really her. Her long black hair, the pride of the family, was gone. Her blue eyes were bloodshot. She reeked of alcohol and still looked half drunk.

Virginia braced herself for a slap in the face, like the night she got arrested for riding the horse naked. But it didn't come. Her father grabbed her and hugged her.

"I'm just glad you weren't kidnapped," he said, "I was afraid I'd never get to walk you down the aisle some day."

Patrick and Tony couldn't hear any of this, but things seemed to be going OK for Virginia. Her mother cried and hugged her, running her fingers through her short, short red hair, shaking her head. Then Mr. von Beirhart snapped his fingers at Virginia's brother, who was off to the side sulking by the police trophy case. He came over and gave her a side hug.

The attorney for the brewery was at the main desk talking with Detective Kurtz. He pulled a document out of his brief case and Kurtz signed it. Under the secret terms of the deal, Virginia would cooperate fully with the investigation—if there was one—and be named only as the "unindicted co-conspirator." As a courtesy, the brewery would also supply free von Beirhart beer for the annual police picnic in perpetuity.

"Looks like Kurtz is happy about something," Patrick said.

"Yeah, he wants us, not her." Tony said. He sat down to do some tactical thinking.

Patrick kept watching her. His bride started to walk away with her family. He waved to her, but she didn't see him. He wanted to say goodbye. Patrick pushed back the table and headed for the door. He twisted the knob. But the cold doorknob refused to turn. It was locked. He darted back to the window and *looked*.

But she was gone.

Except for her shoes. He only got a glimpse of her sneakers—the same sneakers that had climbed the staircase with him just an hour ago. She disappeared from view, and Patrick drifted over and sat next to Tony.

"I've been doing some thinking about our next move," Tony said.

"Tony—"

"Yeah?"

"Please don't say anything right now."

"Sure, I understand. I'll be quiet and let a man think. You're right. I'm gonna shut up."

Tony sucked in some deep breaths and exhaled the toxins from a day of partying. He was thinking about his own parents now, and how it would go with them. His mother would cry. His father would be stern. And a season of shame would come over Tony. And probation would probably follow. But, life would still be good. Besides, he was already formulating a plan to get out of the whole thing, which he didn't want to tell Patrick about yet.

Tony looked over at Patrick. He was still sitting with his eyes closed thinking about Virginia. Poor Patrick, Tony thought. He just wanted to stay in his room and write a paper, and I brought all this on him. But, hey, he told himself, be proud of all you've done to help Patrick. Look at him. A little sad, perhaps, but he's a new man. He's learned things you can't get in books. And, if Patrick was searching for God, at least now he has some *real* sins to confess, so God won't be bored with him.

There was a knock at the door. Detective Kurtz open the door and called for Tony.

Tony wiped the shine off his face and squared his shoulders. He patted Patrick's shoulder as he got up. "We'll be seeing you, man." Then he walked through that door like everything was going to be fine. Tony's mother in her bathrobe and curlers cried and hugged him. When his father shook his hand,

Tony wondered. Why no lecture? No scowl? No talk of grounding? Why such calm eyes? Then Tony noticed his dad was wearing shoes without socks. No socks. Of course! That was a dead giveaway. His parent's had been in bed, probably having sex when they got the call. No wonder he was in a good mood.

The ride going home was not rough like Tony thought it would be, either. His mother blew her nose and said he had been foolish, but his father was sanguine and philosophical.

"Ah, Tony, sometimes youth has to learn for itself. Have you learned?"

"Yes, sir."

God what a great man, Tony thought. How good to be arrested just to feel such love. Such wisdom. No wonder I can have better sayings than all my friends, he thought. Half of my sayings come from him. Tony didn't know it yet, but the two of them would end up working together on Tony's paper all Sunday afternoon, with Tony's dad speed-reading the book on the bird, and telling Tony what to type out. He would get an A-minus on the project.

Patrick's dad finally came to get him. Like Tony's dad, Patrick's dad didn't make a big show. He was calm. He shook hands with Patrick like an executive instilling confidence in the whole company. The company of his family. This wasn't the first time he'd picked up his kids at the police station. He signed the usual forms and waited until they were in the car to give his usual talk. "You're still a part of this family, Patrick, but this is no small thing. You're going to be punished, and I want you to go to confession."

"OK."

Patrick didn't tell his dad or mom about Virginia, or about getting married in a field, or how he almost lost his virginity. He let them think that he just drank a few beers and caught a garage on fire. It was best not to trouble them with all the hardships of his life. After all, they were under a tremendous strain, raising such a big family.

Chapter 35

TONY STEPPED OUT of the shower—steaming hot naked—and dried off with his back to the mirror. He was hungry, and that was good. Maybe God would notice that he had skipped breakfast and was as hungry as John the Baptist. Once, during Lent, Tony went an entire six weeks without ice cream, and then ended up with a new bike. These things were all mysterious and beyond comprehension, but as he dried off, he thought of the little speech he would give the homeowner, Mr. Henley, as he put on his best blue suit and tie and polished his shoes. The poster of Sophia Loren with her abundant bosom and longing eyes watched him dress, but he refused to flirt with her as he usually did, or blow her a kiss. With no one looking, he shut the door and knelt by his bed to ask God to give him a break and bless his plan and get him and Patrick out of trouble with the police.

Patrick arrived in his best suit, too, and they walked down the street together to talk with Mr. Henley so maybe he wouldn't press charges. Patrick was tired and also hungry, not from fasting, but from oversleeping. He barely got dressed in time.

"What are you gonna say?" Patrick said, sticking his finger between his neck and collar, pulling at the tie.

"I'm gonna tell him we'll *work it off*. We'll help them build a new garage, carry wood, nail boards, anything it takes, and then cut his lawn for free, and rake his leaves for free, anything it takes for a whole year or longer."

"Is he a forgiving man?"

"I don't know. I hardly know him."

When they arrived at the house, Mr. Henley was out back by the rubble of the garage talking with a man who was holding a clipboard taking notes. Loretta's car was visible beneath some charred timbers. It looked like a black charcoal briquette on wheels. The rubber was all melted, the windows were black, and all the yellow paint had burned away.

"The resale value on that car is going to be nil," Tony whispered as they approached the two men.

Mr. Henley turned around and saw the boys. He recognized Tony and only nodded. No smile. That was a bad sign. Mr. Henley signed a paper for the insurance adjuster and walked up to the boys. He was a thin man, with a gaunt face like a killer gunman in a spaghetti western.

Tony and Patrick both gulped. Tony worked up a smile mixed with sorrow and shame. He had practiced in the mirror before he took a shower.

"Mr. Henley," Tony began, reaching out to shake hands, "I'm really sorry about your garage."

Mr. Henley didn't shake his hand but side-stepped Tony and hurried past him toward the kitchen door. "Hurry up, inside."

Tony dropped his fake smile and looked at Patrick with dread.

"Does he own any guns?" Patrick whispered as they slow stepped toward the house.

"I don't know. Let's just keep near the door at first, and if he goes for a gun, we can—"

Suddenly, the back door busted open and the boys stopped dead. Mr. Henley was standing there in the doorway. His hand moved fast. Something shiny in it. He pointed it at the boys.

"Don't shoot!" Tony yelled, as they dove to either side. When nothing happened, the boys looked up. Mr. Henley was holding a pancake flipper.

"Come on in. I had to flip the pancakes before they burned. We don't need the house to burn down, too." He smiled. As the boys got up and dusted off their suits, Patrick and Tony smiled back, a little. They looked at each other and Tony nodded, so they went in. Pancakes were cooking on the griddles, and a whole row of bacon sizzling in a skillet. It was as if he was expecting them. Both boys stood by the door.

"Mr. Henley, we're here to work," Tony said.

"Work?" Mr. Henley said, "OK, set the table and have a seat. This'll all be done in a minute."

Never taking their eyes off him, Tony and Patrick set the breakfast table along the wall across from the stove. The same table where some of the gang had been playing cards the night before. The cards were no where to be seen. And everything was in order. Not a beer can in sight.

As Mr. Henley turned the bacon, he shook his head, and said, "You boys must've had quite a blowout."

Tony pulled the cuffs on his shirt out beyond the edge of his suit sleeves to look sharp, as he sat there to give his prepared speech. "Yes, sir, I won't lie to you. We had a little party."

Mr. Henley put the bacon atop a paper towel on a plate to soak up the grease and turned another row of pancakes while he listened.

"The thing of it is," Tony continued, "we want to say we're sorry—very sorry—and we'd like to work our way back into your good graces. We'll help to rebuild your garage, cut your lawn, rake your leaves. We'll work, work, work to prove ourselves to you." Tony widened his eyes and nodded his head sideways toward Mr. Henley, his signal for Patrick to say something good, too.

"That's right, sir. We can be very hard workers," he added.

"Let's eat first."

Mr. Henley served up the pancakes and bacon, and poured them both a glass of orange juice, then got some himself and sat down. They waited for him to take the first bite, or say something to signal how things would go. But he was quiet as if he was praying. The pancakes were steaming and their eyes and noses were sending electrical dispatches to their empty stomachs that something good was about to happen.

"Did anyone get hurt?" Mr. Henley asked.

They told him no.

"Did anyone do anything more than sleep in those beds upstairs?"

"Oh, no sir," Tony said. "I mean, we were hoping . . . but me and Patrick, we just don't have the organizational skills to have an affair."

"I see." He took a bite of his pancakes and the boys started eating theirs. Mr. Henley then told them about his trip, how he got to see the fall colors while visiting his daughter and her husband in the country. "My daughter's going to have a baby. I'm going to be a grandfather. She told me so yesterday. I am so happy. I only wish—" He got choked up and looked over on the wall alongside the breakfast table at a picture of his wife. "I only wish my Jeanne had lived to see these days. God has been very good to me, though. I was young and crazy like you boys once. Pass the butter, would you?" He blew his nose and put some more butter on his pancakes, which the boys didn't think needed more butter since they were swimming in it already. But he needed something to do to compose himself.

Feeling braver now, Tony decided to get down to business. "Now, about our offer," he said putting down his fork to negotiate a settlement. "Me and Patrick want to do all we can to pay for all this."

The doorbell rang. Mr. Henley got up and wiped his face with a napkin. Patrick and Tony watched him cut through the living room and open the door. Sunlight came in on the rug, as clean as if the party never took place. They saw Mr. Henley unlock the screen door. "Please, come on in, Detective Kurtz. Have a bit of breakfast."

"Shit," the boys said in unison as Detective Kurtz walked into the living room. He was standing just off to the side and couldn't see them at the table.

"Thanks, Mr. Henley, but I'm here on official business. I need you to swear out a complaint against those two boys who burned your garage."

Patrick froze and listened.

Tony wolfed down the rest of his pancakes and some of Patrick's while he wasn't looking. He figured it might be his last good meal for a while.

The boys kept quiet as Kurtz did his best living room job ever, telling Mr. Henley how these were boys with criminal leanings who could do society some real harm some day if they weren't finally caught and punished.

"All you need to do, Mr. Henley, is sign your name to this and the police will take care of the rest." He assured Mr. Henley he would be doing the right thing, to show delinquent boys throughout the community that the law has to be obeyed, and when the law is broken, someone has to be punished. Someone has to suffer.

"Well, I don't know . . . my daughter is having a baby. I'm going to be a grandfather."

"Congratulations, sir, but please, this is a separate case. You have to make them pay for what they did."

"But it's already paid for. The insurance man told me himself. I'm covered."

Tony got so excited he flipped the piece of pancake off his fork, which hit a plaque on the wall alongside the table. It hung there for a second, and then slowly dragged down the plaque. Tony grabbed a napkin and wiped off the evidence so there wouldn't be any trouble. Patrick looked at the plaque. He read the words, but it just seemed like one of those plaques old people are always hanging everywhere.

"Not by works of righteousness that we have done, but according to His mercy He saved us."

Tony straightened the plaque and dusted off the picture frame of Mr. Henley's wife while he was at it.

"Are you sure about this?" Sargeant Kurtz asked.

"Yes."

"But these boys are evil. They've got to be stopped."

"I think they've stopped. They'll grow up to be fine citizens some day. It's just hard to be young."

Mr. Henley wished Detective Kurtz a good day and thanked him for all his hard work in the community. Then he reminded him that he was going to be a grandfather and showed him out the door.

Their gracious host came back in and sat down and they all three ate some more pancakes, bacon, and drank coffee. Mr. Henley talked about his own youth, how he wanted to get rich, but never made it. Instead, he said, he got married and he and his wife raised a daughter. Now he was retired and going to have a grandchild, and a new garage, and there were things to do. The yard needed cleaning, and maybe a new swing set was in order for when the grandkid would come over. Tony offered to do all the work for free, but again, the old man surprised them. He insisted he would pay them for their work, that he didn't want them to be able to boast that they got out of trouble by their own efforts. And then the most amazing part happened. Right as they were getting ready to leave, Mr. Henley asked Tony how much money he owed him for watching the house.

Was he crazy? Patrick couldn't believe this old guy. Tony paused on his way out the door, thinking a little cash might come in handy for beer, but he remembered there wouldn't be any beer for a long time, because he was going to be grounded for weeks and weeks. And so would Patrick. Tony looked at the garage rubble and then smiled at Mr. Henley.

"You don't have to pay me for this one. It's on the house."

Mr. Henley got a big laugh out of that. He was in such a good mood, having a grandchild coming. He shook the boys hands and told them to stay away from the police, and to stay out of trouble.

"We're gonna be new men," Tony said.

Patrick nodded and they left. It was a beautiful sunny day, the air fragrant with autumn leaves and burnt garage

Chapter 36

AFTER A LONG, HARSH winter, it was suddenly May again, the night of the Father and Son Sophomore Banquet at St. Aloysius. Patrick and Tony went, along with their dads. It was a night for marking the halfway point of their high school career, a night for awards and thinking about the future. The cars arrived on the parking and the fathers and sons got out and put on their sports coats in the warm breeze. Everything was green again. Daylight Savings Time was back, and Brother Hannigan, the superintendent of Grounds, was way out on the football field on his red tractor cutting the grass in the honey-colored twilight. For their crimes the previous fall, Tony and Patrick had been grounded every weekend until the end of the school year. Instead of drinking beer on weekends, they had been studying and writing papers. Their grades had gone up in the process. Plus, they were both in the running for one of the awards to be given this evening: Most Improved Sophomore.

The crowd filed in past the sports trophy case, every boy checking his hair in the reflection. Many boys had not had a haircut since the October forced clippings, and they were looking wild again and ready for summer. The statute of St. Aloysius stood guard by the drinking fountain, still staring out with his fervent, plaster eyes at the passing crowd. The fathers and sons all went into the library, which was dark, except for the candles on the long tables covered with brown tablecloths, the school color. Everyone sat down and Father Woerstbrauth stood at the podium to lead them in grace. There was not a woman in the room, only fathers and sons and Jesuits. Father Woerstbrauth said something about how "we've all been through a lot" this year, which, he meant scholastically. Through it all, though, Patrick stared at the candle flame in front of him and thought about Virginia.

It had been seven months since he had seen her walk out of the police station, and they had not spoken or written since. It was forbidden. An attorney for the brewery had contacted his dad and Tony's dad, warning them that any effort to contact Virginia von Bierhart would result in litigation seeking an order of protection.

So, that's the way was. The Industrial Age had won.

He still thought of her every day, though, and wondered if she still thought of him. How could she not? They were married. You can't get married in a field and just forget it. On the other hand, maybe she would agree with Tony. Tony had often told Patrick to move on, think about the future.

"What happened that weekend was like a fever," he would say. "Sophomore fever." And now the fever had broken, and a lot of time had passed—Halloween, Thanksgiving, Christmas, New Years, St. Patrick's Day, Easter. But some victims of an illness or fever never get over the symptoms of what they went through. Some walk with a limp their whole life.

Patrick thought of Jane and Nate. They were still limping along. Jane still kept the fever going, maybe even Nate did, too, in his own way. If Jane still loved Nate, maybe Virginia still loved Patrick. Who knows? Perhaps even right now in her bedroom at the von Bierhart estate, Virginia was sitting there in a corner chair thinking about Patrick, writing his name down over and over again, or trying to draw a picture of his fading face. Or maybe she was out on a date with another guy from a better family, a better school, some future captain of industry. There was no way to know. All Patrick could do was sit at the banquet and wait. That was the ethic of the Industrial Age for sophomores everywhere: Wait.

"And the nominees for Most Improved Sophomore are . . . Patrick Cantwell . . . Tony Vivamano . . ."

Patrick heard Father Woerstbrauth say his name and snapped back to the program. Tony elbowed him and said good luck. Patrick's dad looked at Patrick. "No matter what, you'll do all right."

"And the winner is . . ." Father Woerstbrauth lingered to build some tension. "Barney Haladay!"

Patrick and Tony looked at each other and mouthed, 'Barney Haladay?' Even so, along with everyone else, they clapped. Barney stood up and headed for the podium. Barney Haladay, who had negotiated a secret B-average for the first semester in lieu of cutting his hair. Barney Halady, who had buckled down, worked hard, and rocketed up to a B-plus average during the second semester. He had even cut his hair. Voluntarily. The long-haired guy who had married Patrick and Virginia in the field now looked like a junior executive ready for the future.

Everyone sat through a few more awards: Father Dunelli for Teacher of the Year. And Matt Baimbridge, whose grandmother had donated half a million dollars to the endowment fund, was named the St. Aloysius New Man of the Year. He bounded up to the podium to take his award, amidst thunderous applause. His Spanish teacher, Father Ortega, resisted the temptation to stick out his shoe and trip him.

"This school has taught me a lot," Matt said. He gave a short speech and took his trophy and went back to sit next to his dad. It had been a successful year for all of them, even for those who hadn't won an award, Father Woerstbrauth said, because everyone was maturing and learning to "conquer themselves," and be moral leaders in society.

Finally, the lights came on and all the fathers and sons drifted onto the parking lot, guys with loosened ties and sports coats slung over their shoulders. The stars were out and it smelled like a summer night, the kind of night for drinking beer on the golf course or pool hopping .

"Well, we got through it," Tony said. "Starting this weekend, we're ungrounded. How do you feel, Patrick?"

Patrick looked back at the school, then at Tony. "I feel like I was pretending the whole year."

"Pretending? Pretending what?"

"I don't know . . . pretending to be wise, when I'm really just a fool."

Tony smiled and shook his hand. "Don't feel bad. We're all fools in the end."

With that, Tony loosened his tie. Then he yanked it off, and unbuttoned his shirt.

"What are you doing?"

"My final sophomore lap."

He starting running across the dark field, throwing off clothes as he ran. Some of the other boys chased after him. Dads stood in suits shaking their heads. Patrick dropped his sports coat and tried to stop him. But it was no use. Tony was fully alive on his favorite planet, Earth. Soon he was butt naked, and all the sophomore boys from the banquet were running laps around the football field, tossing off clothes, chasing behind Tony and laughing. The school year was over. As best as they could be, they were new men.

The End

𝕬𝖈𝖐𝖓𝖔𝖜𝖑𝖊𝖉𝖌𝖊𝖒𝖊𝖓𝖙𝖘.

Some of this stuff really happened, so I better not thank any of my high school friends by name. They are all reformed now and hold respectable positions in the world. But they all remember. It was fun to be young together trying to figure out life on weekend nights in the 1970s. I scored an incomplete on the project.

When I was a sophomore at De Smet Jesuit High, my English composition teacher, Jeanne Smith, read some stuff I had written on my own and told me to keep on writing. Smith was a great encourager of young writers, but she was also tough. I remember her saying, "Killeen, you're just playing with words here." She was right. And I still am. A few years after I graduated, I heard Jeanne Smith had died. And that was a real shock. She was still young.

So I thanked her posthumously in the acknowledgements page of my first novel, *Never Hug a Nun*. That was that, and I hadn't thought of Jeanne Smith for a long time, and then something strange happened.

After working for weeks revising this book—and getting my brain thoroughly marinated in the world of high school—a package arrived for me at the office from New York. I opened it and read the first line of a letter inside.

"I am Jeanne Smith's brother."

Thunderstruck, I read on. Her aging brother, whom I had never met or heard of, said he was downsizing and couldn't bear to throw out his late sister's teaching books. So, he sent them to me.

Why me?

"Your public 'thank you' to Jeanne made me feel as if she was here," the note said. "She would be humbled by your 'thank you' and cheering you on."

Jeanne Smith had done it again. And her timing was uncanny. It was as though my old high school teacher knew somehow I was writing a book about a high school and wanted to cheer me on. I looked inside the package and found several 1970s paperbacks, smelling sweet and musty. Jeanne Smith's own handwriting filled the margins of *Huckleberry Finn, The Grapes of Wrath, Sophocles, The Great Gatsby,* and *Death of a Salesman.* What a gift. Thanks to Jeanne's brother, Michael Ladish, and to Jeanne, too.

Thanks also to some current friends who helped get me motivated—sometimes over cold cans of Stag beer—with their own memories of high school: Jim and Renee Howard, Melissa Vahlkamp, Brian Kelly, Chris Mihill, Jane Dueker, Keith Juzwicki, and my brother, Dan Killeen. He was a wild one.

Special thanks to J.B. Forbes and his daughter, Taylor Forbes Wicker, for their expert advice on horses.

Thanks to my editor, Donna Essner, who kept this book alive and on schedule, and who encouraged me with many kind margin remarks and suggestions.

And most of all, thanks to my family. I need family. Thanks to Nancy and our kids, Katie, Kevin, Jack and Emily.

And speaking of Emily, she's a high school sophomore now. Don't get any crazy ideas after reading this book, Emily.

About the Author

Kevin Killeen was born in St. Louis, Missouri in 1960, the second oldest of a Catholic family of eight children. With so many siblings, Killeen learned to eat fast if he wanted seconds. His experiences at strict schools run by nuns or Jesuits, and his frequent juvenile entanglements with the law, became fodder for a series of four comic novels about growing up. At this printing, all of the previous books have won either national or regional awards for humor. Killeen is married with four children and works as a journalist for CBS Radio KMOX in St. Louis.